T0286649

Don't Eat Me

Don't Eat Me

COLIN COTTERILL

SOHO CRIME

Published by
Soho Press, Inc.
853 Broadway
New York, NY 10003

Library of Congress Cataloging-in-Publication Data

Cotterill, Colin
Don't eat me / Colin Cotterill.

A Dr. Siri Paiboun mystery ; [13]

ISBN 978-1-64129-064-7
eISBN 978-1-61695-941-8

1. Paiboun, Siri, Doctor (Fictitious character)—Fiction.
2. Coroners—Fiction. 3. Laos—Fiction.
4. Murder—Investigation—Fiction.
PR6053.O778 D66 2018 823'.914—dc23 2017055447

Printed in the United States of America

10 9 8 7 6 5 4 3 2 1

With my uneaten thanks to Brian W, Gordon C, Hanneke N, for their selfless efforts to protect the world's remaining wildlife. To David L, Lizzie S, Rachel, Bambina, Darouny, Dad, Kathy R, Ulli and Magnus, Kate and Bob, Leila S, Micky M, Shelly S, Susan P, and to my wife and best friend, Kyoko.

And, under pressure from the real think tank at Colinland, my long-overdue thanks to Sticky, Gogo, Beer, Psy, Nut, Nah, Chip and Pink and all their not-so-lucky brothers and sisters on the streets here in southern Thailand.

TABLE OF CONTENTS

CHAPTER ONE
Nineteen Eyes

This whole thing started and finished with her. She was in a crate. A compact coconut wood coffin with narrow slits for air. She'd screamed over and over to no avail. She'd tried to make sense of it. She'd counted the unblinking eyes. Nineteen of them. One eye too many or one too few, but nineteen by every reckoning. And even though there was no light beneath the thick tarpaulin those eyes glowed deep yellow like dying stars.

When she came around that last time she thought she was still in the nightmare and in a way she was. Her knees were tucked up tightly against her chest and there was no more than a shoebox of space at the foot of the crate, but the creatures—the nineteen-eyed creatures—had contracted somehow and packed themselves together so closely there would be no contact with her. Not yet. She could feel their hot breaths against her bare toes. She could hear the wheezing in their throats. But they stared at her, unmoving, waiting for her to lose consciousness again because it was inevitable she would. They would bide their time until she had no more fight in her. Then, and only then, they would devour her.

CHAPTER TWO
The Smugglers

Life sped by in Vientiane like a Volkswagen van on blocks. The streets were crusty with red dust, the uneven sidewalks sprouted half-hearted weeds, and the people neither smiled nor raised their voices for fear of drawing attention to themselves. You could never be sure who was listening. They all knew of someone who'd fled the country and at least one person who'd disappeared. Many had relatives in refugee camps on the Thai side of the border. Many more had ambitions or dreams or plans to join them but lacked the spunk.

This was year five of a socialist experiment that had failed the People's Democratic Republic of Laos in many ways. The Communist vessel was holed and on its way down. The rice collectives program had collapsed. Government workers went unpaid for months. And Thailand had once more closed its Mekhong border due to pissy spats over trespassing and accusations of insurgencies, and, never forget, good old historical animosity. The river guard patrols on both banks had been doubled, but it was a vast river and still the midnight rafts of smuggled Thai goods floated diagonally north on the current, crisscrossing disgruntled Lao heading south on their rubber inner tubes.

So it was a surprise to many on one humid night in August when two elderly Lao gentlemen were spotted paddling their bamboo raft in a northerly direction toward the country everyone wanted to leave. They were dressed in ninja black, but their grumbling and coughing destroyed any pretense of stealth. Between them was a balding cross-eyed hound and a mysterious large object wrapped in a nylon parachute. The latter was roughly the size and shape of a grenade launcher and would certainly have led to the old boys' being shot on sight if they were discovered. Smuggling weapons of war was not a wise pastime for men in their seventies.

"Did they not teach you to row?" asked Dr. Siri, the stockier of the two.

"I was a politician," Comrade Civilai replied. "They only taught us how to bail."

"Then that explains why we're going around in circles," said Siri.

The river ran high and fast at the end of the rains, and the current would have taken them far beyond Vientiane if they didn't lean into it with some enthusiasm. But paddling always appeared easier than it was, especially with a heavy cargo. From somewhere to the north they heard the crack of a river guard's rifle but no accompanying scream. Neither the rifles nor the men who bore them had any accuracy. The old boys were not intimidated by the sound because they knew how little chance there was of being hit.

"And going around in circles would aptly describe the direction of our policies these past five years," said Civilai, mostly to himself.

"Save your breath for a final push," said Siri. "There's our signal. We don't want to overshoot."

From the dense foliage ahead, two lights—one white, one red—flashed intermittently.

"My heart can't take this," said Comrade Civilai.

"Then rest your organs and put your back into it."

All at once they seemed to be surfing the current rather than fighting it. They gathered speed, charging toward the lights. Remarkably, they had timed their trajectory perfectly but not their velocity. Theirs was not a dignified landing. Ugly the dog, sensing danger, abandoned the vessel five meters from the bank and swam home. The corner of the raft snagged in a tree root so the vessel spun around and hit the bank at speed and in reverse. Dr. Siri was thrown to the deck. There was a loud thump when his head hit the bamboo, but his was a hard head. Civilai wasn't so lucky. He was jettisoned head first into the river mud where he sank immediately until only his legs were visible. To his credit he did not kick or wave them pathetically. They merely jutted heavenward like a victory sign. He was rescued by the reception committee. Mr. Geung and Madam Daeng took a leg each and yanked him out of the mire. He emerged with a slurping sound like a large snail being pulled reluctantly from its shell.

"Well that all worked out quite well," said Siri.

The next day, Chief Inspector Phosy arrived at Madam Daeng's noodle shop shortly after the morning rush. There were never enough stools to accommodate all the customers who traveled out of their way to eat the best homemade *feu* noodles in the country. Madam Daeng, never satisfied with shop-bought noodles, had taken to making her own beneath a corrugated tin roof behind the shop. Yet despite all the personal touches and time and effort the woman put into her dishes, and in the face of much criticism from her husband, she refused to increase the prices.

"The poor . . ." she would say, ". . . have as much right to eat food of quality as do the more advantaged."

Even the drivers of the black Zil limousines used by the senior Party members had to wait their turn to be served. Their bosses thought they might add a few extra kip as an incentive to jump the queue, but Madam Daeng would have nothing of it. Comrade Civilai often said that hers was the only example of functioning Communism in the republic. She replied that there was nothing political about it. She was just being fair.

"Is he in?" the chief inspector asked.

Madam Daeng saw a familiar scowl on his good-looking face. Since his promotion to chief inspector two months earlier, Phosy had discovered a lot to scowl about. Many members of the central committee considered him too young at forty-six to have been handed such responsibility. But Madam Daeng, twenty years his senior, knew there was nobody more qualified or able to take on the role. She left Mr. Geung to clean the noodle tubs and walked slowly over to the policeman.

"I'm very well, thank you, Chief Inspector," she said. "And you?"

Madam Daeng had been a freedom fighter in the clandestine war against the French imperialists, and she was well aware that she still intimidated even the most confident of men. In fact, her short shock of snow white hair and her piercing hazelnut-colored eyes gave her even more of an advantage. Phosy stood no chance.

"I'm sorry, Daeng," he said. "It just seems that your husband is intent on making my impossible job even more impossible."

"My goodness, what's he done now?" asked Daeng.

She poured the policeman a glass of iced tea and they sat at a table overlooking the river.

He sighed. "You know very well," he said.

"What kind of policeman would assume a wife knew every move her husband made?"

"One who knew she was an accomplice in a criminal act?"

They drank their sweet tea and watched Ugly the dog at the river's edge catching crabs.

"I'm offended," she said.

"You need to work on that inscrutability, Daeng. Not convincing at all."

"And what particular crime am I accused of accomplicing?"

"We'll start with smuggling."

"Oh, Phosy. Smuggling? Really? Twenty years ago that would have been called foraging. Nothing to eat in the village so you head off into the jungle and return with enough game to feed the family. Laos is being slowly starved to death by the Thai embargos, so it's only natural her inhabitants would forage."

"Foraging across a national border is called smuggling," said Phosy. "And if Siri had merely been paddling back from Si Chiang Mai with beans and roast pig I wouldn't be here."

"Then why are you here?"

"We have an eye-witness account of Dr. Siri and Comrade Civilai importing weapons."

She chuckled. "And what witness would that eye belong to?" she asked.

"I'm not at liberty to say."

"Of course you are. Until they get around to finishing the constitution we won't have any laws to speak of. Your liberty to say is arbitrary."

Phosy sipped his tea and followed the progress of a cloud. "A river guard," he said at last.

"A river guard saw Dr. Siri importing weapons?"

"Yes."

"Then why didn't he shoot him?"

"What?"

"Why didn't the river guard shoot Dr. Siri and his accomplices and be done with it?"

"It's delicate."

"Would it be because the river guards have splendid weapons produced in the Soviet Union but that for the past three months, due to some blip in the paperwork, none of them has been issued with ammunition? That in the event of seeing a suspicious craft on the river, our guards have been instructed to set dry bamboo tubes alight because that explosion makes a similar sound to the firing of a rifle and it may just discourage smugglers? The guards do however have marvelous flashlights and permission to shine the beam on suspicious objects. None so far has been silly enough to do such a thing. Thai smugglers are invariably armed and it would be suicidal. Therefore, no river guard on a cloudy night would have the faintest idea what Dr. Siri—if he even were to be on the river—might or might not be smuggling."

Phosy put down his glass. "He recognized all of you," he said. "He even identified the dog. He was in a tree not far from your reception committee. He's a regular customer here."

"Then he should be ashamed of himself," said Daeng. "What's become of loyalty to one's noodle shop?"

"Daeng . . ."

"We often go for a little paddle and a frolic of a night when it's too hot to sleep. Mistaken identity, no doubt. I'll have a word with him. What's his name?"

"Daeng."

"Yes?"

"What was on the raft?"

"There. That's the first thing the old Inspector Phosy would have asked. This new chief inspector's already tangled up in words."

"And if I had asked that question sooner I wouldn't have learned what classified information you have regarding our river guards, would I?"

"Damn, you got me."

"So?"

"So what?"

"So, what was on the raft?"

CHAPTER THREE
The Girl with the Meatless Skeleton

Vientiane was not Cannes. No wealthy European mogul ever planned to winter there. No international film star would establish a second home with a mistress there. Those few visitors from outside agreed it was a thoroughly boring place. The ghostly whitewashed colonial buildings stood stained and weather-beaten, but there was no budget to tear them down and rebuild. The morning market was so lacking in vitality that nobody bothered to call out their wares or invite shoppers to sample what few goods they had. Most families were at home and preparing for bed long before curfew. But that isn't to say it was a city free of crime or corruption. The Lao were poor and poor people are easily seduced.

It was one of the many problems new Chief Inspector Phosy had on his plate. He headed a police force of just over two thousand men, many of whom were hopeless. The women in the force were too few to raise the standards. A police academy had been established at Ban Donnoun, but the intake was largely uneducated, and there were dramatic problems with changing the mindset of the ex-guerilla soldiers who studied there. The lessons were conducted in Russian and Vietnamese with interpreters who hardly understood the material being taught. There were several hundred Vietnamese agents operating as security and surveillance personnel, but they were beyond the influence of the new chief inspector, and he certainly could not recruit them for his own purposes. Experienced Lao police officers in the field were based mostly in Vientiane and the surrounding districts. Those in remote provinces were hard to supervise and many were already laws unto themselves. As their Thai neighbors had demonstrated after many years of experience, being a police officer could be a most lucrative profession. And with the Lao monthly salary set at five dollars, it was hardly surprising Phosy dedicated much of his time to matters of graft.

Thai public officials owed allegiance to their king, which was an incentive to do their jobs well. But Laos had sent its monarch and his family to toil in a labor camp, and its citizens had fought one another for decades in the interminable civil war. With over forty ethnic groups corralled together by an intolerant French administration, modern Laos had yet to create a sense of national pride. And as there were not enough police uniforms to go around, many of Phosy's men still wore their military fatigues. The chief inspector was charged with the task of making his officers proud of uniforms they didn't yet have.

The sergeant who sat before him at the police tribunal that morning had been recruited by Phosy's predecessor, Oudomxai. Sergeant Wee was a cocky middle-aged man with what Nurse Dtui—the chief inspector's wife—referred to as a Jerry Lee Lewis hairstyle. She was a fanzine aficionado. Wee was one of the lucky ones who had been allotted a uniform, but he'd made certain alterations to it.

He had a gold braid hem on his short sleeves and meaningless metal air force wings on the pocket. His trousers were ironed to a paper cut crease and his boots were crocodile skin.

"Sergeant Wee," said Phosy, "do you know why you're here?"

"Yes, brother," said Wee.

"I'm not your brother, Sergeant."

"In a little country like this you can never be too sure," said the sergeant.

"Should I assume you'll be foregoing standard politeness and respect protocol for this tribunal?" Phosy asked.

Wee leaned back on his chair and linked his fingers behind his head. He looked one by one at the five senior policemen sitting opposite, trusted men handpicked by Phosy but unknown to the sergeant.

"Why pretend?" said Wee. "You're going to have me shot anyway. Might as well hang on to the last threads of dignity."

"Why should I have you shot?" asked Phosy.

"Oh, don't."

"Don't what?"

"Pretend this case isn't already ploughed and planted. You got a report from my captain. Every man in the unit signed it. I'm a goner."

"I have it here," said Phosy, flipping the pages on his clipboard. "You were part of an anti-corruption team set up by Chief Inspector Oudomxai. Why do you suppose you were selected to join that team, Comrade Wee?"

"I don't know."

"Yes you do. It was because your family's in the trafficking business."

"It was my uncle."

"Family's family. And they've been trafficking Lao labor to Thailand since before the takeover. Men to building sites. Girls to brothels. The men thought they'd be getting a living wage. But they arrive at the site, and they're informed they have to pay back the agency fee out of their salaries, so for six months they get nothing. Then they're fired. The girls thought they'd be working in hotels and restaurants so it comes as something of a shock when they're locked in rooms without windows and are forced to service a dozen men a day."

"Look," said Wee, "you know all this and I know, so why don't you just put on the black hood and get it over with?"

"Be patient, Comrade," said Phosy. "We're just getting to the interesting part. You were given a place on the trafficking team because, it says here, you suffered remorse over what your family—"

"Uncle."

". . . what your uncle had been involved in and you wanted to help clear out the trade. So you went south, all the way back to your hometown in Khammouan and you started to inform on the traffickers. But, according to this report, you were providing our team with false information. You were diverting our police away from the trafficking routes and implicating people who had nothing to do with the trade. Your uncle was never arrested because you tipped him off."

"What can I tell you?" said Wee. "Reports never lie."

"That's all you have to say?"

"Look, brother, I've been in this system long enough to know how it works."

"What did you think of your captain?"

"I'm sure he's kind to his grandchildren."

"Nothing else?"

Wee stared blankly into Phosy's eyes. "No," he said.

Phosy looked at his fellow officers and smiled then turned back to Wee. "What would you say if I told you your captain, Viseth, was downstairs in a cell?" he asked.

"Eh?"

"Captain Viseth is awaiting a tribunal of his own."

"What?" said Wee, baffled. "Why?"

"You know why. As soon as his team got down south he teamed up with your uncle and had his men run the traffic. They sent a nice little monthly stipend to Oudomxai here at police headquarters. I've disbanded the unit. All the others are up on charges. There was only one officer in the team who protested. Refused to be a part of it."

Wee's confident act crumbled and he slumped in his chair. "So, I'm not . . . ?"

"Going to be shot?" Phosy smiled. "Not by us. There may be some fashion unit that'll take objection to your dress sense, but I doubt they'll execute you."

"So, why am I here?"

"When you found out what your captain was up to you could have run or you could have joined him. But you didn't. You stuck around and tried to sort it all out by yourself. You put yourself in harm's way. You could have been killed. You're an honest man. That's why the captain made up the report about you. I want you to run your own unit. We've put together a team for you."

"Me?"

"Yeah. The traffickers are still operating. You've been around your uncle long enough to know how it all fits together. Start with him. We'll see how it goes."

"What would I be . . . I mean what can I do? We haven't got any laws."

"Just shut him down and bring him in to us," said Phosy. "We can classify his activities as anti-state; treason, something like that. And it's across borders so we can get him on all kinds of . . . look, I don't know. But we do have to make a big deal of it. We want all the other traffickers to see this example and know we're serious. So, we'll get him on something. Leave that to me."

Dr. Siri and Comrade Civilai sat in the room that had once hosted an illicit library on the second floor of Madam Daeng's noodle shop. There were no books now. They'd been destroyed in a fire. Victims of arson. Or perhaps they were victims of Dr. Siri's proximity to disaster. The old fellow attracted crises like ants to a greasy pork sausage. But, as they stared at the magnificent beast that stood in the center of the room they could both feel the moths of darkness fluttering out of their lives. Before them was a new beginning; the tadpole of a life they'd both dreamed of since their study days in Paris. Here was their passport to world domination.

"Perhaps we should have asked them for a manual," said the doctor.

"When procuring stolen goods one does not push one's luck," said Civilai.

The old boys were seated on a bench eating banana baguettes, just . . . ogling. They usually preferred to take their lunches down to the Mekhong and cast aspersions on the Thais opposite, but they had become fixated with their new toy. They had not yet dared twiddle with it. The dials and levers were daunting enough, but the potential it held was overwhelming.

"We'll work it out," said Civilai. "How hard can it be?"

"I'm told in California they have six-month courses in its operation," said Siri.

"And how could you possibly know that?"

"The dealer told me."

"He wasn't a dealer," said Civilai. "He was a crook. A common thief. He would know no more about this wonder than I know about space exploration."

"It is magnificent, isn't it?" said Siri.

Before them stood a hardly used Panavision Panaflex Gold movie camera with a super speed thirty-five millimeter lens on a genuine steel tripod. It had literally fallen off a truck during the filming of a Hollywood movie called *The Deer Hunter*. They'd seen the movie, of course, dubbed in Vietnamese in a café in Hanoi. The natives didn't come out of it too well, but Siri and Civilai had admired the film from a cinematic rather than a historical viewpoint. When the camera fell off the truck on a potholed road in the north of Thailand it had still been in its packing crate, so it wasn't damaged. The driver continued on his way oblivious to his loss. The locals who had witnessed this miraculous gift from the gods carried the crate into the village, disguised it with liana fronds and palm leaves and began the process of selling it. They were offering it for the very reasonable sum of a million dollars.

To their surprise, nobody in that impoverished province had a need for a cinema camera. The villagers toyed with putting an ad in the national newspapers but were afraid they'd be caught in their theft. The longer they went without a buyer, the lower the asking price dropped. It fell past half a million dollars, paused briefly at the two-hundred-thousand mark, then came to rest in the region of "make me an offer." Still nobody bit. A year went by, then two and the crate had become a village landmark. They fired rockets from it at the rain-making festival and burned candles on it for the Loi Gratong celebration—almost losing the whole thing in a fire.

But word of the village with a movie camera finally reached Nong Kai and the ear of No Nose Looi. Looi, among other things, was a travel agent and entrepreneur. Before fleeing his native Laos he'd been a fan of Madam Daeng's noodles and an admirer of Dr. Siri. He knew of the doctor's fascination with cinema and wondered whether he might be interested in making a film of his own. Madam Daeng had passed on the news rather casually to her husband whilst on the verge of sleep. Siri sat up like a spring lock.

"They've got a what?" he asked.

"A cinema camera," she said. "And twenty reels of film."

Siri hadn't slept a wink that night. He was too full of wonder. What a dream it would be to make a film of his own. He spooled through the unwritten screenplays in his mind, and at 3 A.M. he left his sleeping wife, climbed on his bicycle and with Ugly trotting beside him, he rode out to kilometer six and Civilai's house. He and the battery on his bicycle lamp were almost dead by the time he arrived. The old politburo man had taken some rousing, but once he was on his feet and responsive, it took absolutely no work at all to involve him in the venture.

A year earlier there had been an incident that resulted in the old boys coming into possession of some drug money. Quite a sum in fact. Siri had invested much of his in charitable acts while Civilai had smuggled in some delicious but rather expensive wines, a new lounge suite and a car—not new but classic. Yet still they had not completely used up their ill-gotten gains. In fact they had enough not only to buy the camera, but also, with a little budget tweaking, to produce a modest film of their own. As the thieves who had stolen the camera had received no other offers they reluctantly accepted two hundred dollars in cash and agreed to take it to the river on an agreed date and time. As the crate weighed more than the equipment, they removed the camera and wrapped it in an old parachute canopy. Getting it to the Lao side would be Siri's problem.

And there it was. Fifteen thousand dollars' worth of camera. Enough to keep a family of twelve fed for a decade. And twenty reels of film. Four hours of footage if they could get every take right the first time.

"How do we develop the film?" Civilai asked.

Siri laughed.

"Old Brother," he said, "on the eve of the race does the marathon runner worry about what drinks will be available at the winner's reception party? No. He takes one step at a time. First we need to put together a screenplay that is worthy of this beautiful camera."

"Couldn't that take a long time?" Civilai asked.

"Not necessarily. I already have one."

"What? You never told me that. Where is it?"

"Right here," said Siri, tapping the side of his temple with his index finger.

"There's room in there with all the ghosts?"

Admittedly there was a lot going on in Siri's head. To shorten a very long story, and through no fault of his own, Siri was possessed by a number of spirits. There was a dog in there for one, and Siri's dead mother who never spoke, and a number of soldiers he'd saved in battle but who had gone on to lose their lives regardless. There was Yeh Ming, a thousand-year-old Hmong shaman and, to Siri's chagrin, there was his spirit guide: a transvestite fortune-teller by the name of Auntie Bpoo. She was a cantankerous and thoroughly annoying presence but there was no getting rid of her. Siri was plagued by visitors from the other side and still he hadn't learned how to manage them.

"It's a different department," he said. "Screenplays come under "files—hyphen—genius.""

"Can't say I've ever associated you with order and organization," said Civilai. "What's it about?"

"Imagine this, if you will," said Siri drawing a rectangle in the air in front of him. "A Lao version of *War and Peace*. Not quite as long as the Bondarchuk production, which I believe topped the scale at four hundred and fifty minutes. More so the Audrey Hepburn version but without all that upper-class family relationship nonsense. We'll keep the heroic nationalism and the struggle against the French imperialists."

"Sounds a tad . . . ambitious."

"Not at all," said Siri. "You'd have to see it written down to appreciate it."

"And who do you have in mind to play the lead roles in this extravaganza?"

"We have a great tradition of storytelling in Laos," said Siri. "We just have to find the players and minstrels that wander the land and convert them to the big screen. We Lao are masters of pretense."

"You do know we don't have an infinite budget?" said Civilai.

"Ah, there you are as pessimistic as ever. Why do you think I've chosen *War and Peace* as our inaugural launch?"

"Because you have delusions of grandeur?"

"Because China has all but declared war on us and, as a result, the Soviets have become our best friends on the planet. They fund our military, equip our hospitals . . ."

". . . send us to the Olympics."

"What a junket that was. And how hard do you think it would be to secure funding from a vibrant Soviet art and culture community—especially as we'll be adapting one of their most beloved books."

"They'd throw money at us."

"An embarrassment of rubles."

"Siri, you're a devious man. How long will it take to transfer your head screenplay to paper?"

"What day is it?"

"Friday."

"Unless I'm distracted by the spirit world I could have a first draft down by Tuesday."

"Champion," said Civilai.

They finished their baguettes and washed them down with coconut water, smiling at their Panavision.

"I wish we had a manual," said Siri.

Chief Inspector Phosy had a wife and a daughter. It was his second attempt at building a home. His first family had taken advantage of one of his many absences to boat across the river and find passage to somewhere far away. He'd entered this second marriage to Dtui, a chubby nurse, with the confidence of a man who had failed miserably. Initially it had been a pragmatic arrangement. He'd slept with her and she'd fallen pregnant with their daughter, Malee. He'd agreed to marry her because, well, she was a friend and it was the decent thing to do. He hadn't expected to fall in love with the red-faced girl from the rural north, nor to adore their daughter. But both miracles had occurred. He'd only recently begun to tell his wife of his feelings although he had yet to find suitable language in which to wrap his thoughts. When he told her he loved her, even though the sentence left his mouth with the utmost sincerity, it always seemed to arrive like a "Have you eaten yet?" or an "It looks like it's going to be hot today."

"Have you eaten yet?" asked Dtui.

"Not actual food," said Phosy. It was eight in the evening and the earliest he'd arrived home all week. He found Nurse Dtui playing poker on the floor with Malee. Still they were staying in the police dormitory, twelve cell-like rooms and a shared bathroom. As the chief inspector, Phosy had the right to choose a dwelling more appropriate for his rank. His predecessor had moved into a two-story concrete house out by the Soviet hospital. He had a maid and a gardener and a security man who checked the credentials of visitors and opened and closed the remote-control gate. Eight of the twelve rooms had air-conditioning. Not a bad home for a man on fifteen dollars a month.

To Dtui's regret, Phosy had rejected the mansion and had decided to await the completion of a block of police apartments on the way to the airport. He was a man who led by example. Most of the lower ranks thought he was insane. He unbuttoned his stiff shirt and sat on the edge of the bed.

"You don't think it's a bit soon to be teaching her to gamble?" he asked.

Their daughter stood to hug him without letting go of her cards then returned to the game.

"It's lucky we aren't playing for money," said Dtui. "She's cleaning me out."

With the closing of the morgue at Mahosot Hospital, Dtui had been transferred to the old Lido Hotel, currently a nursing college. She was teaching basic everything to country girls for whom "basic" was "advanced."

"Lose any students today?" Phosy asked.

The previous day a girl had fainted at the sight of a liter of blood in a bottle. She was three months away from graduation. Dtui had suggested to the college director that the lass was probably better suited to growing turnips. As ever, the director shuffled the false teeth around inside his mouth with his tongue and reminded her there was a drastic shortage of nurses in the country.

"I had a girl suture her finger to a patient's leg wound this morning," said Dtui.

"I hope they'll be very happy together," said Phosy.

Malee put down a seven, an ace and a three. "Three crocodiles," she said.

"Two elephants," said Dtui, putting down a pair of queens.

Malee laughed and picked up all the cards.

"You do know you're only two years old?" said Phosy.

"Yes," said Malee, shuffling the deck.

"When did she learn 'crocodiles'?" Phosy asked.

"She just soaks it all up," said Dtui. "There's no stopping her. She tied a shoelace today."

"I couldn't tie shoe laces till I was twenty-seven," said her husband.

"That's 'cause you were running barefoot through the jungle till then."

"Bed," said Malee.

"Okay," said Dtui.

Their daughter kissed them both, crawled onto the bed roll and was asleep almost immediately. She gave a little burp to signal the fact she'd shut down for the night. They sat watching her sleep.

"She was just waiting for you to come home," said Dtui. "The nights are getting later."

"The new job's getting heavier," said her husband. "With all the paperwork and formalities, I hardly have time for police duties. Yesterday morning they sent me off on a wild goose chase to the airport to welcome the Cambodian police chief. Even gave me a bunch of flowers to give him. Of course, he wasn't on the flight."

"So, where are my flowers?"

"Sorry, I didn't have time for breakfast."

"You ate my flowers? Where's the romance in our relationship?"

"Are you free tomorrow afternoon?"

"A date?"

"Sort of. I'd like you to do an autopsy for me."

"Passion comes in so many disguises."

"I tried to talk Dr. Siri out of retirement, but he wasn't interested," said Phosy. "He said there was no need to recruit him because I'm living with the best forensic detective in the country."

"An unqualified one," said Dtui. "I'm just a glorified lab assistant."

"We all know you're more than that. If it wasn't for me and motherhood you'd be on your second year of forensic pathology in the Soviet Union."

"I wasn't that interested."

"You spent a year learning Russian medical terms."

"Hobby."

"Okay," said Phosy. "Then I'll get Dr. Mot to do it."

"Okay."

"Okay."

They sat cross-legged on the plastic carpet. There was the buzz of conversations from the neighboring rooms. Dtui corrected homework. Phosy took files from his briefcase and browsed until he felt his wife's eyes on him.

"You'd really get Dr. Mot to agree to do this autopsy?" she asked.

"No choice," said Phosy.

"He did three weeks of pathology in East Germany," said Dtui. "He didn't even spot a hand grenade sewn into some poor bugger's insides."

"We make the most of what we have available," said Phosy. It had become a tired mantra in the People's Democratic Republic.

There was silence inside the room again apart from the purring of Malee in sleep.

"What's the case?" asked Dtui.

"No, it's all right," he said. "Dr. Mot will—"

She climbed on his back and wrestled him to the ground. "Tell me, or I'll rip your arm out of its socket," she said, holding her pen to his ear.

"All right. Put the pen down and we'll talk."

She tossed the pen but stayed on top of him.

"It's a skeleton," he said.

"Oh well, that counts me out right away," said Dtui. "I don't know a thing about bones."

"Siri said you do."

"I might be able to identify knife and gun wounds on them but none of that age, height, origin, historical stuff."

"Nothing historical," said Phosy, crawling out from under her. "It's quite recent in fact. There are even parts still attached."

"What sort of parts?"

"Ligaments, tendons, hair. The ligaments are holding a lot of the skeleton together."

"What sort of hair?"

"Long. Very long. Black. Even if the Party hadn't forbidden men from wearing their hair long it's clearly female."

Dtui looked at her daughter.

"Any clothes?" she asked.

"None at all."

"Where did you find it?"

"At the base of the Anusawari Victory Arch. Four o'clock this morning."

"No cover? No note? No witnesses?"

"Not a lot of action at four A.M.," said Phosy. "Still curfew hours. One of the night patrols noticed it when they were passing. All they saw was the skeleton propped up against a wall."

"But if she was delivered there must have been a car or a truck. There's so little traffic on the road someone must have heard an engine. Some insomniac might have seen it pass."

"Nobody we've found so far. We're interviewing."

"And why would they put it at the arch?" Dtui asked. "Do you think—"

Malee called her mother but it was from the depths of her subconscious and she was soon back in her dreamland.

"Do you think it was symbolic?" Dtui asked. "They were trying to make a point? Something political?"

"They certainly wanted it seen," said Phosy. "There's one electric light bulb at the foot of the arch and she was sitting there in the lamplight. But right now, all we have is the body. So, I'd really like it if you could take a look and see if there's anything that might tell us who she is."

"Phosy, something terrible's happened to this girl."

"I know. And we'll find whoever did it to her."

"Where is she?"

"In the freezer at the morgue. We put the power back on this afternoon."

"I'll need help."

"Madam Daeng's given Mr. Geung the weekend off. And I've cleared it with the hospital director. You can take as long as you want."

"I wish I were more qualified."

"You'll do a good job. You always do."

Dtui arrived at the Mahosot morgue on Sunday afternoon. Dr. Siri's WELCOME mat still greeted visitors, and Mr. Geung had been there all morning sweeping and mopping. Geung had been the cornerstone of the morgue in its heyday. He'd carried corpses with respect, he'd cut them open and sewn them back together. He'd weighed the internal organs and put all the fluids in plastic bags—all the time talking to the spirits who'd stuck around to make sure their old bodies were being well taken care of. Siri often wondered whether this paranormal chitchat might be his fault in some way. Had he tuned the young man in to the wavelength or had Geung always carried the gift? One thing for certain was that as their relationship progressed, Mr. Geung's awareness of that other dimension strengthened. Those outside the loop assumed the lab assistant was talking to himself, perhaps an offshoot of his condition.

"Those Down syndrome folk are a weird mob," Civilai would say.

Like Dr. Siri, Mr. Geung usually preferred to keep the secret to himself. But on this day in the morgue, there was a premonition Mr. Geung needed to get off his chest.

"Any guests today?" called Nurse Dtui as she entered the cutting room. It was a long-standing joke question that never failed to tickle Mr. Geung.

"One g-g-g-guest in room one," said Geung.

The skeleton lay in front of him on the zinc table. Her hair lay to one side of her scalp as if she hadn't had time to fix it before the coroner arrived. The bones were a yellow grey, not the blanched white of a skeleton left in the sun. Tufts of tendons and ligaments clung to the joints. There was no skin on her face and most of her fingers and toes were missing. Those remaining had no nails. The deterioration was in its early stages, yet there was no flesh. How had the woman's meat been so completely removed from her bones?

"How are you, Geung?" Dtui asked, checking through the equipment.

"I'm f-fine," he said, "and you?"

"Sparkling," said Dtui, eliciting another laugh from her friend. "And how's Tukta?"

Mr. Geung went silent, which was unlike him. He was usually delighted to discuss his Down syndrome lady friend. He and Tukta had been working at the hospital: he in the morgue, she in the canteen. At first they'd resented each other for being more competent, more popular, more . . . Down's. But chemistry had triumphed and they'd formed a union based entirely on love. It was possible neither was completely sure what that word meant but, as Siri told him, none of us really is.

"I need to t-talk to you," said Geung.

"About Tukta?"

"Yes."

"Is there a problem?"

"Work first," said Geung who didn't like to keep a body waiting.

So Dtui went to work. It wasn't the type of autopsy she'd ever been a part of. There wasn't much left to allow her to follow procedures. All she had was a basic structure in front of her. The scalp was intact, connected to a lock of well-cared-for ebony-black hair. Dtui could smell sweet coconut oil on it. Some mothers applied oil to their daughters' hair as soon as it started to grow. The hair hung loose. There was no rubber band or hair tie to enable her to work without the hair getting in her eyes. Perhaps it was lost.

The bones and tendons fascinated her. If the flesh had been cut from the body as one of Phosy's colleagues suggested, there would have been numerous knife tracks. Not even the most competent butcher could cut meat from a bone without scoring it here and there. But the marks on the bones and tendons were neither regimented nor neat. They didn't suggest any order. There was no evidence of slicing or sawing. The marks on the bones were abstract, random, chaotic puncture marks and scratches. To her mind, it looked more like a frenzied attack than calculated butchery.

There was a peculiar chemical scent emanating from the corpse. It was a confusing smell, as if two conflicting odors were competing for her attention.

"What do you smell here?" she asked Geung.

"Insect spray," he said as if he'd been waiting for the question.

"That's it," said Dtui. "And that explains something that's been worrying me. There's no evidence of insect damage, no maggots. She spent at least one night out in the open. But why would anyone go to the trouble of spraying a dead body?"

Once she'd isolated the scent of the repellent the second scent became recognizable. It was disinfectant. Not so obvious as to suggest that the body had been washed in it but clearly the skeleton had been in contact with a strong disinfectant.

She used Siri's old magnifying glass to examine the marks on the bones in detail. She looked especially at stains and dark deposits here and there. She leaned close and smelled them, attempting to isolate those scents from the chemicals. And after half an hour she was confident there was only one explanation for the state of the corpse. It was impossible for her to say whether it was a pre- or postmortem act, but the lady with the nice hair had apparently been eaten by animals. It was an awful thought.

"Any communication with the spirit?" Dtui asked.

"It's all hi-hi-higgledy piggledy," said Mr. Geung.

"Really? Care to explain that?"

"No."

"Fair enough. I suppose we should put her back in the freezer, don't you?"

They were carrying the skeleton on a flattened cardboard box used like a stretcher when Dtui remembered Mr. Geung's request.

"Would you like to talk about Tukta now?" she asked.

"No."

"Awful lot of no's today, Geung."

"I . . . I'm higgledy piggledy too," he said and that was the end of it.

"Animals?" said Chief Inspector Phosy. "What type of animals?"

"Small ones I'd guess," said Dtui.

It was supper time and the smell of instant noodles stalked the police dormitory corridor like an unpopular cousin. With the markets almost empty and salaries unpaid for three months, the officers in Dormitory 3 and their families had to live on non-perishable stock and vegetables they grew themselves. Those with nets caught fish. Those with slingshots knocked shrews from the trees. Poor people off in the countryside ate better than city dwellers.

"You mean like mice?" said Phosy.

"No, bigger," said Dtui. "Perhaps cats."

"Our victim was eaten by cats?"

"Something about that size, yes."

"We don't see a lot of cat packs roaming the streets of the capital," said Phosy.

"I know. It's odd. I went to take a look at the base of the monument. I'm sure she wasn't attacked there. The crime scene would have been a bloodbath."

Malee was already asleep inside and her parents sat outside the window of their room in a small vegetable garden. It was cooler there. They burned lemon eucalyptus oil to keep off the late-evening mosquitoes. The sky was an inky ocean speckled with stars.

"What I can't understand is why anyone would bother to transport the body," said Dtui.

"I'm assuming it was to draw attention away from the actual location," said Phosy.

"But they clearly wanted it to be found," said Dtui.

"And that's another mystery," said her husband. "There is no end of places to dump a body. If they had just wanted to get rid of it, they could have buried it out in the jungle somewhere. They could have cremated it in the kiln at some deserted temple."

"They could have put it on a chair after a Party seminar," came a voice.

They looked up to see Siri standing inside their room looking out through the window.

"And we'd all assume she'd died of boredom," he continued.

"Who let you in?" asked Phosy.

"Security is virtually non-existent here," said Siri.

"Evening, doc," said Dtui.

At that point, Ugly arrived through the thick grass that surrounded the allotment. He'd follow his master anywhere as long as it was outside. For some reason, he was petrified of buildings. He accepted a single head pat from Dtui and lay beneath the window. Siri sat on the sill.

"I knew you wouldn't be able to keep your nose out of this one," said Phosy.

"Just curious," said Siri.

Dtui gave him a summary of her findings and suspicions from the autopsy, and Phosy added the loose ends he'd been unable to tie thus far. Nobody had reported a missing friend or relative in Vientiane. It would be a few weeks before he'd receive any such reports from the provinces.

"My estimate is that she's been dead for less than a week," said Dtui. "Probably three or four days."

"And in that time I've had no reports of wild animal packs roaming the city," said Phosy.

"I have to admit I do enjoy a mystery," said Siri.

"Good, then you can help us solve it," said Phosy.

"No need," said Siri. "The most competent couple in the county is already on the case."

He climbed down from the window sill and started off through the vegetable garden with Ugly at his heel. But then he stopped suddenly and the dog walked into him. His eyes weren't so good.

"There is one thing," said the doctor.

"What?" Phosy asked.

"Well, I'm sure you've considered this already, but the patrols said they didn't see anything out of place after the curfew."

"That's right."

"Then we'd probably be looking for something that wasn't out of place."

"What do you mean?" asked Dtui.

"Unless the skeleton was delivered on foot, which is unlikely, there had to be a vehicle of some kind. We have so few cars on the roads anything that wasn't supposed to be there would have stood out like a goiter. But you said the earlier patrol saw nothing when they circled the arch."

"The boys doing the patrols aren't always totally reliable," said Phosy. "But whoever put the skeleton there found the only functioning light bulb. The patrols couldn't possibly have missed it."

"Assuming they actually did the patrol as they were supposed to," said Siri.

"They have control boxes all through the route," said Phosy. "They have to log in at ten locations. They merely drop a printed card with their names on it into a slit in the top of a box. They're encouraged not to go from one to ten in order. That way nobody knows where they'll be at what time. I checked. They logged in at all ten boxes. One of those boxes is opposite the arch. One unit passed there at three-fifteen. They did the rounds they were supposed to. A different unit found the body."

"Then the body was delivered sometime between three-fifteen and four," said Siri. "The driver of the delivery vehicle couldn't possibly have known exactly what time the patrol would pass the arch. So, there was a strong possibility he would have been spotted. But he didn't care. That can only mean one of two things. Either he was extremely daring . . ."

"Or he was in a vehicle the guards expected to see," said Phosy.

"And as private cars are not permitted on the streets after curfew, our delivery man had to be in a government or military vehicle," said Dtui.

"Or, on special occasions, an embassy vehicle," said Phosy. "We also have a dozen assorted cars, old trucks and jeeps in our car park at police HQ. I have a man watching them overnight. I didn't assign anyone a vehicle that night."

"Are the patrol units required to record any government vehicles they see on their route?" Siri asked.

"No," said Phosy. "They're just there to scare people back into their beds."

"Then I think a meeting is called for to test their memories of the night of the skeleton," said Siri.

"It's astonishing," said Civilai.

"Thank you," said Siri.

"I mean I'd never have known you had it in you. I wasn't even aware you could write. In all these years, I can't say I've ever seen you put a pen on paper before. Thought you were illiterate. Yet here you are with a grammatically correct, well-spelled rather splendid work of literature."

Siri and Civilai were sitting on a log on the bank of the river in front of Daeng's shop. They were eating baguettes and drinking pomegranate juice and Siri had been forced to keep his mouth shut for two hours while Civilai read the screenplay.

"Did you copy it from someone?" Civilai asked.

"Copy it?" said Siri, offended. "How many other Lao do you know with the ability to put together a full-length screenplay?"

"It's truly wonderful," Civilai gushed on. "And what a storyline. Two visionaries, not unlike our young selves set off in search of truth and enlightenment. We . . . I mean, *they* travel the world, get an education, meet brother Ho Chi Minh in Paris, become Communists and come home to their beloved country to drive out the usurpers and help establish a republic that is fair and prosperous."

"Plus sex and a little violence," Siri added.

"Unavoidable," said Civilai. "If only we could get Rata-naporn Intarakamhaeng to play the part of Madame Daeng."

"Civilai, there is no Madame Daeng in this movie. And, even if there was we won't be bringing in a Thai movie star to play the part."

"But the brassy young girl freedom fighter who selflessly gives her all for the revolution?"

"The character's name is Saylee."

"I know that, but of course she's based on Daeng. We're

all in it. You can't deny that. You've compressed our lives into one hundred and twenty minutes and resisted the Hollywood urge to give it a happy ending."

"Yes, I'm sorry I killed you," said Siri.

"I deserved it," said Civilai. "And I'd sooner go on the silver screen than in a government nursing hospice. Just think how many lovely young girls will be crying into their handkerchiefs as they watch me take my last breath. My character's amazing. All the characters are."

"You don't think the not Dr. Siri character is a little too—I don't know—too Kung Fu?"

"Oh, Siri. It's 1980. Cinema goers expect a bit of violence. There are no limits. We can do what we want. But . . ."

"But what?"

"There is one issue we might have a little problem with."

"What's that?" Siri asked.

"Well, is there any way we can shoot the entire movie inside?"

"Inside what?"

"Inside—the opposite of outside."

"Civilai, this is thirty years of revolution we're talking about. Famous land battles. French invasions. American bombing. And how can we make a Lao movie without footage of the Plain of Jars, of That Luang monument, of the caves of Houaphan? We don't even have a studio. Should we make our entire movie in a bathroom? The water trough doubling as the mighty Mekhong? Little paper boats in a Thai armada?"

Civilai looked disturbed. "It's just . . ." he said.

"What?"

"The Ministry of Culture."

"What about it?"

"If we're in the open air shooting a movie, somebody's going to spot us and report it. You can't disguise a full-size film camera."

"So what are you telling me?" said Siri.

"We need permission to make the movie."

"We need permission to sell a pig. There are ways around it. I know people in these ministries."

"Yes, and they don't like you."

"That's not true. Not all of them."

"Siri, you've antagonized every head of department in every ministry and government office. Everyone above a clerk grade-two level."

Siri sulked for a while. "I have a lot of friends in grade one," he said.

"That's true, you do," said Civilai. "And sellers in the market, and street cleaners, and vagabonds. But none of them will give you a license to make a movie."

"You're ex-politburo," said Siri. "You must still have some influence."

"All the people I used to know at the Ministry of Culture are dead."

"Culture's a dangerous business," said Siri.

"Actually, they died of old age and boredom. That whole generation of autocrats is fading out. Now everything's decided by committee."

"Then that's perfect," said Siri. "We'll just put in our request and as soon as it gets bogged there in the slush of committee formalities we'll start shooting. By the time they get around to it we'll be in post-production. Don't worry, older brother. I know how these things work. Bureaucracy has its good points."

◙ ◙ ◙

That afternoon, Madam Daeng typed up a very vague request to make a film and Siri went off on his bicycle to deliver the document with Ugly trotting alongside him. He parked in front of the flaky-walled single-story building that currently housed the Ministry of Sport, Information and Culture. Ugly watched the bicycle. Upon entering the building, Siri deliberately turned onto the Sports wing, found nobody in the clerical office and buried his request under a very tall stack of documents. He'd done his duty. One day in the future they would find his request, and they'd know he'd followed the rules. The error would be entirely that of the ministry.

So, it surprised all of them when Siri came downstairs the next morning to find a slightly built man in a Boy Scout uniform standing in front of the noodle shop.

"What's he doing there?" Siri asked Daeng.

"He's waiting for you," said Daeng.

"Is he a time traveler?"

Daeng thought about the question. "No, I give up," she said. "Why would he be a time traveler?"

"The Boy Scout movement was disbanded in '75," said Siri. "'Bourgeois, decadent elitist cronyism,' they called it. Where's he from?"

"Culture."

"What?"

"You did bury the request deep?"

"As dirt."

"Then it's probably just a coincidence," said Daeng. "Good luck."

She went off to deliver her tray of noodles leaving her husband in limbo. The Boy Scout man turned to look at him and gave a salute that looked like something from the Hitler Youth Movement. Siri shrugged and went to meet him.

"You wanted to see me?" said Siri.

"Comrade Phooi from the Ministry of Culture," said the man, holding out a hand for Siri to shake.

Siri could not resist asking about the uniform. "I thought we'd banished the Scouts," he said.

"Scouts?" said Phooi. "Yes, most certainly we have. This is the new uniform of the Socialist Youth Movement."

"Looks like a scout uniform to me," said Siri. "Have a lot left over from the old regime, do you?"

"Perhaps a similar color," said the man. "But you'll notice the scarf is red and the only badge is the portrait of our esteemed prime minister."

"My mistake," said Siri. "What can I do for you?"

"I'm here about your request to make a film," he said.

Siri's teeth shuddered. "I didn't expect you to get back to me so soon," he said. "I thought there'd be a discussion and meetings."

"Usually there are," said Phooi, "but they're usually of a more academic nature. We don't have a lot of actual projects to discuss. In fact, your proposal is the first we've seen for quite some time."

"Marvelous," said Siri, feeling everything but. "So, do we have permission?"

"Ah, Comrade Siri. Would that it were so simple. Now don't get me wrong. We're excited, really we are. The thought of producing a feature length film about Lao history and its latter-day awakening to the dawn of socialism would be a dream come true. What a dream, Comrade."

"Then you think we can do it," said Siri. He could feel the quicksand of bureaucracy dragging him down to reality.

"Oh, I hope so, Comrade Siri. I really do. All we need is to approve the screenplay."

"You need to what?" said Siri.

"Don't worry, Comrade Siri," said Phooi. "It's purely routine. We'll have a small group of experts browse through the—"

"Experts in what?" Siri asked.

"I'm sorry?"

Siri knew there were no experts in his country. Anyone with a claim to being an expert in any field had long since left for the camps on the Thai side and was already running a grocery shop in Cabramatta. Any scholars from the old regime who chose to stay would be keeping a low profile.

"I'm just curious as to the qualifications of the experts who would be assessing the appropriateness of my work," said Siri.

Siri had raised his voice and Daeng could tell he was about to undergo another bureaucratic meltdown. She whispered something to Mr. Geung and went to the aid of her husband.

"Are you sure you wouldn't like to sit with us and enjoy some noodles?" she asked Phooi.

He ignored her and addressed Siri. "As you know," he said, "all of the output of our ministry, whether fictional or non-fictional is directed by the minds of Comrade Marx and Comrade Lenin. They taught us the truths and our film should reflect those truths."

"Our film?" said Siri.

"Perhaps a glass of ice tea?" said Daeng.

"Of course," said Phooi. "There are no individuals. A work of art is a creation not of one person but of the society that molds that person. So perhaps you'd be kind enough to give me a copy of the screenplay?"

Daeng looked into the face of her overly flushed husband. Were he a tea kettle he would have been a few seconds from popping his rivets. It was exactly the moment when a man needed a wife.

"I would not . . ." Siri began.

"The doctor would not expect for one second to make a film without the guidance of brothers Marx and Lenin," she said and took her husband's hand. From a distance it might have seemed to be an intimate gesture but Madame Daeng had a grip that could grind gravel to dust. Siri let out a small yelp.

"So," she continued, "I've taken the liberty of having my worker put a copy of my husband's script under the seat of your motor scooter."

She nodded in the direction of the scooter where Mr. Geung was in the process of lowering the seat. He gave a thumbs up sign. Siri's eyes were watering.

"I do hope you'll like it," said Daeng.

"I am excited beyond words," said Phooi, and he jogged back to his scooter.

CHAPTER FOUR
Curfew

"Don't tell me," said Siri. "Let me guess. It has something to do with air-conditioning."

"I have no idea to what you are referring," said Auntie Bpoo.

She was wrapped warmly in a beautiful white polar bear skin. The head and claws were still attached so there was no doubt about the origin of the fur. The head hung behind like a hood. Siri was wearing a Moscow Olympic T-shirt and his undershorts. He'd worn them to bed not expecting to be thrust into an arctic blizzard. He had to shout to be heard.

"We both know these dreams are symbolic," Siri yelled.

"Have I not explained to you the difference between dreams and disappearances?" said Bpoo.

"You have," said Siri. "It's just that I usually enter this state when I'm asleep and leave it when I wake up. There are those who might see that as a dream, better still a nightmare."

There was one real difference between Siri's dreams and his disappearances. During the latter he could only be in one place or the other. When he was with Auntie Bpoo he could not be with Madam Daeng. His wife awoke often to find his side of the bed warm but empty. All she could do was await his return with stories from "over there." Every now and then he'd leave her in broad daylight. She'd turn to him at the market and there'd be nothing but a shopping basket on the ground. She'd be beside him at a cultural event and have to fight to keep others from taking his seat. Woe betide he should return to the lap of an unsuspecting music lover. And there she was, 3 A.M. and alone. It wasn't even legal grounds for divorce. But she had no intention of leaving her husband. He was the only man she'd ever loved; warts and all.

They'd talked about it of course. They wondered whether they were merely senile. Whether Siri imagined he had a spirit life and Daeng, due to poor eyesight, could not see her husband who was clearly there beside her. Only Siri was witness to the tail that Madam Daeng had grown in return for a cure for her rheumatism. Did that mean it didn't exist? Were they both mad? And, after a while, they concluded that they didn't care. Their ridiculous life was a constant joy. Every elderly person deserved a period of insanity to combat the boredom of decay.

Siri had known Auntie Bpoo when she was alive and he hadn't liked her any better then. He hadn't selected her as a spirit guide. She was an uncalled-for interloper. Siri had only recently learned of his ancestral connections to the spirit world, and it had been only a matter of months since he'd learned how to communicate directly with his supernatural lodgers. He had no choice but to speak to them through Bpoo, the least convincing transvestite ever to cross over to the other side. And she made even less of an effort to take care of herself in the afterlife. On this occasion she sported three-centimeter-long false eyelashes and a ten-day-old beard.

"Are you going to tell me what all this damned snow is about?" Siri asked. "You've been dragging me through snow drifts and skating me across frozen lakes ever since I got back from Moscow. Everything's white here. I need variety in my symbolism. If I'm supposed to learn anything during this particular stage of my training, I'll need a little more color."

"What about a poem instead?" said Bpoo.

"No. No, not that. Not another poem. They're meaningless. You're a terrible poet."

But the scream of the blizzard drowned out his words.

Daeng heard an icy tinkling sound and a chill sped through her veins, and there beside her was her husband with icicles on his bushy white eyebrows.

"I think I-I-I urgently need warming up," he said.

She wrapped herself around him as best she could and felt for signs of frostbite in his extremities.

"You aren't cold at all," she said.

"Not physically," he confessed.

"Did she have you back in the snow?" Daeng asked.

She knew that a successful marriage was one in which couples shared all their supposed supernatural experiences.

"I don't get it," said Siri. "She runs the inside of my head like a military training academy. I pass one test and she gives me another. This whole snow scenario has been going on for a month. She just sits there looking at me. Waiting for me to have an epiphany. I try to bait her with insults but she doesn't budge."

"No clues?"

"Usually not, but today I got a poem."

"Oh, no."

"Yes. She wrote it in the snow in urine."

"You poor man."

"All those hours I've spent trying to decipher her poetry. I thought there might be subliminal messages but keep coming back to the conclusion she's just a lousy poet. Her latest has that same *je ne sais quoi* about it. He retold it in his most dramatic voice.

They roamed the earth
Birth, death, dignified
And if they died
There was a fitter beast survived
Then comes us
No fuss. We shot and trapped and knifed.
Bereft
Except for those behind bars.

"Sounds serious," said Daeng. "Did she give you a hint as to who 'they' might be?"

"I don't give them much hope whoever they are," said Siri. "I asked her, 'Can't we just forget the snow and move on to the next test? Put me down for an *F* for this class, and I'll make it up in the next.' She said before I walk on I have to learn how to see."

"It must be beautiful though, all that snow," said Daeng.

"You'll see it one day, Daeng. We'll go skiing in Switzerland on the proceeds from my first movie."

"That would be nice," said Daeng.

"You know what?" said Siri. "I think the feeling is returning to the nerves in my extremities."

"It would appear so," said Daeng.

◙ ◙ ◙

"I'm sorry to drag you out of your beds so early," said Chief Inspector Phosy, "but I need your collective memories of the night we found the skeleton at the Anusawari Arch."

He was speaking to fourteen young men the military referred to as failed cadets. They'd applied for military service but been rejected on various grounds: poor eyesight, non-symmetrical limbs, weight issues, and so on. But they'd been given a second chance to prove their worth. If they could excel as curfew patrollers they would be reconsidered for an army posting.

For thirty years anyone with functioning legs had been accepted into whichever army unit they applied to. The royalists had put US-funded weapons into their hands and prodded them northeast to fight the Communists. The Pathet Lao had put Chinese and Soviet weapons into their hands and prodded them south to fight the corrupt drug lords in royalist uniforms. But peace had led to a trimming down of personnel to fit the budget and now young men and women had to apply and be trained.

Phosy stared at the sorry-looking but enthusiastic group in front of him. Each unit comprised two boys on a motorcycle with the pillion rider holding a gun that was not necessarily loaded.

"Comrades," he said, "you know why you're here. A terrible thing happened that morning so I want you to think back to everything you can recall, no matter how irrelevant you think it might be. Just spill it out."

A young man with half a mustache put up his hand. Phosy nodded.

"I had to stop our motorcycle in front of the Lane Xang

Hotel at about one P.M.," he said. "My ma had made us stew and it had frogs in it. I hate frogs. I threw up half a dozen of the little bastards in the flower beds."

"And that's as good an irrelevant start as any," said Phosy.

And it seemed to set the trend for the next hour. Young people had been caught on the river bank pursuing some nooky-like activities. One unit calmed down an old couple fighting with meat cleavers in front of their shop house. They all reported some crazy Indian running naked across their paths, but it was such a common event they'd learned to ignore it. When it came to vehicles there had been a couple of army jeeps and one old camouflaged military truck with a slipping cam shaft belt early in the morning sometime after 3 A.M. There was one embassy car with a coat of arms on the front but the boys didn't recognize the country code on the diplomatic plates. That had been around 2 A.M. But by far the most common road users after curfew were those in black Zils—the official vehicles of the government. There had been seven curfew units out on the night and morning of the skeleton and all of them had seen at least two Zils apiece. There had clearly been some late official function that night.

"I always assume they're out on some matter of national importance," said one young patrolman. He was describing his encounter with a Zil very early in the morning. "We leave them alone. But that morning it was all I could do to get out of the way of this one limo. We weren't even safe on the pavement. It drove right off the road and almost hit a wall. The window at the back rolled down a crack and someone yelled for us to get out of the way. I have no idea what he was playing at. Maybe the steering went."

"Any idea what time that was?" Phosy asked.

"We started our patrol at two A.M. so that must have been about two-fifty A.M." said the boy.

Two other units had seen a Zil driving slowly through the southern suburbs and the sleepy downtown area, zigging and zagging as if the driver were drunk. As nobody dared take down the number there could have been more than one erratic limo driver that morning but Phosy doubted it. And even if it had been an official limousine that delivered their Jane Doe, nobody, not even the boys on the curfew patrol, would report such a thing. Privilege set its own rules. Phosy knew he had to talk to the Zil drivers directly in an informal setting and he knew the very place.

Nurse Dtui had agreed to meet Mr. Geung at a café behind the morning market. He didn't drink coffee. He said it made him hyperactive and stupid. But in his own way he appreciated the tradition of clandestine meetings in coffee houses and Dtui was eager to hear her friend's important news. She'd been running through the possibilities in her mind ever since the aborted disclosure in the morgue.

He was there at a shadowy rear table when she arrived. He was wearing sunglasses so she was sure he couldn't see much. He certainly couldn't recognize her against the glare from the street.

"May I sit here?" she asked.

"No . . . it's f-f-f . . ." he began, then lowered his shades to the end of his nose.

"Dtui?" he said.

"That's me."

The rusty metal stool squeaked when she sat on it. The

vinyl covered tabletop was a map of decades of coffee rings, and there were daddy longlegs dangling above them like paratroopers ready to drop. Dtui raised a finger to the girl at the coffee trolley. The girl knew her. Most people knew most people in Vientiane.

"You bring me to the loveliest places," said Dtui.

"It's pr-private," he said.

They waited for her chewy brown coffee to arrive and for Dtui to churn the condensed milk around in it. She had a taste for it, but she agreed it was like drinking sweet sump oil.

"Go!" she said.

His stammer was more pronounced than usual.

"I . . ." He couldn't get out a second word.

"I have to go to work in half an hour," she said.

"I'm . . ."

"Yes?"

"I'm going to b-b-b-be a . . . a . . . a daddy."

Despite the heat of the coffee, the glass froze against Dtui's bottom lip. Her eyebrows clambered up her forehead.

"What?" she said.

"I . . . Mr. Geung . . . am g-g-going to be a daddy."

He looked so proud of himself Dtui didn't know how to begin with her many questions and observations. She knew she should take it all slowly.

"Why do you think so?" she asked.

"Eh?"

"Why do you think you're going to be a daddy?"

"I . . . I . . . I put my penis in—"

"That much I guessed," said the nurse.

Her coffee was too hot, but she drank it anyway and put up her finger for a second cup.

"My first question is . . ." she searched for something simple to begin with, "when did you start?"

"Start what?"

"Start to put . . . to have sex with Tukta?"

"The second," he said.

"The second? Of this month?"

"Yes."

Dtui smiled. "Then you can't possibly know," she said.

"I . . . I know," said Geung.

"Darling, we've talked about this before, remember? With your condition you both have much less of a chance to . . . to make babies than other couples. The odds are really against you. You have more chance of being selected to play in goal for the Lao national football team. Sorry to say this, but I don't want you to build up too much hope."

He laughed at her football joke. He laughed at all of Dtui's jokes, even if they weren't funny. She looked into his watery eyes and felt a stomach churning sadness for Geung she'd never experienced before. In Laos, even if by some miracle Tukta fell pregnant, the baby would have a thirty percent chance of survival and if it did, a seventy-percent likelihood of having Down syndrome like her parents. As Dr. Siri said, somewhere back in history these Down syndrome people must have really pissed off the gods.

"I don't want you to expect too much," she said.

"I ex-expect to be like Nurse Dtui and Com-Comrade Chief Inspector Phosy and and and Malee," he said.

A chunk of melancholy lodged in Dtui's chest. "Now that's exactly what I mean when I say you shouldn't expect too much," she said. "Geung, you've both been given a lousy deal in life."

"I . . . I know."

"It's very possible you won't have a baby."

"We will."

"Geung, I—"

"Pornsawan."

"What?"

"That . . . that's her name," said Geung with a smile. "Pornsawan—a g-g-gift from heaven."

"My friend, it's a lovely idea. I really wish it could happen. But you have to—"

"I've m-m-met her."

"Who?"

"Our Pornsawan."

"Where did you meet her, Geung?"

"In In Mahosot. In n-n-n-nine months."

"It was a dream?"

"No. It was . . . it was real."

"Oh, Geung."

CHAPTER FIVE
Culture Shock

"All right," said Civilai, "this is what we do. We take notes. They'll go through the screenplay and suggest alterations here and there. We'll nod, write things down, and generally agree with them. Where possible, without lessening the thrust of our project, we'll incorporate their suggestions."

"Over my dead body," mumbled Siri.

"If necessary," said Madam Daeng.

"Siri, listen," said Civilai, "all we have to do is convince the Culture people that we agree with their opinions. They won't be with us the whole time checking on what we do. Once they think we're all on the same page we can jump off the page and write our own book. All I hope, and I need the Lord Buddha's back up on this, is that you can keep your mouth shut. With your cooperation we'll get that rubber stamp at the bottom of our script, provided by a content, unoffended Minister of Sport, Culture and Information. We'll all laugh together, wish each other luck, and we'll walk out of there after forty minutes with a document giving us unrestricted permission to produce a work. That work will put our nation on the world cinematic map and us up there with Bergman and Truffaut."

"And it all depends on you minding your temper," said Madam Daeng.

They were sitting in Civilai's car at 1:40 in the afternoon. Their appointment with the minister was at two and even though they were all Lao they intended to show respect and enthusiasm by being there directly on time.

"We need you to promise," said Civilai.

"Promise to let those mor—?"

"Yes," said Daeng.

She held out her pinky and Siri stared at it as if it were a grenade pin. She glared at him and smiled so sweetly his heart retook control of his mind. He linked his little finger with hers and they shook. It was a contract more binding than the Warsaw Convention.

"He's probably at lunch," said an untidy man who sat at the receptionist's counter. He was plucking hairs from his nostrils with tweezers.

"What do you do here?" asked Madam Daeng.

"Oh, I'm not here," said the man, looking up from his mirror, "I'm a football referee. We have a meeting sometime this afternoon."

"Shouldn't you be at the other end of the building?" asked Civilai.

"Yes, Comrade," said the referee, "but there's nobody over there either. This isn't one of your most . . . urgent ministries. You know what I mean? Not like Interior or Foreign Affairs."

Civilai and Daeng looked at Siri, whose face was more waxen than old Lenin's in his tomb. The three of them sat on a bench and waited. It was 2:45 before the first ministry officials arrived. They were sweaty and had towels around their necks. Madam Daeng left the bench to talk to a woman who seemed quite at home behind the reception counter. The first thing the woman asked was whether Daeng had seen her mirror.

"Do you actually work here?" asked Daeng.

"Yes," said the woman.

"We had an appointment for two."

"The petong tournament ran a bit over," said the sweaty receptionist.

Daeng smiled in the manner of all affronted Lao.

"You must be fighting a deep urge to apologize," she said.

"I don't understand," said the woman.

"And I doubt you ever will," said Daeng. "Where might we find the office of Comrade Many?"

The office door of Comrade Many was closed with a padlock. But the familiar form of Comrade Phooi came trotting along the corridor. He was no longer in uniform but had a towel around his neck and looked flustered.

"My friends," he said, "thank you for coming. Dr. Siri, I can't tell you how enjoyable we all found your screenplay."

Siri nodded.

"And so professional," Phooi continued, "scenes and dialogues and all that stuff. Really well done. A rare talent."

He rattled the padlock on Many's door and agreed it was locked.

"Big petong tournament today," he said, trying keys from his own bunch one by one in the lock. "We didn't win. Never do. You'd think as we share a building with Sport that something would rub off. But no."

"Why then did you make an appointment with us for two P.M.?" asked Civilai.

"They probably forgot the tournament," said Phooi. "Never mind, eh? We're all here now."

The visitors sighed and watched the man work his way around the key ring.

"Your manuscript is in here," he said. "The version with Comrade Many's corrections."

Siri looked at Daeng.

"Corrections?" she said.

"Just a few, you know, historical errors," he replied. "Wrong places, wrong names, wrong dates. It's to be expected. A writer can't possibly be accurate all the time. The mind of an artist can be a little cloudy sometimes. But don't worry; we've sorted it all out without spoiling the story. It's still a wonderful thing."

The last key on the ring opened the padlock. The room smelled of old paper.

"Is there a reason why Comrade Many—your expert in Lao literature—isn't in his office?" Civilai asked.

"He can't make the meeting today," said Phooi. "He's writing a Lao-Ethiopian lexicon. But he did give your script a thorough going over before he left."

Phooi found Siri's screenplay amid towers of documents and waved it triumphantly.

"Will anyone be meeting us?" Daeng asked.

"That's what's so exciting," said Phooi. "The vice minister has taken a very strong interest in our project. We'll be meeting him personally."

"After his rattan ball competition?" said Civilai.

"He doesn't play rattan ball," said Phooi, mystified. "But he should be back from the petong tournament by now."

Indeed, the Vice Minister of Culture, a tall happy man in his fifties, was sitting at his desk doing nothing. He too was wearing a towel around his neck. He stood when the visitors arrived.

"Brothers and sister," he said. "I'm so pleased to see you. I can't tell you how excited I am to embark on this project with you."

The drawer of his desk took some persuading but eventually it yielded to his tugs, and the vice minister took out an unusually fat wad of papers.

"This will be our working script although I haven't added Many's corrections yet," he said. "Phooi, we'll need another two chairs here."

The room had barely enough space for the two guest chairs crammed up against the desk. It was stuffy and the shutters were closed. The overhead fan rotated at the speed of limestone erosion.

"Don't you have a meeting room?" Daeng asked.

"Yes," said the vice minister, "but it's Thursday and Sport gets it on Thursdays."

So Phooi squashed in two more chairs and they sat in a very intimate circle with their knees touching. The vice minister addressed the gathering.

"My name, as you probably know, is Vice Minister Kinim. The minister would have liked to have been here himself to meet you but he's on a cultural tour of Havana. But I've included his comments and corrections into our almost-finished document here."

He lifted the wad with a smile as if the weight of it were a triumph in itself.

"Our mimeograph girl is making copies for all of you, but I'm afraid they won't be ready in time for this meeting," said Kinim. "But I'm sure, as this is our first editorial meeting, as they say, I can just talk you through the more important changes."

At this point, Dr. Siri, who had said nothing thus far, reached into his shoulder bag and produced pencils and notepads. He handed them to Daeng and Civilai and kept a set for himself.

"That's the spirit," said Kinim. He peeled off the first dozen pages of the manuscript and lay them to one side.

"You didn't like the beginning?" Civilai asked.

"Haven't got there yet," said the vice minister. "Those were just the credits pages."

"Credits for what?" asked Daeng.

"Personnel of the ministry who have been or will be involved in the production," said Kinim. "Of course, the minister will be the executive producer with myself as deputy and so on down through the ranks."

"In short, everyone who works here," said Daeng.

"Not everyone, of course," said Kinim. "We didn't include the canteen staff."

Kinim and Phooi laughed at the joke but the visitors wouldn't have been at all surprised if everyone down to the gate guard had made it into the credits.

"Of course, we'll be adding the names of dignitaries from other ministries as a courtesy, but you don't need to concern yourselves with those matters," said Phooi.

"But let's get down to the story," said Kinim. "I must say we were very impressed with Dr. Siri's opening. It was most imaginative. The son of rich merchants goes to school in Vietnam and the poor village boy studies at a temple in Laos. Wonderful contrast. And then they meet in Paris and establish a lifelong friendship. Very clever."

"Brilliant," said Phooi.

"Thank you," said Civilai on Siri's behalf.

"But, I'm afraid, after careful consultations, we decided to cut it," said the vice minister.

"Cut which part exactly?" said Civilai.

"All of it," said Kinim.

Siri was busily taking notes.

"Comrade Many and the minister decided it was unrealistic," said Phooi, "and it detracted from the whole point of the film."

"What do you mean?" asked Civilai, whose shirt was already soaked through with sweat.

"We decided it was more beneficial to follow the lives of the men whose philosophy gripped the consciousness of the world," said the vice minister. "We'll be looking at the boyhood and youth of Comrades Marx and Lenin."

"Don't you think the Soviets might be better equipped to make a movie about their own heroes?" asked Madam Daeng.

"Oh, goodness me, yes, most certainly," said Kinim. "Once we've introduced the founders of our doctrine we turn to the rise of socialism and the struggle of the peasants and how our own beloved leaders led the charge to independence and freedom from Western tyranny."

"Just out of interest," said Madam Daeng, "do the main characters from the original script make an appearance at all?"

"Oh, yes," said Phooi. "But they're no longer the unlikeable, unruly youths who see life as a joke, drinking and carousing through their formative years. What example would that set for our own new generation?"

"We have refashioned them as role models," said Kinim.

"Ideal socialist man and his comrade. In fact, the lives of our two heroes would more closely parallel those of our prime minister and our president."

"So, I doubt there'll be a great deal of romance," said Civilai.

"Comrade Many has suggested, and quite rightly, that your script leaned rather heavily into the romantic comedy genre," said Phooi. "That, the minister decided, detracted from the reality of our struggles. We want our film to be an accurate record of the revolution and the men who brought us to the utopia we have today."

"And women," said Daeng.

"What?"

"We can live without romance but we cannot live without recognition," she said.

"Naturally there will be women in our film," said Kinim. "Our leaders benefited a good deal from the efforts of our girls. But I don't see any of them in a . . . major role. Oh, I wish I could give you copies of the completed screenplay right now. You'll see how magnificently it all comes together. But we'll have to wait for our next meeting."

The visitors completed their note-taking, shut their books and smiled.

"Well, that was a most enlightening meeting," said Civilai. "We can't wait to get cracking. So, may I say, while we're waiting for the copies of the screenplay I suggest we do a few location shots around the city. Background stuff, I'm sure you understand."

"Splendid idea," said Kinim. "Splendid."

"Then perhaps you'd be kind enough to issue an official note to that effect," said Daeng.

"A what?"

"A note. A chit. An indication that we are filming on behalf of the Ministry of Culture," said Daeng. "We don't want to get arrested, do we now?"

"No, of course not," said Kinim, "but I . . . I can't sign anything without the minister's consent."

"But you have an official ministry stamp, don't you?" said Daeng.

"Well, yes . . . but . . ."

"Then there's no problem," said Civilai. "I took the liberty of typing up a short notice of our intent. It reads, "The barer of this note is doing preliminary filming for a Ministry of Culture project."

"Right . . . well, that seems . . ."

The vice minister was clearly flustered. The room was hot as a bakery.

"No signature needed," said Daeng. "A nice, non-committal permission slip. Nobody needs to take direct responsibility."

"Yes, right," said Kinim, and he wrestled open his drawer and took out a stamp and an ink pad. He smiled unsurely, stamped the paper and handed it back to Civilai.

Meanwhile, Dr. Siri had stepped over to the closed shutters and was prodding at the frame.

"Those things have been stuck since I moved in here," said the vice minister. "The builders say it can't—"

Siri aimed a kick with his old leather sandal at the center of the shutters. One flap burst open to give a view of lush bushes and blue sky. The other dropped and was left hanging by a single hinge. A blast of fresh late afternoon air flooded in through the window.

"Oh, my goodness," said Kinim. "Yes, thank you . . . I suppose."

CHAPTER SIX
As Drunk as a Judge

"Chief Inspector. Congratulations on the new job. Don't see you around here too often these days."

There were two Zils parked on the riverside opposite Madam Daeng's noodle shop. It was 7:40 A.M.. The drivers usually ordered one spicy number three to eat in and one more to take away for their bosses. Phosy was sitting opposite old See. He'd been a military supply vehicle driver during the wars and had been driving the secondhand Russian limousines since their donation in '75.

"The wife usually insists on me eating at home," said Phosy. "With this job we see precious little of each other. But some days I come down here for seconds."

"Don't suppose there's a restaurant on the planet that makes noodles like Daeng does," said See.

"How's work?" Phosy asked.

"Ah, you know. Stop and start. Meeting to meeting. Drive a little bit. Sit in the car for a couple of hours. Drive a little bit. Vientiane's not exactly a sprawling metropolis. Ten k out to the pedagogical institute or the forestry department is about as far as they'll let us take the limos.

Those Zils are thirsty, bloody beasts. Mostly for show. Any long trips and there are vans and trucks, you know?"

Phosy was always surprised at the amount of information that spewed forth from his countrymen with the slightest prompting.

"But you get plenty of overtime," said the chief inspector.

"You must be joking," said See.

Their noodles arrived at the same time. There were condiments on the table, but nobody ever added them. Daeng's noodles weren't to be trifled with. The two men had to wait for the steaming dishes to cool down before they could start.

"You don't get paid extra for nights?" Phosy asked.

"Like you, we work for the government so we're on a flat rate," said See. "But there aren't a lot of places to go after dark. Mostly diplomatic stuff, birthdays, wakes. Any excuse really. Whatever the event, the boss usually ends up being shit-face drunk. Not the old fellows so much anymore but the younger bucks. There's a lot of what we call rice-whisky diplomacy that goes on after the curfew."

"I believe it," said Phosy. "One of our curfew boys said he was almost killed by one of your mob running him off the road last Saturday morning."

The noodles hadn't cooled much but you could only stare at a spicy number three for so long. They risked serious lip burns but they both chowed down and conversation was put on hold. They smiled as they spooned in the last few mouthfuls of broth.

"What were we talking about?" said See.

"Hmm, can't remember," said the policeman. "No, wait, I was telling you one of the curfew patrols was almost wiped out by a limo the other morning."

"I heard about that," said See. "It was the morning they found the skeleton."

"Really?" said Phosy. "The same morning?"

"No doubt about it. You rarely get two newsworthy events on the same day in this dead hole."

"You know what happened?"

"There was a dinner at the Soviet residence. Their justice secretary was in town. They invited all the Lao with justice connections, past and present, to come for a knees up. I wasn't on that night but the boys said there was a long line of limos out front. Being a Soviet do there was a lot of vodka, and all the Party uncles arrived back at their limos a bit the worse for wear. Could hardly walk some of them. The incident you're referring to involved a certain Party member who decided halfway home that he'd prefer to drive himself the rest of the way. We have a genial enough relationship with the bosses, but some of them, when they get a few drinks inside, they can get a bit stroppy if you know what I mean. You do your best to talk them out of suicidal activities but it's not worth losing your job over. So, the limo driver that morning let the boss take the wheel and the driver very wisely climbed into the back seat."

See looked at his wristwatch.

"Shit," he said, "I'm going to have to get moving. I've got a politburo passenger today."

He was about to put his small pile of banknotes on the table but Phosy insisted on paying for both bowls. He walked out with the driver.

"So, what happened?" he asked.

"First thing that happened is the boss put his foot on the accelerator instead of the brake and sent the limo up on the sidewalk, stopping just in time before running over your curfew patrol. The driver shooed the boys away and tried to convince the boss to give him back the wheel."

"Are the bosses allowed to drive their own limos?" Phosy asked.

"Against regulations," said See, "but there have been occasions. You can't really argue with a prime minister if he feels like taking a Zil for a spin. Some of them are good drivers. But that boss the other morning wasn't one of them. He stalled. He crunched gears. He couldn't tell the road from the grass verge. At one point, he pulled out the ignition key and dropped it on the floor. And the driver took advantage of the lack of movement to hop out. He decided his job was to drive for them, not die for them."

"And the limo found its way home?"

"By some miracle, yes. It was in the compound with all the others when we started work that day. Barely a scratch on it."

"But every other Zil out that night had an official driver?" asked Phosy.

"As far as I know."

"And did any of the drivers see the skeleton?"

"If they did they're not talking."

They reached the Zil and Mr. Geung raced across the street with the driver's forgotten takeout.

"Thanks, boy," he said.

"You're w-w-welcome," said Geung.

"All this talking and I almost forget the boss's breakfast," said See, unlocking the car door.

"There's one more thing," said Phosy.

"What's that?"

"I'm afraid you're going to have to tell me the name of the boss who kicked out the driver that morning."

"I'd get in trouble if I did that," said See.

"You wouldn't believe how much more trouble you'd be in if you didn't."

It wasn't so much a network, more an industry. On the Thai side of the river, just a short paddle away, was austerity and opulence. Their TVs said so. The magazines with the four-dollar models wearing thousand-dollar fashions said so. You could get a job in a restaurant in Ubon and make enough in a month to keep your family in Laos alive for a year. What was left would still be enough for a good time in Thailand. Women in their twenties would come to the village and tell the wide-eyed girls, "A few years ago, I was just like you. No money. No opportunity. No future. Then I met Uncle Thongkum. I didn't trust him at first. How could you trust someone who makes promises beyond your dreams? But I was desperate. He arranged me passage to Ubon and got me a job in a restaurant. The owner was nice. She was a Lao married to a Thai. At first, she had me working in the kitchen. And even there I was making two hundred dollars a month. But she said I had a nice personality and that I should try out as a waitress. I still had my two-hundred-dollar basic salary, and I got tips in the restaurant. Some nights I'd make a hundred dollars. It was like being in a dream."

And the village girls, thirteen, fourteen upward, sat in front of her spellbound like dogs waiting for a cat to fall from a tree. And one by one they followed this fantasy to Thailand and put their youth and their lives in the hands of Uncle Thongkum. And in Thailand they ripened too fast and fell from the tree too soon. Uncle Thongkum didn't care either way. He had a nice house, a major wife who supervised his kitchen, two minor wives on a rotational basis in the bedroom and enough money to shut everyone up. Living in a poor country was a crooked man's dream.

And then he was dead. He was sixty. He'd had regular health checkups. He didn't drink or smoke. He even exercised which was most uncommon on the Lao side. None of that had prevented his death. His wives were at the funeral, his sons, their wives, representatives of the local council, his employees and his nephew, Wee, the policeman.

The topic of conversation in the temple was how they'd make up for this loss of income, how the uncle's wealth would be distributed, and, for that matter, where exactly the trafficker might have kept his money. There were no lawyers. He lived fifty kilometers from the nearest bank branch. There was nothing under the mattress. It was as if a sink hole had opened under the family business and everything had vanished into it. Nobody expressed their sorrow for the loss of Uncle Thongkum. Sergeant Wee certainly felt no regret. In fact, his job had just become a lot simpler. He no longer had to think of a way to drag the old man screaming all the way to Vientiane. His mission had been accomplished in the neatest way.

"And, action!" shouted Siri.

The handsome young man fought his way through imaginary vegetation peering left and right in case a French patrol might pounce upon him. He looked sensational. He was a Lao Marlon Brando: firm of jaw and proudly built.

"A dead ringer for me," said Civilai.

"You never looked like that even in your dreams," said Siri.

They stood beside rather than behind the Panavision because they still hadn't worked out how to operate it. It seemed in need of power of some kind, but they couldn't imagine the makers of *The Deer Hunter* running a twenty-kilometer cable out to the location sight. They'd been students in Paris when technology amounted to lighting a gas lamp and starting a car with a crank handle. They'd returned to the jungles of Laos where there were no telephones and most of their learning came through watching newsreels and feature films on reel-to-reel projectors powered by diesel engines. Neither of them was stupid but just looking at the camera gave them migraines. They knew there had to be some sort of battery component and some way to charge it. They'd played with all the buttons and levers and had evoked no response from their large toy. They'd been to the Fuji Photo shop and asked the owner whether his expertise extended to the Panavision. He told them he was rather limited to Instamatics and Zenits but he had a cousin in Sydney who might know somebody. He said he'd keep them informed. So, they used their magnificent camera as a prop to see how their would-be actors responded in front of it.

"And your line?" said Siri to the Lao Brando. But the boy continued to flex his muscles and gnash his splendid teeth without speaking.

"Didn't I give you the script?" asked Siri.

"Yes, comrade."

"Then . . . ?"

"I can't read," said the boy.

As Siri and Civilai weren't about to set up literacy classes for their actors they were once again reminded of what a monumental task they'd set themselves. They were currently advertising for actors through word of mouth at the market. They daren't place ads in the Pasason Lao newsletter because there was a remote possibility someone at Culture might read them. And the ministry had taken on the task of recruiting actors itself from its own staff. What Siri and Civilai really wanted was a nationwide search for actors and anyone who could turn on a camera.

"I'm beginning to think we've climbed on the back of a buffalo that doesn't realize it's a buffalo," said Civilai.

Siri pondered that concept and, although he didn't understand it, he certainly couldn't refute it.

"Don't you think we're being too ambitious?" he asked.

"In what way?" asked Civilai.

"Attempting to make a full-length movie without technicians, actors, funding, support or the ability to turn on the camera?"

"Those aren't the thoughts of the Dr. Siri I know," said Civilai. "Haven't we attempted the impossible before?"

"Yes," said Siri, "usually without success."

They gave Lao Brando three-hundred kip for his time and spent another half an hour attempting to activate their camera. Then gave up and went for a drink at Two Thumb's bar behind the morning market. A lot of problems had been solved there but none as titanic as this.

Judge Haeng was the head of the Public Prosecution Department at the Ministry of Justice. Dr. Siri described him as "a spotty, immature little runt who got his education on the back of his wealthy father's funding then got promoted to the position of judge because there was nobody else in the running, and every country needs a judge or two."

The assessment may have been a little cruel, but that didn't make it any less accurate. After some stormy initial encounters, Siri and his team had gathered enough dirt on the man to have him off their backs and house-trained. Chief Inspector Phosy knew enough about the judge to dispense with formality and politeness. He could drop by his office any time without an appointment and expect a warm welcome.

"Chief Inspector Phosy, my dear friend," said Haeng when he saw the policeman in the doorway. He hurried over to him and took Phosy's hands in his like a kickboxer in gloves.

"I was so very pleased to hear about your promotion," said Haeng. "I would have loved to have attended your ceremony, but I had urgent ministry business in Vang Vieng."

Phosy rescued his hands and walked into the room. He knew the head of public prosecution's staying away from the inauguration was a political decision. The judge had his own nominees for the position; men who would serve him without question. The only business Haeng had in Vang Vieng was a retired nightclub singer with a penchant for chocolates.

"The morning of the twenty-third of this month . . ." said Phosy.

"Would you like some tea? Coffee?" asked the judge. He closed the office door and walked to his desk. He didn't sit. Neither did Phosy.

"Something stronger?" asked Haeng. "A twenty-year-old scotch to launch your new career?"

"On the morning of the twenty-third of this month you were driving home from an event at the Soviet residence out by Ammone Temple at around two-fifty A.M.," said the policeman.

"I'd have to check my diary," said Haeng.

"That's not necessary," said Phosy. "I can tell you for certain. At one point, you decided you'd like to take over the controls of your Zil."

"I . . ."

"Despite your obvious state of inebriation."

"Oh, I see what this is." The judge smiled. "It's probably based on a statement by my driver, right? Yes, I'm sure it is. I put in a complaint about his driving skills. He stood to lose his position. This sounds like revenge to me."

"That may or may not be so," said Phosy. "I have no knowledge of your relationship with the driver you had that morning. I haven't talked to him. My information comes from our curfew patrol. You almost killed them."

"That's nonsense, Phosy."

"In fact, by coincidence, there were two patrols on that stretch of road when you decided to kick out your driver and take the wheel yourself. They recognized you."

Phosy had never hesitated to cling to a good lie if it brought out some truths.

"Inspector, you're taking the word of uneducated, unsophisticated youths. And what is this all about anyway? Surely the national police chief isn't on the streets investigating a drunk driving case?"

"No, Judge. I'm on the streets investigating a murder."

"Well, that's more like it."

"I'm following up on all the vehicles seen around the Anusawari Arch between three and four on Thursday morning."

"And you think that might include my limousine," said Haeng indignantly.

"I'm asking," said Phosy. "All I need to do is confirm that the patrol guards weren't lying about the incident."

The judge walked to the far wall and looked up at the louver windows as if he could see a canopy of lush vegetation outside. In fact, they were too dusty to see anything at all.

"All right, Phosy," he said, putting up his hands. "You've got me. It was the Soviets. They seemed to have a quota of vodka to get through a night. It flowed like the Mekhong. I'm sure you know how pleasant it is to drink expensive alcohol for free. You don't even notice it going down. But by early morning you're shaking hands with garden statues. That morning I was so drunk I really needed the driver to tell me to pull myself together. But, yes, Phosy, it's true. I did order him out of the car. I did attempt to drive that clumsy black beast. And at one stage, when the car stalled, I did give the driver permission to desert. I'm very lucky I wasn't seriously hurt. At one stage I came around, and I was heading toward the river with no idea how I got there."

"Then it's conceivable you drove to the arch," said Phosy.

"God, man, have you never been drunk? At one point I became paranoid. I was certain I was about to die. I drove the limo back to the Zil parking lot in first gear, left the key in the ignition and staggered home. But the Anusawari Arch is forty-nine meters high. Even in the condition I was in I'm sure I would have noticed it had I passed it."

Phosy removed a map of the city from his briefcase and unfolded it on the judge's desk.

"Perhaps you could show me the route you took from the Soviet residence to the parking lot," he said.

"Are you serious?" said Haeng.

"If you're that certain you didn't pass the arch you must have an idea of how you avoided it. It's only two blocks from where you left the car."

Haeng went to the desk and looked at the map.

"This would be a guess," he said and he trailed a finger from the residence to the point where he parted company with the driver. "I remember passing Sok Paluang Temple on the way. From there I hit the river road somehow. Don Chan Island was looming there in front of me."

Phosy could see that the most direct route would have been to pass the arch, but Haeng insisted he did not. Instead he pointed out a winding trail west along the river, somehow skirting the old palace before driving into town past the telephone exchange and doing a circuit around the football stadium. Somehow, illogically, he arrived at the car park from the north.

Phosy told the judge he'd be seeing him again very soon and returned to his department jeep. He drove to the Soviet residence and followed the route the judge claimed to have taken. It was possible to arrive at the Zil parking lot from the north but the road leading there was no more than a dirt track with pot holes deep enough to emerge in Peru. The area was unlit at night and required a certain amount of skill to negotiate. Even in daylight in a jeep it was a challenge. Phosy pulled up at the parking lot and switched off his engine. Haeng's convoluted story seemed to have only one purpose: to place the drunken judge as far as possible from the arch. Why would he bother to do that if his only crime was driving under the influence? But what connection could there have been between the judge and the skeleton? Haeng was devious but he wasn't stupid. He wouldn't have risked being seen dragging a corpse to the base of the arch not even whilst three sheets to the wind.

As he sat there looking across at the black limousines, two certainties took a bow on the stage of Phosy's mind. The first was that Judge Haeng had not been as drunk on the morning of the 23rd as he pretended to have been. And the second was that Judge Haeng had lied about not passing the arch. Whether he'd merely seen the skeleton displayed under the lamplight or had been involved in its placement were matters the detective would work on at a later date.

As chief inspector, Phosy was not expected or encouraged to be conducting investigations himself. The politburo would have him sitting at his desk ten hours a day signing documents. But he wasn't that sort of chief inspector. He drove back to police headquarters, where he'd scribble his name on fifty report sheets, cancel a few mindless appointments and head off again to find the Zil driver Judge Haeng had replaced on the morning the skeleton was found. Phosy knew that without results his tenure would be a short one, so he had to be sure any investigation, particularly that of a judge, was accurate and the outcome indisputable. And there was no doubt in Phosy's mind that he was the best man for that sort of job.

CHAPTER SEVEN
Civet Shit

It was Nurse Dtui's day off and she and Malee went to the zoo. It was likely that her daughter, upon reaching the age of sixteen, would look back on her family outings and realize they all coincided with criminal cases her parents were working on. As her mother's daughter, she'd probably be more proud to have been used than be offended. And on this sunny but breezy day all she knew was that she was going to the zoo, where she would see animals.

In her backpack, Dtui had soft drinks in screw-top bottles, lots of peanuts, and two human bones. She'd done her homework before embarking on this adventure. The zoo they were visiting had been established in the '60s in Dong Paina by a Frenchman called Yves Proman. He'd charged very little for entry because, as he said, this was an educational opportunity, a chance for Lao, young and old, to learn about the wildlife of the region. He let it be known that he did not want to take advantage of the poor people in his adopted country. To all appearances, he lived frugally with his wife and took delight in the smiles on the faces of the visitors.

He also took delight in the vast wealth he amassed over

the years. If any visitors returned regularly to the French-man's zoo, and if they were observant, they would have noticed some oddities. Firstly, how their favorite pan-golin changed its markings with every visit. The snakes lengthened and shortened as the mood took them. The orangutan became five months pregnant in the space of a week. Then, the aware visitor might also hear animal cries emanating from an area beyond the public boundary of the zoo. And these howls were not those of well-fed, con-tented beasts but of hunger and illness and fear.

For over ten years, Proman was the leading trafficker of Southeast Asian wildlife to Europe, Japan and the Ameri-cas. He'd used the zoo as a front for his nefarious business and a conduit for the trade, which, in Laos, had very few legal controls. The French and the American colonists had more profitable interests to police than the shipping of a few monkeys. Legal restrictions would only be imposed when and if the livestock arrived at their destinations.

"But now, as you see, it's just a zoo," said their guide.

Malee was in her element. She toddled free-range from cage to cage waving at the gibbons and the crab-eater monkeys, throwing peanuts for the sunbird. Dtui let her set the pace while she held back to talk with Comrade Sisouk, the current director of the zoo. He was a barrel-chested man whose uniform badly needed letting out. He had a little mustache which reminded Dtui of the villains in the old Chinese operas whose facial hair was painted on. Sisouk carried a cane more as a prop than a walking aid.

"We were shocked when we heard of Proman's doings," said the director. "Of course, he'd fled by the time we took over, but we were hurt that he should have single-handedly shipped such an incredible volume of animals overseas. Those of us who were brought up in the countryside loving the wildlife had learned to respect nature. Certainly, there was hunting. That was nature's way. Take no more than you need, you know? There was always plenty to go around. And, of course, we humans were on the jungle menu too. It was a balance of respect. Juxtaposition of hunters and hunted.

"But Proman's people came to our villages and paid the locals to catch game. He had middle men all over the region. He was shipping our finest animals to die in zoos in Europe. For every puma that arrived in one piece in France, thirty had succumbed to disease and starvation in transit. But he didn't care. He relied on volume you see? If one golden panther makes it to the zoo they'd pay enough to fund the capture of another fifty."

There was a knot in Comrade Sisouk's throat even though Dtui was sure he'd given the same talk many times. His eyes watered and she was afraid he might burst into tears.

"Proud, beautiful animals," he went on, "abused and demeaned. I wish I'd met him, the Frenchman, I really do. I'd have shown him how I felt."

Such a high-level, emotional tour of the zoo was not available to every visitor. But Dtui had arrived with a letter from the head of the police department saying that she was a very close aid to the chief inspector as well as an expert in forensic anthropology—a term she and Phosy had looked up the night before. The director himself insisted on showing her around, and he arranged for his longest serving keeper to help with her rather odd request.

Dtui didn't see herself as qualified to doubt the

director's sincerity, but even though these animal prisoners in their concrete and wire mesh cages were "the lucky
ones," she couldn't help but feel sorry for them. Their eyes
seemed to see another life—a life that was losing clarity
and focus. And those beasts that had been there the longest could see only wire mesh and concrete. All memories
of the past had drained from them. They sat on their logs
and their rocks, their heads slowly scrolling left and right
like dementia patients, mesmerized by the passing visitors
but not at all interested in them.

"Ah, there he is," said Sisouk.

Ahead was an old dark-brown man in khaki shorts
and no shirt. There wasn't a trace of fat on him. He had
a fine head of silver hair and not a single tooth in his
mouth.

"This is Chong," said the director. "Our longest-serving
keeper. He's the only one left from the Frenchman's days."

The old man put his hands together in an overly
respectful *nop*.

"No need for that," said Dtui. "I'm not the queen of
Thailand."

Chong laughed and his lips caved inward.

"He's a bit stuck on some of the old ways," said Sisouk.

"It's very kind of you to arrange this for me," said Dtui.

"We're constantly trying to erase the horrors of the zoo's
past," said Sisouk. "Anything to show we are with and for
the community is as much for our benefit as yours. And of
course, we're most pleased to help the police."

Chong was still standing with his nose on his fingertips.

"If you have more important things to do I can talk to
Comrade Chong alone," said Dtui.

"I wouldn't dream of it," said Sisouk. "This will be an

education for me. Never too old to learn, I say. Chong, you tell this lady everything she wants to know."

"Yes, sir," said Chong.

"Hello, Chong," said Dtui.

"Hello, Your Ladyship."

"There's something I'd like you to take a look at," said Dtui.

Before removing the bones from her bag, she looked back to see whether her daughter was missing her at all. Malee was sitting cross-legged in front of a caged slow loris, and she seemed to be teaching the animal numbers. They were at two. Dtui knew she'd be there for a while. The nurse took the two bones from her pack and held them out to Chong.

"That's a person," said Chong, taking a step back.

"That's correct," said Dtui, impressed that the old man could recognize human bones so quickly. "I'd like you to look at them."

He took another step back. There were many fears about contact with the dead, beliefs that the spirit might pass from the body to the handler. But she'd never seen anyone quite as afraid of human bones.

"Chong, what are you doing?" said the director.

"It's all right," said Dtui. "You don't have to touch them. Just look. There are bite and scratch marks on them. I was wondering if you might be able to tell me what type of animal made them."

Chong leaned forward. There was something of a lost past in his eyes too. He studied first one bone, then the other.

"There's one or two possibilities," he said. "Teeth are pretty much the same on the smaller carnivores. But that . . ."

He nodded toward the dark stain on one of the bones. He leaned closer and took a sniff and smiled.

". . . now that's civet shit, without a doubt."

"Really?" said Dtui.

"Having a keen sense of smell in a zoo can be a curse, Your Ladyship," he said. "I can identify about forty different types of shit. I can sleep through an air raid but smells keep me awake. I can see you aren't convinced."

"It's just . . ." said Dtui.

"That's all right. Hard to believe. You need a bit more proof. How about this? You've been drinking orange cordial, not juice, the sweet muck from Thailand. And you've been eating peanuts. You wash with Lifebouy soap and you're using some sort of mango shampoo on your hair. Probably homemade."

"I'm convinced," said Dtui.

"There's just one thing," said Chong.

"What's that?"

"In all my years I've never seen a civet attack a human."

There were two men sitting in front of Chief Inspector Phosy's office, and he was undecided as to which he should see first. If his country had coins he would have tossed one. Both interviews promised to be uncomfortable in their own ways. So he left it up to Comrade Manivon, his new secretary. She'd been the clerical assistant at the justice ministry for the past five years before getting kicked out by the same Judge Haeng that Phosy was investigating. She was delighted to be invited to work for the policeman and said it was refreshing to be treated like a human being again.

"Bring me the one who seems least nervous," said Phosy,

and she arrived with Sergeant Wee. His pompadour stood even higher than at their last meeting, and his dress sense was even more inadvisable. Wee apparently had yet to grasp the concept of plain clothes.

"You do know the point is to blend in," said Phosy.

Wee sat on the guest chair and crossed his legs. He tapped the cigarette pack in his top pocket. "Smoke?" he asked.

"You're a clown," said Phosy.

"Blending in just makes you obvious," said Wee. "Plain-clothes police look like police in plain clothes. You can pick 'em out a mile away. How do you ever blend in at a village where everyone's been together for generations? Your only option is to be an outsider that nobody suspects. You'd be surprised how insignificant people think I am."

"No, that wouldn't surprise me," said Phosy.

"Mind if I do?" said Wee, tapping the pack again.

"Nervous?"

"No, just addicted."

"But you do have every reason to be nervous," said Phosy.

"How so?"

"Your family business."

"Did I not take care of that?"

"In your own sweet way," said Phosy. "I have some questions about your methodology."

"It was a heart attack."

"So they tell me."

"Are you accusing me of killing him?"

"No, I just have a problem with coincidences," said Phosy. "You and your team had done a good job of shutting down his business. You stayed undercover as a corrupt cop so you could follow up on prospective successors. Nobody there knew you were working for us. All your team had to do was arrest your uncle and bring him to Vientiane. They broke into his house and there he was, dead on the bathroom floor. The local medic said it was a heart attack."

"So?"

"No record of ill health. No symptoms leading up to his death."

"Just think what you like."

"There's that attitude again," said Phosy. "Listen, boy. You're a team leader. I'm your boss. I might very well be the only honest person you're ever going to work for. This is a debriefing. I'm a busy man. I'm giving you ten minutes. And in those ten minutes I have to establish whether you're out of control. I'm good at what I do and I got where I am by being thorough. So why don't you just tell me what happened?"

"Look," said Wee. "I'm not a doctor. Who knows whether it was a heart attack. The local medic had about ten weeks of training. I doubt he could tell herpes from a hernia. It could have been anything. I saw the body. There were no wounds, no signs of a struggle. When you live out in the countryside there's any one of a hundred ways to die. A liver fluke can have you in the grave in a few hours. There was nobody to do an autopsy so, no, I can't tell you. All I can say is I'm sorry he didn't leave this earth in a more unpleasant way. I'd like to have watched him die slowly. Sorry you don't like coincidences. But that's not my problem."

Phosy looked at the sergeant's impassive expression. "Okay," he said.

"Is that all?"

"Sorry, I didn't catch that."

"Is that all . . . sir?"

"I think it is. Please pass on my congratulations to your team. My secretary has new orders for you on her desk. You can pick them up on your way out."

Sergeant Wee walked to the door and was about to leave the room, but he stopped, took a step back and saluted. Phosy returned the salute and frowned. Wee was going to be a hard horse to break, but if he ever sorted out his head he'd be one hell of a good policeman. Phosy opened his notebook and wrote a reminder to send Siri to the south before the cremation. The chief inspector didn't leave anything to chance.

He looked at the clock on the wall. It was seven hours late to the second and, therefore, reliable. He didn't dare alter it for fear it might stop. The knock on his door was so tentative he mistook it for the sound of a lizard beating a moth against the window. He shouted, "Come in!"

The man shuffled in. He was short and had a permanent bad-smell scrunch to his nose. He took a seat and Phosy looked at him. Zil drivers were, through necessity, faithful to their bosses. There was no end to the secrets they were sworn to keep. Breaking that trust would inevitably result in the termination of a comfortable job and a trip to a re-education camp. But every man had his own fears of why a senior policeman might want to see him. Sometimes all Phosy needed to do was stare. He gave Uthit enough time to come up with his own defense.

"I had no choice, comrade," said Uthit.

Phosy glared.

"The judge was drunk," Uthit continued. "Never seen

him so drunk. I know. I know the regulations. I should have sat there and resisted but . . . well, he's a judge. What could I do? He was insistent. I have seven kids. It's not a job I can afford to lose."

"What time are we talking about here?" said Phosy.

"Must have been a bit before three. Can't be certain. I haven't got a watch."

"When you got out of the limo, what did you do?" Phosy asked.

"I headed back to the dormitory. It was ten odd k. I had to be up at seven for another job."

"Did the car pass you again?"

"No. Didn't see nothing."

"And you weren't concerned about the plight of the Zil and its new driver?"

"Oh, I worried about it," said Uthit. "I worried about it all the way home. I thought about what shit I'd be in if the judge ran it into the river and drowned. It'd be my fault, right? Didn't get any sleep."

"What made you think I wanted to talk to you about that morning?" Phosy asked.

The driver stared at the hands on his lap.

"Well?" said Phosy.

"The judge was talking to me today," said Uthit. "He said you'd probably want to see me about that incident."

"And what was his advice?"

"Just to tell the truth. He said he was the one at fault so there was nothing to worry about."

Phosy watched him squeeze his hands together.

"So what are you worried about?" Phosy asked.

"I . . . I don't know."

"He told you to tell the truth, right?"

"Yes, but . . ."

"There's no but."

"Well, comrade, me getting kicked out of the Zil wasn't the only odd thing to happen that night. But I don't think the judge knew about it."

"Tell me."

"I dropped him off at the Soviet residence and me and the other drivers were in the empty lot opposite having a smoke and a chat. And one of the boys tells me one of my front tires is soft. We all have foot pumps in the trunk. It was hard work but I didn't have much else to do. So, I went to get the pump. But when I took out the key ring, the trunk key wasn't on it. It's always there. In fact, it's hard to get off. I felt in my pocket, looked on the mat under the steering wheel. No sign of it."

"Does anyone else have access to the keys?" Phosy asked.

"No, well, when we put the limos to bed at night we drop off the keys at the office by the lot. The guard there signs the car in and puts the keys on their hooks. But only the drivers and the guard can sign the cars in and out."

"And when was the last time you'd used the key to open the trunk?"

"The previous morning," said Uthit. "I was at the ministry waiting for the judge and I used the squeegee to wipe the windows."

"Could you have dropped it then?"

"Like I say, the keys were really hard to take off the ring. Nothing else was missing from the bunch. I suppose it's possible. But that wouldn't explain how it came back."

"It came back?"

"When I went to see what damage the judge had done to the Zil the next morning, I stopped at the office to get the keys. I was relieved they were there and not at the bottom of the Mekhong. And the limo was in good nick too. I'd forgotten about the key being missing and instinctively I went to the trunk to check everything was there. It was only then that I remembered. The key was back on the bunch."

"No way you could have just missed it the previous night?" Phosy asked.

"There are five keys," said Uthit. "I can count to five."

"So, the judge had returned the limo and five keys at the end of his hell ride?"

"Not returned exactly," said the driver. "He parked outside the lot halfway up a grass verge and left the keys in the ignition. He shouted for the attendant to come and get it and he vanished."

"He could walk?"

"At speed by the looks of it."

Phosy was taking notes in his book.

"All right," he said, "back to the previous day. You met the judge at the ministry in the morning. Where did you take him?"

"We had to go to the airport to pick up some VIP."

"Who?"

"Don't know."

The memory came back to Phosy. The chief inspector had gone to the airport to meet the Cambodian on the same day. He remembered seeing the judge arrive at the airport in a Zil. The judge had lowered the window and nodded as Phosy passed.

"But for that day you were the judge's personal taxi service?" said Phosy.

"No, it's not like that. The Zils are for special occasions.

Judge Haeng is one of a dozen high-rankers I take around. We're usually reserved for state functions and, you know, high diplomatic stuff. The prime minister and president have their own limos available all the time but down through the politburo and below they have to book. There are only twenty-four Zils in all. We don't do milk runs."

"So it was unusual that the judge would have you twice in one day?"

"Yeah, he'd have to book it in advance. He wasn't that fond of being driven. He preferred his motor scooter. But the justice ministry insists sometimes."

"What time were you at the airport?"

"Nine for the nine A.M. flight from Hanoi. It arrived at eleven-fifteen."

"What did you do for those two hours?"

"Drank coffee in the canteen."

"Alone?"

"I knew people there. We talked."

"Did the judge join you?"

Phosy noticed a brief hesitation before the answer.

"No."

"Where did he go?"

"No idea," said Uthit.

"And where was your car?"

"In priority parking in front of the terminal."

"And the keys?"

Another hesitation.

"With me," said Uthit.

"Never out of your sight?"

The hesitation was even longer this time.

"No."

"You sure?" said Phosy.

"Yes."

"All right. And where did you take your VIP?"

"Which one?"

"The one you went to the airport to meet."

"Oh, he didn't turn up," said the driver. "Missed the flight."

"Who told you that?"

"The judge."

"Weren't you surprised about that?"

"Not really. Happens all the time. If anyone ever arrived on the right flight at the right time there'd be nobody there to meet them. Air travel. It'll never catch on."

CHAPTER EIGHT
Loved and Lost

"Civets?" said Madam Daeng. "Can't say I've ever heard of civets hunting in packs."

With all their respective duties and hobbies, Dr. Siri's group of crime fighters had not been able to get together for a while. But that evening they were all there at Madam Daeng's noodle shop: Chief Inspector Phosy, Nurse Dtui, Siri, Daeng, Civilai, Mr. Geung and his lady friend, Tukta. Ugly the dog kept watch outside.

The imbibement of choice for all those apart from the Down syndrome representatives was vodka, duty free from their trip to Moscow. Siri and Civilai had become rather fond of the Stolichnaya and this was their last bottle. But they reluctantly agreed there were worse things in life than running out of vodka: being eaten by civets, for one.

"The keeper was confident," said Dtui, "and he gave me a little demonstration of his nasal capabilities that left me in no doubt."

"Then our mystery woman was eaten by large rodent-like mammals," said Civilai. "Any idea where the beasts pounced?"

"I'm guessing it was inside," said Dtui.

"Why's that?" Siri asked.

"Just a hunch," said Dtui. "If she was attacked in the open air I'm assuming larger animals would have soon carried away the bones to gnaw on. And I don't think the skeleton was exposed to sunlight. There was no bleaching at all. The keeper had never heard of civets attacking a person. They usually live on insects and smaller mammals. So, something tells me the animals and the girl were trapped together."

"The civets were st-st-starving," said Mr. Geung.

"Is that a guess or Mr. Geung's psychic intuition?" asked Dtui.

"I know," said Geung.

"But even so she could have fought them off," said Civilai. "They're just little pussy cats."

"Assuming she was conscious," said Siri.

"I wonder if she was being tortured," said Madam Daeng. "I've seen men thrown into animal pits at the end of a rope. Their only chance to be pulled back to safety is to give up their secrets."

"All right, let me sum this up," said Phosy. "You have a young woman thrown into a room full of starving animals to make her confess to something. Perhaps she's already been beaten so she doesn't have the strength to fight them off. She dies. Why then do her torturers not dispose of the body discreetly?"

"And what's Judge Haeng's role in all this?" asked Siri. "The evidence is mounting against him. He had the transport. He had a locked trunk. He was alone and he had plenty of time. But why would he go to so much trouble to make sure the body could be found? Even with all the planning, he took a serious risk of being caught."

"I'm rather impressed," said Civilai. "I wouldn't have credited the man with the type of mind to come up with such subterfuge."

"But we have no evidence that he was involved at all," said Phosy.

"We have to account for those two missing hours at the airport waiting for his imaginary VIP," said Daeng. "That was the only time he could have put the body in the trunk."

"But what was the skeleton doing at the airport in the first place?" said Dtui.

"That's my homework for tomorrow," said Phosy.

"You do know you're the chief inspector of police?" said Siri.

"It's written on my door," said Phosy.

"Then you have a police department at your disposal," Siri continued. "You shouldn't be out there using up shoe rubber interviewing people. Don't you think it's time to delegate responsibility?"

"Siri, I've officially been in the job for two months," said Phosy. "I've done some culling, but I haven't yet got around to firing all the officers I don't have faith in and if I did it would be a very vacant police department. I have a dozen men I'd trust with my life and a few hundred I think I can rely on. Of the rest, I don't know who's loyal to me or who Judge Haeng has planted there to keep an eye on things."

"Then it looks like the noodle shop justice league will be back on the streets," said Civilai. "And now that you have control of the cash register we might even get paid for our services at last."

Mr. Geung and Tukta thought that was hilarious.

"You are irretrievably *Civilai*," said Daeng.

Like the entertainer between acts of a play, a bat swooped in through the door, scooped up a mouthful of moths from the aura of the overhead light and swooped out again.

"And what news of your film?" Phosy asked.

"Oh, you know," said Siri, "it's not the easiest thing in the world to make a movie with a grenade launcher."

"Haven't I apologized enough for that?" said Phosy. "Smuggling is smuggling, be it a weapon of war or a cabbage. You endangered yourselves and your friends. You're lucky I didn't lock you all up."

"Then you wouldn't have any allies at all," said Civilai.

"Was it worth the danger?" Phosy asked.

"It will be," said Siri.

"You haven't started yet?" said Dtui.

"We are scouting out locations," said Siri. "We are fine-tuning the best light and sound settings for our camera."

"But they can't turn it on," said Daeng.

Only Siri and Civilai failed to see the funny side of that comment. When the laughter died down Siri produced a wad of papers from his shoulder bag.

"We have a script," he said. "We are two thirds of the way there."

"We're hanging on to our script for dear life," said Civilai. "The Ministry of Cultures and Pond Life would have us turn it into a propaganda newsreel."

"Plus, we're a bit short of actors," said Siri.

"We don't have any," said Civilai.

There was another trickle of laughter.

"Why don't you go to the women's union?" asked Dtui.

"Do they know how to use cameras?" Civilai asked.

"It wouldn't surprise me," she replied, "but I'm thinking

more of their network. You're looking for performers. You know from experience how fast the ladies can spread information. I'm sure you'd have a queue of budding film stars at your door."

"It's worth a try," said Civilai.

"And if anyone can get the Ministry of Culture off our backs it's the union," said Daeng. "They could take it on as their own project."

"But they'd want all the main roles rewritten for women," said Civilai.

"And what's wrong with that?" said Dtui, Tukta and Daeng simultaneously.

Mr. Geung didn't turn up for the morning shift at Madam Daeng's noodle shop and Tukta wasn't there to wait tables. It was the first day's work they'd missed in all the time anyone had known them. Given the couple's diligence and reliability, their absence could only have meant that something terrible had happened. Mr. Geung occupied the room behind the shop. His bed hadn't been slept in. Tukta sometimes joined him there overnight when they would listen to music and "dance." But Siri jumped on his bicycle and headed on over to Tukta's aunt's shop house, where Mr. Geung's girlfriend kept her belongings. The old woman hadn't seen her niece since early the previous morning.

Siri hurried back to the noodle shop, where he found the customers in the same heightened state of anxiety as Daeng and himself. Madam Daeng was working. There wasn't a chance she'd abandon her shop. Some customers had volunteered to wait tables and wash dishes in the absence of Geung and Tukta. Daeng ladled her noodles into bowls with no need to watch what she was doing. Nothing was spilled. At the same time, she was handing out instructions. She was the general.

"Mu," she said, "can you go via the new museum along Samsenthai? The prime minister's old place. Swing by the stadium. Ask around."

Mu, one of Daeng's most regular customers, finished his noodles and was off without a word. Siri stood back to let him pass. He knew better than to interrupt his wife when she was abuzz. She continued to dollop noodles, add ingredients to the broth and dice vegetables, but it was all through instinct. Her mind was dicing the city into grids. By the end of breakfast, she'd have someone in every square.

"Foo," she said.

The old soldier stood and saluted. "Yes, comrade?" he said.

"Can you take Tai Ngyai Market? Geung likes to get his river mussels there."

"Yes, comrade," said Foo, and he took off to his bicycle. There were no limos that morning. Most of Daeng's troops were on foot or on bikes. But nobody objected to being given these tasks. Daeng noticed her husband at the shop front.

"Any luck?" she asked.

"She hasn't seen them," said Siri.

"Damn."

"Are the hospitals covered?" he asked.

"May and Mai went without their breakfasts," said Daeng. "They're over at Mahosot now. They're good nurses. Experienced. If anything bad happened overnight they'll take care of it."

"And the Soviet hospital?" asked Siri.

"I can take that," said a young man in a white shirt buttoned to the top. He was well-groomed and confident. "I have a motorcycle."

"You a doctor there, son?" Siri asked.

"Yes, comrade," said the man.

"I've never seen you here before."

"I'm just back from East Germany. A friend recommended this place. It's my first time. Won't be my last. This is the old Laos I missed."

He stood to leave but something behind Siri caught his eye. The other customers followed his gaze. Siri turned to see Crazy Rajhid standing in the road, buck naked and semi-erect. Around his neck he wore the seat of a Western-style toilet, probably washed up from the Thai side of the river. The Indian was as iconic to Vientiane as Nelson's column was to London but perhaps less photographed. He was a young man in fine shape until you reached his mind. In the past five years, only three people had heard him speak. Siri was one of them.

"We can't find Mr. Geung and Tukta," said Siri.

Rajhid looked around the busy morning restaurant pointing at his penis, as if anyone had missed it.

"Jogendranath," said Siri, using the Indian's given name.

Rajhid's chest heaved and he gagged as he tried to free something from his throat. Siri was about to perform the Heimlich maneuver but it wasn't a chicken bone stuck in Rajhid's wind pipe. It was a sentence. He walked to Siri, hugged him, and whispered in his ear.

"I know where they went," he said, and suddenly he was Lassie. He ran a few meters along the road and stopped.

He wagged his bottom and cocked his head. The noodle shop customers had come to the street to see what was happening. Even Daeng abandoned her post at the noodle trough.

"I think he wants us to follow him," said Siri. "He knows where Geung went."

"How do you know?" asked Daeng.

"He told me."

Siri climbed on his bicycle.

"How reliable is the word of a crazy man?" said an elderly customer with the adventurous spirit of a filing clerk.

"He's never let us down before," said Daeng, "but we shouldn't put all our fish balls in one strainer."

So, Madam Daeng returned to direct her noodle troops and Siri, with Ugly at his side, went off in pursuit of Rajhid. The Indian would run thirty meters, stop, wag, and sniff the ground. There had been many moments such as this in Siri's long, peculiar relationship with Rajhid. There were times when Siri believed it was all an act, that the man had scripted these scenes just to give the appearance of being a madman. He was sure the day would come when the performances came to an end. Rajhid would take a bow, be lauded for his interpretation of insanity and they'd all go for cocktails. But that day never came. The show never ended.

They'd been following him for thirty minutes. They'd left the river and were proceeding along Luang Prabang Road. Every rainy season left the street potholed. They'd fill the holes with gravel and call it road works then be surprised when the holes came back the following year. It was the only road to the airport, a great welcome to visitors.

The fledgling Ministry of Tourism announced 1980 would be Visit Laos Year but they didn't do anything to make it happen. So, nobody came.

Rajhid ran remarkably quickly for a barefooted man. Once he'd left his comfort zone of the river bank more people shouted at him, old ladies chased him with brooms, dogs snapped at his ankles. But he ignored all this and soon they were at the turn off to Wattay Airport. Rajhid refused to enter. Siri and Ugly caught up with him.

"What do we do now?" Siri asked.

Rajhid smiled. It was that frustrating trained dog moment that Siri had seen so many times in the movies; the point where the dog barks and her owner knows what it means. But Rajhid didn't bark and real life didn't come up with easy answers.

"What is it, Lassie?" said Siri. "What are you trying to tell us?"

But in Rajhid's mind his work was done and Siri watched him run off in the direction from which they'd come. Siri looked at his Olympic wristwatch. Despite all the drama of the day it was still only 7:30 A.M. The first flight wouldn't be departing until ten, or whatever time it chose to leave. He wheeled his bicycle into the airport grounds. There was no guard at the gate. Siri knew from experience there'd be a night watchman somewhere behind a locked door and you'd not be able to rouse him until the official opening time. The terminal building was quiet with an empty car park in front of it. Some night creature had overturned a bin and spread garbage all around. The sun had risen but three electric light bulbs still burned at the front of the building.

Siri wheeled across the car park and wondered why

there were a hundred spaces marked on the concrete when there weren't even a hundred functioning vehicles in the capital. Ugly peed against a concrete post that held a government announcement speaker aloft. Siri had taught him to do that.

"Good boy," he said, and patted the dog's head.

Sure enough, the doors leading to the airport interior were locked. The terminal had an open-fronted waiting room not unlike that of a rural train station in France. There were wooden benches at its center and Siri sat on one of them wondering why Crazy Rajhid had delivered him there. The unfortunate young man was the eyes and ears of the riverfront community, but why would he think Geung and Tukta might want to come to the airport? Ugly soon got bored and went off in search of another speaker post leaving Siri alone, or so he thought. There came a groan from one of the empty benches behind him. Siri jumped to his feet and took a few steps back. What he thought was a shadow beneath the bench slowly developed a form and somebody rolled out.

"Bugger it," came a voice.

"What are you doing down there?" Siri asked.

The shape cracked a few knots, groaned and got to its knees. It was a man of about thirty with medium length but disastrous hair that sprung off in every direction. He was skinny but carried his bones well. He wore a grey safari suit common among public officials.

"Benches aren't wide enough," he said. "I'm a sleep roller. Kept falling off. So, I moved to the ground floor. Can't fall off the ground, can you?"

He stood, shook hands with Siri and they sat on the front bench.

"Siri Paiboun," said Siri.

"Sommad Somlith," said the man.

"You work here?" asked Siri.

The man laughed. "I've spent enough time here to consider it work," said Sommad. "But no, I'm deputy director of the Pakse education department."

"Then what brings you to a bench in Vientiane?" asked Siri.

"I'm in transit. I've been in transit for six days."

"Where have you been?"

"Just here so far."

Ugly had sensed human contact and returned to protect his master by lying down on his foot.

"That yours?" asked the man.

"Probably more accurate to say I'm his," said Siri. "Where are you supposed to be going?"

"Luang Prabang. I had my bookings confirmed; arrive Vientiane ten-fifty, leave for Luang Prabang two-twenty. That was six days ago. But I got bumped."

"Who by?"

"A whole queue of people. You know. The usual. Every day it's the same. People of influence. And then there's flights cancelled 'cause of crop burn offs. Sometimes a wheel falls off. The pilot's too drunk. No end of reasons not to travel. And I couldn't get a flight back to Pakse, so I'm stranded. What about you?"

"I'm just here looking for some friends," said Siri. "You might have seen them."

"What flight were they on?"

"They weren't on a flight, or . . . I don't know. They might have been. But it's unlikely."

"Then what were they doing here?"

"I don't know."

"What do they look like?"

"They look like two people with Down syndrome."

"Geung and Tukta," said Sommad.

Siri leaned back. "That's right," he said. "You talked to them?"

"Too true. We had a nice long conversation."

"Did they say why they were here?"

"Said it was top secret," said Sommad. "Spy work, they called it."

"And where did they go?"

"Well, they obviously weren't planning to fly anywhere. They arrived about seven P.M. yesterday. The last flight had left. The truck arrived about eight. I assumed that's what they were waiting for."

"They went somewhere on a truck?"

"I'm guessing they did. When it arrived they went to check it out. They were gone for about twenty minutes. When they didn't come back I walked around a bit to see where they'd gone. When you're in permanent transit there's not a lot to entertain you. A few trucks arrive at night with cargo for the next day. They just leave the crates and packages and stuff out there behind the terminal. The night watchman comes out and counts the boxes and he and the driver exchange signatures. So anyway, I stood and watched. The truck was unloaded but I didn't see any sign of Geung and Tukta. I suppose they could have gone off somewhere else. When it was empty, the truck drove out."

"Do you remember which crates were unloaded?"

"Yup."

They walked around the building to an untidy ghetto of

boxes and packing cases. Some were covered in tarpaulins, others open to the elements.

"These," said Sommad, pointing at five large crates. Two were big enough to hold three or four motorcycles, the others were the size and shape of coffins. They were wooden, probably coconut, and solidly constructed. But on the sides, there was a gap of a few centimeters between the slats. There was no sound or movement from inside the crates, but Siri could sense life . . . and death.

Dtui had told him of the chemical smells from the skeleton, and here at the loading bay the stench of disinfectant and repellent was overwhelming. But more natural scents reached out from the crates. It wasn't just the odor of bodily functions and rotting flesh; once it has submitted to fatality a body gives off a scent of defeat. That's what he could smell. Recently he had become used to the sight of the spirits waiting for their moment—for the paperwork to clear so they could move on. He'd seen the soul of his old dog Saloop, but he often wondered why he'd not seen the spirits of cows and monkeys. Creatures were dying all around him. Every day he'd pass by the skins of snakes, the corpses of rats, the broken birds that flew into the windows. And the insects. Millions died in light bulb genocide every night. He'd swatted flies and mosquitoes with no qualms whatsoever. Why did they not all come back to haunt him? Why were his sightings only of the spirits of people? And why, now in the shadow of Wattay Airport, did the spirit of a Malay bear appear to him? It lay on its back on the top crate with its legs in the air. It ground its haunches into the rough wood as if it were taking care of a lifetime of itches.

"What do you suppose is in there?" asked Sommad peeking in through the slit.

There was no answer. The transit man turned around only to find himself alone. His new friend had disappeared.

If ever Siri took control of his other world the first thing he'd do was fire his transvestite spirit guide and hire someone less complicated; someone who gave straight answers to questions, someone less prone to imagery.

Siri was on the ice-cube shelf of a huge refrigerator. The door was shut but the light was on, which showed Auntie Bpoo had done no research at all on refrigerators. The spirit guide was in there with him, still in her polar bear skin coat. It was starting to go green with mildew. She sat cross-legged between the beers on the door rack.

"I've lost Mr. Geung and Tukta," said Siri.

"None of my business," said Bpoo. "Seems like you're losing a lot of things."

"Like what?"

"At your age your body mass is being replaced with flab, your gums are receding, your prefrontal cortex is shrinking, you're losing fifty-thousand brain cells a day, half your taste buds have gone. Now I don't know where to start about your sexual performance."

"Then don't. Just tell me how to find my friends."

"That's not what I do."

"Be helpful?"

"Find missing morons. I'm not a lost and found officer."

"What is it you do, exactly, apart from insult people?"

"I take your crumbly old hand and lead you one step at a time through the precepts of the other world. You barely passed the first test, that of *taking control of your own destiny*, and here we are still stuck on *awareness*."

"I'm a very aware person."

"You think you are, but you're not."

"Test me."

"Shut your eyes."

Siri did so.

"What's the brand of the beer on either side of me?" asked Bpoo.

"Heineken. Easy. Next question."

"Perhaps it was too easy," said Bpoo. "Open your eyes."

"There," said Siri. "Heineken."

"Look more closely."

That was when Siri saw the label on the beer bottles. Where there should have been the letter "n" was the letter "m." The beer was Heimekem. Siri had failed. Bpoo turned her back on the doctor and shook her head. The bearskin coat was turning black at the edges.

"Damn," said Siri.

"No awareness," said Bpoo.

CHAPTER NINE
The Airport Connection

The director of Wattay Airport, Comrade Maysuk, reminded Phosy of one of the fancy curtains that used to hang in front of the opium dens of Vientiane during the old regime. What you saw from the outside was high class and attractive but there was almost certainly something seedy and sinister behind it. Maysuk put up a thirty-two tooth smile as soon as Phosy arrived and it didn't let up. It was the type of smile that must have cost money to piece together in some overseas dental clinic. The skin on his face was flushed pink, either from exposure to the sun or embarrassment, and he wore a tie and a short-sleeved white shirt like the CIA.

"I'm not sure I can help you," he said, pouring Phosy a glass of water. "When everyone arrived this morning, all was as it should have been. I have no idea why your friends should be here after dark. There's nothing to see, nobody to meet. We have watchmen and neither of them reported seeing any late-night visitors apart from truck drivers. No, I tell a lie, there was one transit passenger camping out in the waiting room. Apart from that . . . nothing."

Siri had briefed Phosy on his pursuit of Crazy Rajhid

and his conversation with the transit man. But it was almost midday before the chief inspector could get away from his office.

"I'm told your guards sleep all night," said Phosy.

"Nonsense," said Maysuk without losing grip of his smile. "They patrol every thirty minutes. When there's a delivery they sign the drivers' log books and have the drivers sign their arrival sheet. There's a guard room with coffee to keep them alert all night."

"If you don't mind, I'd like their contact information," said Phosy.

"They'll be back this evening," said Maysuk.

"Regardless . . ." said the policeman.

The smile was annoying Phosy. He wanted to paint graffiti on it. The director pressed a button on the machine on his desk and a voice said, "Yes, comrade?" Phosy decided he'd like one of those for himself. Maysuk told his secretary to bring in the home addresses of the night guards.

They sat silently for a while. Phosy couldn't help but notice the director's altar. It was astoundingly ornate for a representative of a supposedly atheist administration. Smoke wafted from a cluster of incense sticks in front of a vast curtain call of deities and Buddha images and small wooden characters elaborately carved and painted. On one of its shelves sat a half bottle of rum, a pack of cigarettes and a fresh banana. The director obviously called on every aid to keep his planes in the air.

"There's one thing I don't understand," said the director as they waited for the list.

"What's that?" said Phosy.

"Aren't you a little too . . . high ranking to be investigating a missing person case?"

"If that's all this was I'd have to agree I'd be better off sending a colleague to interview you," said Phosy. "But I have several cases that seem to be overlapping and the loose ends are flapping around. I'm rather good at loose ends, and I'm starting to believe these aren't several small cases but rather one big ugly one."

"Fascinating," said Maysuk. "And how does my airport fit into this?"

"Well, Director, obviously I can't go into details, but I have a feeling that all roads lead here."

"I certainly hope you're wrong," said the director, "but you know I should be delighted to help your investigation in any way. Cooperation is the keystone of progress."

"I'm very pleased to hear that."

The secretary knocked on the door and the director beckoned her in. She was unnecessarily attractive. She gave Phosy a flirtatious look as she handed the document to her director. Maysuk browsed it briefly before passing it on to Phosy.

"Thank you," he said.

"Is there anything else I can do for you?" asked Maysuk.

"In fact, there is," said Phosy. "You know? I pass through this airport often on my way here and there but I've never taken any time to enjoy the place. How about a little tour?"

The smile waned.

"What would you like to see?"

"Let's start with the cargo bay."

Actually, there wasn't much in the cargo bay. There were a few large cartons on pallets, a crumpled crate of air conditioners that seemed to have been dropped from a height, two large busts of the prime minister destined for the south, but no animals.

"Where's all the stuff that arrived last night?" Phosy asked.

"We've had two cargo flights this morning," said Maysuk.

"Where to?"

Maysuk turned to his transport manager, a short man in spotlessly clean overalls. He held a dirty clipboard.

"One domestic to Xiang Khouang," said the manager, "and one Aeroflot to Moscow."

"And where did the animals go?" asked Phosy.

The director looked at his manager then back at Phosy. "What animals would that be?" asked Maysuk.

It was the wrong response but one Phosy had been hoping for.

"The animals either sedated or dead that were delivered in five crates at around eight last night," he said.

"Was there an animal shipment last night?" Maysuk asked his manager.

The manager looked confused as if he didn't know which answer to give. A small nod from the director helped.

"Yes, sir," he said.

"Ah, that's right," said Maysuk. "There was a shipment that went out this morning on the Aeroflot flight. I remember now."

"Do you happen to have a manifest for that shipment?" asked the policeman.

"Not on me," said the director.

"But you do have one?"

"In the office."

"Good," said Phosy. "Then we'll swing by your office at the end of the tour. You wouldn't happen to recall what type of animals they were?"

The manager looked at his boss before answering.

"There might have been a couple of bears," he said. "Some rhesus monkeys probably. I'd have to check."

"And why were they being sent to Moscow?" Phosy asked.

"Transit," said the manager. "On their way to Czechoslovakia."

"Wasn't that trade shut down in the mid-seventies?" Phosy asked.

"The illegal trade, yes, of course," said Maysuk. "Those were terrible days. Inhumane. The regulations have been seriously tightened since then. All the animals are checked by registered veterinarians who issue certification that they're fit to travel. They're given inoculations and powerful sedatives so they sleep through the flight. Basically, they go to sleep here and wake up in a zoo on the other side of the world."

Phosy walked around the bay. He smelled disinfectant and an undertow of something vile.

"Clean up here recently, did you?" he asked the manager.

"Oil leakage," he replied.

"Right," said Phosy. "And do I smell insecticide?"

"You have a good nose," said Maysuk. "The airlines insist on spraying the cargo. They don't want the planes crawling with insects."

"You spray the animals?"

"It's quite humane. Not so strong as to cause any discomfort."

"Let's go and see that manifest," said Phosy.

Comrade Civilai was as concerned as everyone about the disappearance of Mr. Geung and his girlfriend, but in his mind some things were irrefutable. Nothing he was capable of doing would hasten their recovery, alive or otherwise. He no longer had influence, he didn't have Siri's detective mind, and his knees weren't so good. He wasn't about to scour the town for missing people.

So, with Siri and Daeng worrying on his behalf, he took the opportunity to visit the busiest and most efficient organization in Laos. Officially the place was called the National Union of Lao Women but, informally, everyone called it the Lao Women's Union. The one thing Civilai had noticed on his many visits there was that staff were always on their way to or out of meetings. But unlike the politburo, these meetings generally yielded results.

He saw Dr. Porn scurrying toward her office.

"Sister," he called.

A man's unnecessarily loud voice always caused a stir at the union. Conversations stopped, eyebrows raised, and there was some tutting. But once they saw the fellow was elderly and harmless they went about their business. Porn approached him and squeezed his arm affectionately.

"Civilai, you old goat," she said. She was a fit fifty with few wrinkles and no eyebrows. "I was sure you and Siri would have died of liver cirrhosis by now. What's keeping you alive?"

"The thought that every new day we might see the face of one more beautiful woman such as yourself," said Civilai.

"If I had a suspicion you were flirting, you know I'd interrupt the breastfeeding workshop and tell your wife."

"Of all the creatures on the planet, only women see ulterior motives in the declaration of their beauty," he said.

"That's probably because the butterfly has no idea what

you're saying," said Porn. She led him into her office and sat him down.

"My wife's at a breastfeeding workshop?" he asked. "Isn't it a bit late for that?"

"She's teaching it," said Porn.

"Really? I had no idea she was an expert."

"Most men have no idea of their wives' capabilities," she said. "Have you found Geung and Tukta yet?"

"Not as far as I know."

"Why aren't you out there searching?"

"Because I am here at the union making sure you have it all under control."

"And there I was thinking you were here to recruit actors for a movie," she said.

"I don't really need to be here at all, do I?" said Civilai. "There's nothing you don't already know."

"Oh, we like to have visitors."

"I assume you've already sent out the word for thespians," said Civilai.

"We have a room at the back full of people waiting for an audition."

"Really?" he said.

"No," she replied, "but I'll let you know when it happens. It's a project we'd really like to get involved in. I visualize a lot of meaty parts for our sisters."

"All the main roles as far as I remember."

"Excellent."

Only five rooms at the Ministry of Justice had telephone lines and the switchboard was out of order. That suited Judge Haeng because he didn't want to speak to anyone. He'd told the telephonist to take a message, or if it was important, to make an appointment. But if someone significant phoned, someone who might have a positive influence on his career, she was to sprint up the stairs, bang on his door, and he would run to the phone. But on this occasion the telephone operator was standing in his doorway, puffing and blowing, yet she had no name for the man who had called.

"Have you not yet learned?" Haeng asked her. "You simply tell him I'm not here and take a message."

"He was quite insistent," she said.

"We cannot make exceptions just because someone has a louder voice or a threatening tone," he said. "A good socialist speaks calmly but carries a machete. I mean, a metaphorical machete, of course, not an actual—"

"He said I should tell you the word 'Skeleton,'" she said.

Judge Haeng was in a crowded office. The clatter of typewriters and the chatter of clerks made it hard to hear the man at the end of the phone. But he did make out the words, "They know."

"Who? Who knows?" asked the judge.

"The police."

"They can't possibly," said Haeng. "It's all taken care of."

"The new chief inspector; the one you said couldn't last a week on the job, he's been to the airport."

"What did he say?"

"It doesn't matter what he said. He knows. I want him off the case."

"What?" said Haeng.

"One way or another. I want the chief inspector off my back."

"I'm in no position to hire and fire policemen. It's not my responsibility."

"Then find another way."

"I . . . I can't."

"Then you know what's going to happen," said the man.

"What are you saying?"

"It's up to you. One way or another."

He was a watchman at the airport at night but Lampuy's day job was harvesting salt at Ban Bo. The salt seemed to have preserved him in a mummified kind of way. His back and his limbs were stiff and he squinted as if he permanently had something in his eyes. Captain Sihot felt he was interviewing a very tired man.

The captain had worked with Chief Inspector Phosy for a number of years as his sergeant and he knew the ropes. He was a rough old soldier with crumbly teeth but he was honest and totally loyal. That's why he jumped two ranks when his boss got the CI job. Phosy needed men like Sihot around him.

"Nah, didn't see nothing," said Lampuy, looking over his shoulder to see if his foreman was watching.

"That's because you and your buddy took it in turns to sleep," said Sihot. "In fact, you missed all but your first two and last two security rounds. That's the system you had worked out. You did get out of bed long enough to meet a truck."

"That's rubbish, that is."

"Oh, yeah?"

"I never sleep at night."

Sihot already had all the details he needed from the other night guard.

"Look fellah," said the policeman. "I have a job. You have a job. You shovel salt. I ask questions. If they gave you half a coconut shell to fill your sack instead of a shovel, it'd take you twice as long to do your job, right? It's the same if you give me bullshit answers. That wastes my time too. Plus, it really pisses me off. You know what I'm saying?"

"Yeah."

"So, you met a truck."

"Regular delivery."

"How often?"

"Twice a week."

"Always animals?"

"Yeah. They put 'em to sleep so they're no trouble," said the guard. "Stink sometimes but we don't have to handle 'em. We just disinfect the place when they're gone."

"When you were meeting the truck last night did you see anyone that shouldn't have been there?"

"Only the transit guy. He's been there all week. I brought him some bananas."

"Nice of you," said Sihot. "You didn't see a couple?"

"Couple of what?"

"People."

"No. I signed for the delivery and went back to the guard room."

"Did you write down the truck registration number?"

"No. Just the invoice numbers. They're written on the crates."

"Any idea where the driver went next?"

"No."

"You didn't see anything out of the ordinary?"

"No."

Sihot looked into the squinty eyes and wondered if he could see much of anything.

"Look, brother," said the night watchman. "It sounds

heavy, you know? Airport security guard. Uniforms and everything. But it's quiet out there. You can hear a truck coming a kilometer away. The airport building's locked and the cargo in the bay's too heavy to run off with. It's a cushy job. Same thing night after night. No reason not to catch a bit of sleep, am I right?"

"Never any surprises?"

"No. Well . . ."

"Well what?"

"I almost shit myself the other night when the government limo turned up out of nowhere."

CHAPTER TEN
Get Down's and Boogie

By the following evening, Madame Daeng was frantic. Still she worked. Still she organized. The illegal squatters from Siri's official government residence: the abandoned, the lost, the disenfranchised—they all chipped in with free labor so no diner had gone hungry that day. But thirty-six hours of searching for Geung and Tukta had come to nothing. Overnight, Daeng had turned from concerned to angry, and she was already planning what to do if anything had happened to her protégés. The news of the airport visit and the truck had complicated matters. They had no idea where that truck might have gone or whether the couple was on board. To keep herself calm she sharpened a complete set of carving knives to a razor edge. Woe betide the next shank of pork that found its way onto her cutting board.

After the evening shift Madam Daeng took a nap and Siri and Civilai sat at a rear table of the restaurant working out camera angles for all the scenes of their screenplay. They were restricted, of course, by having just the one camera—if that—but Siri said the single camera technique would be to their advantage.

"You go to the theatre," he said, "and you have just the one pair of eyes. But that doesn't stop you enjoying the play, does it? You don't suddenly have an urge to climb up to the royal box to get another angle. Your entire experience comes from that one lens: the one in your head. Ours might be the most intimate film ever to win a Palme d'Or."

To celebrate their future victory, Siri went to the refrigerator and took the last dregs of their vodka from the freezer. He poured two shots and handed one to Civilai. The old man looked forlorn as he stared at his glass.

"What's wrong?" Siri asked.

"Siri, do you think we have . . . ?"

"Yes?"

". . . a drinking problem?"

"Goodness me no," said Siri. "As some famous drunk once said, 'You drink. You fall over. No problem.'" He raised his glass.

"I'm serious," said Civilai. "What if all this drinking shortens our lives?"

Siri laughed. "We're seventy-five, brother," he said. "If drinking has shortened our lives by even twenty-five percent thus far, that means we'd have lived to a hundred apiece. And how many fun-loving centenarians have you met recently? They're all withered and immobile. We're doing a service to our bodies by shortening our lives."

"I don't know," said Civilai. "Dr. Porn was sure we'd both be dead by now."

"Ah, so that's it," said Siri. "You were lured into the enchanted caverns of the women's union where fairy godmother Porn cast her spell on you again. She'd have us eating watercress baguettes and drinking frog eye juice into eternity. The healthiest fossils on the planet."

"It's all right for you," said Civilai. "You're possessed. You have a psychic medical team on board with an interest to keep their host alive. When you go, they're homeless. Nobody cares if I go."

"I care, you grumpy old bastard. Now drink your medicine and focus on the—"

He was interrupted by the sound of a motorcycle. Daeng came running down the stairs and into the street where Phosy sat on his department Vespa with Dtui and Malee behind.

"Any news?" she said, but the dour expressions on their faces answered the question.

"I've had everyone looking for them," said Phosy. "No sign."

Madame Daeng began to prepare them a late supper. Siri and Civilai joined them and listened as Phosy recounted the story of his visit to Director Maysuk and, as a finale, about the Zil that arrived at the airport on the morning the skeleton was discovered.

"The watchman said it arrived around three-fifteen," said Phosy.

"Then it could only have been Judge Haeng's," said Civilai. "By that time all the others were accounted for. Am I right?"

"What was he doing there?" asked Daeng.

"No idea," said Phosy. "If it was an official visit the driver would have had the watchman sign his work document. But this guy didn't even stop at the gate. Who's going to chase after a government limo?"

"And the watchman didn't see who got out?" asked Siri.

"No," said Phosy. "He went back to his office and told his pal there was a limo parked in front of the administration block. The office light was on so they assumed their boss had an early meeting. They're not really encouraged to think too much."

"But if it was Haeng, it would make no sense at all," said Daeng. "If we've got this all worked out right, Judge Haeng arranged to meet this fictitious VIP at the airport the previous morning, so he'd have an excuse to put the skeleton in his trunk. He removed the trunk key from the bunch so the driver wouldn't find it. That night he pretended to be drunk, commandeered the Zil, and left the skeleton at the arch. He'd successfully done what he set out to do, whatever that was. All that remained then was to drive up and down the river and be seen a few times."

"He couldn't have known that the driver would discover the key was missing, or that the curfew patrol would identify him," said Siri, "but basically it didn't matter. Until we came along he thought he'd got away with it."

"So why would he go back to the airport in the middle of all this?" said Daeng.

"There's only one person who can answer that," said Phosy, "and I think the judge has reached his desperation level."

"Why so?" asked Civilai.

"I got this on my desk as I was leaving this evening," said Phosy. He unfolded two sheets of typed paper and laid them on the table. "It's signed and stamped by the Vice Minister of Justice, but I happen to know he's off in Hanoi. It's an urgent request for me to attend a seminar in Houay Xai. There was a plane ticket stapled to it. I checked. There is a seminar in Houay Xai but it's about border demarcation. Nothing to do with me at all."

"The judge is trying to get you out of town," said Daeng.

"So it seems."

"I think it's time for that serious talk," said Siri.

"I have to be careful," said Phosy. "There's no precedent for this. Arresting a judge is in the same category as staging a coup. You're bringing down a pillar of the establishment. You have to be really sure of your accusations."

Siri put down the ministry order and shook his head. "Look," he said, "I don't like the fellow, never have. We've got all kinds of personal smut against him. We've got a certain letter we use to blackmail him whenever we need a favor. So, I suppose you could say that we've kept him in the game. He still has his position because we haven't disclosed what we know about him. That, in an odd way, makes us all culpable for what he does."

"Are you making excuses for him?" Dtui asked.

"Not at all," said Siri. "But I get a feeling he's involved in something that's beyond him. I don't believe he killed the girl or was involved in her torture. He hasn't got the balls for it. And I think there had to be a really good reason why he'd go through all this Zil intrigue. The faked letter from the vice minister is the last straw. Everything's gone wrong for him. He's about to cave in."

"Siri's right," said Daeng, serving up a large bowl of fried rice. "If we don't intervene soon he's likely to do something even more stupid. Don't forget he's not that aware."

"I'll take him in tomorrow morning," said Phosy. "You know I was hoping my first case would be a little less . . . What the . . . ?"

Phosy was looking over Siri's shoulder toward the open shutter. The others turned their heads. Standing in the shadows beyond the doorway were two familiar characters.

"Hello," said Mr. Geung.

"Hello," said Tukta.

Geung's stutter made his stories hard work to listen to. Tukta spoke quite well but rarely and reluctantly. So, they'd developed a technique where one plugged into the gappy dialogue of the other to keep things flowing. The group ignored the fact that the couple smelled of animal excrement after their time on the road. They couldn't abide the thought of waiting any longer for their story and the returnees were most keen to tell it.

"We decided to to . . ."

"To go to the airport," said Tukta. "Geung was full of the spirits of the civets. They were calling him."

"You speak civet?" Civilai asked.

Everyone told him to shut up but Geung and Tukta thought the question was worth a laugh.

"Go on," said Daeng.

"After work we too-too-took a *tuktuk* to the airport," said Geung.

"We talked to Uncle Sommad in the airport waiting room for a while," said Tukta.

"But I I I could hear the civets calling me," said Geung. "There was a a t-t-truck come but that w-w-wasn't where the civets were."

"They were on the other side of the runway under gravel," said Tukta.

"Their ssspirits were sad."

"Geung said there were ten of them. We sat with them for a few minutes. I sang them a song."

"Wa-wa-one couldn't see."

"Some bad person had stuck a chopstick in its eye.

Others were sick. I think it's good for them they were all dead."

"Th-th-th . . ."

"The truck was unloading some big crates," said Tukta. "Two men were throwing them on the ground. Not careful at all. The men went for a smoke. We went and looked. I couldn't see so good but Geung said there were animals in the crates."

"They w-w-were all sad."

"I started to cry. Geung cried too. One bear was dead."

"And we g-g-got on the t-t-truck."

"We squashed in the corners like slugs so the driver didn't see us. It was magic."

"And the truck w-w-went out and w-w-we went out and drove and drove."

"Why?" asked Dtui.

"We we we . . ."

"We wanted to see where the animals came from," said Tukta.

"We drove and drove and drove and—"

"All right, we appreciate the distance," said Civilai. "Where did you go exactly?"

"The sun came up and we stopped in in a little village."

"And the driver and assistant got out and we got out and we didn't know where we were."

"B-b-b-but the driver wen-wen—"

"Went into a house and we see him hand over money to the woman in the house. A lot of money."

"A l-l-lot."

"And . . . but the house isn't a house. It's a big like, market beside and behind. And all these animal noises."

"Un-untidy. Dirty. Smelly. And some other men came and and threw bags and boxes and crates on the truck and and the t-t-truck starts to go."

"And we wonder if we should get back on the truck but it's too late. So, we stay there."

"There's a foo a food shop down from the market and we got r-r-rice porridge and meat."

"The food was horrid. The place was horrid. Everything was horrid. The woman in the shop talked to us like we're little children freaks."

"Like w-w-we're stupid."

"But we have to stay there 'cause we're watching the market."

"And so so so many animals come to that market."

"Hunters and people with rattan cages and myna birds tied together by their feet."

"And they they they're all frightened and sick and they they they called for help but nobody heard them. It wasn't f-f-fair. This is our garden. These are are our animals. They're n-n-not f-for sale."

"How did you get back here?" Daeng asked.

Geung and Tukta looked at each other and smiled.

"The t-t-two-head lizard show," said Geung.

"I don't understand," said Daeng.

"You you remember we went to the T-T-That Luang festival and there was a two-head lizard in a g-glass case?"

"And a both sex monkey and stuffed five-leg dog," said Tukta.

"And what's the connection?" Dtui asked.

"We are t-two head lizards," said Geung, and laughed again.

"We were sitting in the stall drinking coffee . . ."

"I shhhouldn't drink coffee," said Geung.

"And some man comes to the shop and the owner says, 'Here they are. Aren't they cute?' and the man sits and listens to us and the owner says, 'See? They can talk.'"

"And the man aaaahsks if we want a free trip aaaah-round the country with him. And I ask, 'Whhhere are you going?' and he says he's heading n-n-north. And I say, 'Will you p-pass through Vientiane?' and he says 'of course.'"

"Not even offering money," said Tukta. "Just food, like we're goldfish. And I hear him talk to the owner, and she asks for a tip for finding us, and he gives her some kip, and he talks about dirty stuff he wants us to do."

"He thought we were were deaf," said Geung.

"But there you were getting a free ride back to Vientiane," said Siri. "Who's the stupid one in this story?"

"And we slept one night in his van with the stuffed animals with five legs and snakes in bottles and posters of people joined together," said Tukta. "And we ask can we stop off at our shop to get our clothes . . . ?"

"And then we c-c-can be b-big stars in your freak show," said Geung.

"And here we are," said Tukta.

"And where is he?" Phosy asked.

"Outside," said Geung.

Siri and Daeng looked at each other and smiled.

"You or me?" Siri asked.

"After a day like today, allow me," said Daeng. She took off her pinafore, mussed her hair, armed herself with the number five carving knife and headed for the street.

A uniformed officer escorted Judge Haeng along the concrete corridor to the office at the end. For reasons best known to himself, in his hand the judge held a thick copy of *The Communist Manifesto*. The office door was shut which emphasized the fact that the room was air-conditioned. Haeng's air-conditioning had been off for a month. The officer knocked and a faint "Yes?" could be heard through the old teak door. The officer opened it and somehow shoveled the judge inside without entering himself. The chief inspector sat at a splendid desk and looked comfortable behind it. The judge took three frog-march steps to the desk and stood at attention. The door clicked shut behind him.

"Firstly," he said, "I do not come to you. You come to me."

"And yet, here you are," said Phosy.

"Secondly, I may remind you that I am a judge and the director of public prosecution, which means I am your superior."

"Yet I was recruited and promoted by the Ministry of Interior which puts us on different tracks. You aren't my boss and if I have my way you won't be anybody's boss by the end of the week."

"And thirdly—"

"All right, we've had enough counting for one day," said Phosy. "Sit yourself down and we'll get directly to the reason I sent for you and the reason you came."

"I will not have you bully me into—"

"Oh shut up and sit down," came a voice.

The judge turned to see Siri and Civilai sitting on a vinyl couch against the far wall. They were shuffling through a pile of papers on the coffee table in front of them.

"What . . . are they . . . doing here?" said the judge, dramatically.

"All will be revealed," said Phosy, "and as soon as you sit

down and calm down we can start to answer each other's questions."

"I will sit but I want it to go on record that I strongly object to both the manner of this—"

"Haeng, put your puffy back side on that chair," said Siri.

The judge did as he was told. The wooden guest chair swayed a little beneath him.

"I shall begin with the obvious first question," said Phosy. "Why did you go back?"

"I think, in order to play this game, I shall need a little more input," said the judge.

"You'd done it all so efficiently," said Phosy. "The pickup at the airport. The drunken hijack of the Zil. It was almost a faultless performance. But the only thing we can't understand is why you returned to the airport."

"I really have no idea what you're talking about," said the judge.

"Here's what we think," said Siri.

Judge Haeng didn't bother to turn around to look into his accuser's fresh-grass-colored eyes.

"Is he a police officer now?" Haeng asked. "Because if he isn't I don't have to listen to him."

"We think, for some reason, you were forced to do this," Siri continued. "We think someone took advantage of the fact you had access to a government limousine and could travel at night at will."

Siri stood and walked to a position where he had eye contact with Haeng but the judge continued to stare at the chief inspector.

"Hiring senior citizens to do your detective work now?" Haeng asked.

But the judge's eyes were moist and the forceful tone he assumed from day to day to make himself more threatening was teetering.

"You know that we can release a document at any time that would have you kicked out of your position?" said Civilai, "but we haven't done so."

"Because it suits you all better to blackmail me and keep me submissive," said the judge.

"Not, you have to agree, for sinister purposes," said Phosy.

"We only blackmail you if we think you're wandering off the path of righteousness and into the brambles of evil," said Civilai.

"Nicely put," said Siri.

"Thank you."

"But what you did the other night was beyond our help," said Phosy. "You are an accomplice to a murder, and—"

"That's ridiculous," said the judge. A small, barely noticeable bead of sweat had begun to roll down his brow.

"And to make matters worse," said Phosy, "if indeed they could be any worse, you go and falsify a document and use ministry funds to buy me an air ticket to the north."

"That suggests to us that you're desperate," said Siri, "and you're on your way down a very slippery slope. And even though the three of us dislike you a good deal, we are your only hope for redemption."

By this stage, the judge's neck seemed no longer able to bear the weight of his head. Siri went back to the sofa and continued working on the screenplay. From experience, he knew that it took time for a guilty conscience to surface. They waited.

"We were together in Moscow," said Haeng, at last.

They all looked up.

"Some undergraduate work," said the judge, "some language study. But I went on to law and he took public administration. We drank together. We had similar backgrounds: wealthy fathers investing in a socialist future. In our second year I . . . I did something . . . something terrible, and he was a witness to it."

"Should we assume you're referring to Comrade Maysuk at Wattay?" said Phosy.

"Yes," said Haeng.

"What was it?" said Civilai. "What did you do?"

"I will honestly die before I tell anyone that," said Haeng. "I will cut off my own head, rip out my—"

"Okay, okay," said Siri, "we get it. So, what did Maysuk make you do to keep your secret safe?"

"He called me to the airport one day," said Haeng. "We used to drink together in one of the small hangars across the runway from time to time. Talk about the old days. But that day we drank in his office—drank quite a lot, and it wasn't till after dark that he led me to the hangar. He told me he had a secret. He unlocked the door, put on the light, and pointed. That's when I saw the skeleton. It was in a sitting position against the far wall. It was surreal. She had hair but no face. Her bone structure was mostly intact like a lab skeleton."

"So, what did you do?" Phosy asked.

"I had another drink," said Haeng.

"That concerns me," said Civilai. "You find a skeleton and your first reaction is to have a drink?"

"I was already drunk," said Haeng. "The skeleton shocked me. I needed something to steady my nerves. Maysuk asked me how we might dispose of the body discreetly.

He said she'd arrived in a packing case the night before and he—"

"Were there animals in the packing case with her?" Siri asked.

"I believe so," said Haeng. "Maysuk wanted to avoid all the administrative red tape he'd be thrust into if the body was discovered."

"You agreed to dispose of a body to avoid red tape?" said Phosy.

"No, of course not," said Haeng. "Not at first. I positively refused to be a part of it. I am a judge. We have ethical standards. But . . ."

"But what?" said Siri.

"I might have suggested we move the body elsewhere."

"Haeng, you're a disaster," said Civilai.

"I was drunk," said Haeng. "Don't tell me you haven't made dubious decisions when you were drunk."

"Of course," said Siri, "but then the morning comes and you blame your stupidity on fermented rice and you re-enter humankind. You apologize and those you've wronged eventually forgive you. You don't transport dead people when you're sober."

"I know," said the judge. "I know. And the next morning I told Maysuk I wouldn't be involved in a cover up. I said I'd contact the police and not incriminate him in any way. That's when he brought up the incident in the USSR."

"He blackmailed you," said Civilai.

"He said if I didn't keep my word he'd release the evidence," said Haeng.

"So, you agreed to move the body," said Phosy.

"I didn't want the woman's death to go unnoticed," said Haeng. "That's why I chose a public place."

"Talk us through that day," said Phosy.

"Would you like a Fanta Orange or something?" said Civilai.

"Civilai!" said Phosy.

"Sorry," said Civilai, "just showing compassion for the condemned man."

Haeng sobbed just once before describing his day.

"It was three days after our drunken night with the corpse," said the judge. "I'd already booked the Zil for the airport and the Soviet do in the evening. I knew a vice minister from Vietnam was due in for the Soviet event. I also knew he'd not show up because he hates the Soviet justice minister. So, I took the limousine to Wattay early. On that first night with the airport director we'd put the skeleton in a freezer that had a lock. My Zil driver was drinking coffee in the canteen and having a good time with his friends so I went over there and told him I needed the keys. I said I'd been offered a few kilos of leftover Aeroflot meals and some duty-free booze and I needed to put them in the trunk. I said we could share them fifty-fifty. I said that as a government worker he couldn't be seen loading contraband into an official vehicle. There were spies everywhere. I said I'd slip the key to an airport official to load them. The driver promised to keep it to himself and gave me the keys. I took the Zil to the loading bay and we loaded the skeleton. Bits were falling off all the time so we put them in a plastic bag and brought that along too. Maysuk made sure his workers weren't anywhere near.

"I returned the Zil to the priority parking space with a few duty-free tidbits on the back seat for the driver. When I gave him the key ring, the trunk key wasn't attached. He didn't notice. I thought I'd got away with it."

"It didn't occur to you that this was more than a slight overreaction from the director?" said Phosy.

"What do you mean?" said the judge.

"That he'd force you to go to all this trouble just to side-step some administrative bull?"

"Red tape can be debilitating for serious administrators," said Haeng.

"Really?" said Siri.

"At the top level, just the requisition of a ladder can take up to a dozen forms," said the judge. "Can you imagine how much paperwork you'd have to fill out to explain a corpse in your cargo?"

"You really are a fool," said Civilai.

"Why?" said Haeng.

"Did it really not occur to you that the director might have been the one that killed her?" said Siri.

"I . . . ? No," said the judge. "It's . . . no, he couldn't have. It was too . . . too elaborate. She was clearly killed by the animals in the crate."

"You didn't wonder why he involved you at all?" said Phosy.

"What?"

"It's an airport," said Phosy. "There are trucks in and out all day. What was to stop him throwing the body onto one of them?"

"Or even put her in his own truck, drive her off to the bush and dump her somewhere?" said Civilai. "He didn't need you."

"I'm a friend," said Haeng. "He needed advice."

"A friend doesn't blackmail you into committing a whole charge sheet of crimes," said Phosy. "But this all brings us back to the original question. Why did you go back to the airport after you dumped your girlfriend?"

"I didn't," said Haeng.

"The guard saw you arrive there," said Phosy.

"I don't mean I didn't go there," said the judge. "I mean it wasn't after I deposited the body. I went there while she was still in the trunk."

"Why?" asked Phosy.

"From the first moment, I'd been overwhelmed with remorse," said Haeng. "I was ashamed of what I was involved in. I had betrayed the process of the law. I wanted to rewind time, put her back in the hangar with all her parts then call you lot to the crime scene. It was too much for me to bear."

"And why didn't you?" asked Civilai.

"He was there, Maysuk. I wasn't expecting him to be in his office that early in the morning. He heard me arrive and intercepted the car. He told me I was in it too deeply to pull out. That if he got into trouble it wouldn't be nearly as serious as the trouble I was in. I'd moved a corpse from a crime scene and he could claim to know nothing about it. The devils were on my back. I hadn't planned to put her at the arch. I drove back into town. My original idea was to leave her somewhere quiet and dark. But I couldn't be sure she'd be found, afraid the locals would be too scared to report it, afraid the dogs might get her. I wanted her to be discovered immediately. No more humiliation. I wanted the process of law to start there and then."

"So, you put her at the arch under the one functioning light bulb knowing one of the patrols would spot her soon enough," said Phosy.

Haeng nodded. "What's going to happen to me?" he asked.

"You won't be a judge anymore; that's for certain," said Siri.

"But that's the least of your problems," said Phosy. "The big question is whether they'll have you shot or just locked away for the rest of your life."

The little judge lowered his head into his hands and sobbed uncontrollably. And in some peculiar way the three men who'd gone there that day to bully him into a confession felt sorry for him.

CHAPTER ELEVEN
Enough Perverts to Keep Us All Busy

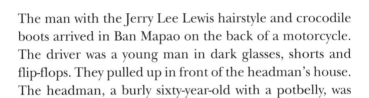

The man with the Jerry Lee Lewis hairstyle and crocodile boots arrived in Ban Mapao on the back of a motorcycle. The driver was a young man in dark glasses, shorts and flip-flops. They pulled up in front of the headman's house. The headman, a burly sixty-year-old with a potbelly, was sitting on the veranda with two other lowlifes.

"What do you want?" said the headman.

"I'm Beung," said the passenger. "I think you're expecting me."

He had a central Thai accent, self-righteous, snotty. He climbed off the bike and brushed the road dust from his tonic mohair suit.

"And who are you?" the headman asked the driver.

"Name's Hok," said the boy. "Motorcycle rental."

"That's class," said one of the lowlifes, laughing, "renting a motorcycle with a chauffeur."

"Never did learn to ride one," said Beung. "Sooner be in a car, me. But your charming country's never heard of car rental. Didn't have a choice."

"All right, boy, you can go now," said the headman.

"I'll need him to take me back," said Beung.

"No, you won't. Sọd off, boy."

"All right," said Beung. He took a leather briefcase from the pannier, reached into a pocket and pulled out a hundred baht note, which he gave the driver.

"Shit," said the headman, climbing down from the porch, "the little punk wouldn't earn that kind of money in a month."

He held out his hand but the driver stood staring at him. The headman slapped the young man in the face and gestured again for him to give up his Thai banknote.

"Unless you've had enough of living," said the headman.

The boy reluctantly handed over his money. The headman reached into his pocket and gave the driver a few thousand kip. It looked like a lot more than what it was worth. The driver trod down on the kick-starter but the headman grabbed his arm.

"We don't like outsiders here," he said. "If you tell anyone where you've been and who you brought to us, we really will kill you. Get it?"

The driver nodded.

"Now bugger off," said the headman.

The boy was shaking so violently he almost went off the dirt track on his way out of the village. They all watched until he was out of sight.

"So, Bangkok, you must be feeling uncomfortable now, right?" said the headman to the visitor. "You're all alone with a bunch of hicks, and there you are with a bag full of money and no witnesses."

Beung laughed.

"Something funny?" said the headman.

"Did you hear about Mu Yor down in Savanaketh?" said Beung.

"No," said the headman.

"There was a fire about four months ago," said Beung. "Lot of people died there. Twelve to be exact. Tragic, it was. The headman and eleven of his men were burned alive. The whole village football team. There wasn't much left of them nor the ropes that tied them together."

"You saying you had something to do with that?" asked the headman.

"Me?" said Beung. "No, no, no. I'm just a business man. But it is the reason I'm here. My predecessor—that means the person before me, just in case you're as ignorant as you look—my predecessor went into Mu Yor with the monetary advance for a deal not unlike the one we're attempting here today. But the headman in Mu Yor decided to make my predecessor disappear, take his money, and pretend he'd never been there. In such a way, the merchandise was still available to sell a second time. But word travels fast down there in the bogs and whoosh, barbequed hillbillies.

"My people know I'm here today. I don't have to be afraid because you look like a man who has an eye to the future. And if this deal goes down successfully you know we'll all be getting filthy rich together over the next few years."

After a couple of seconds, during which the words caught up with the headman's intellect, he smiled, put his arm around his visitor's shoulder and called for something to drink.

The headman walked with Beung up a winding track on a hill behind the village. Three henchmen tagged on behind them. At least one had a pistol in his belt.

"You do know that was just a test?" said the headman.

"A test for what?" asked Beung.

"To be sure you weren't a cop."

"Yeah, really," said Beung, "this is our new standard uniform."

"A cop would have crumpled."

"Give me a break. You know there are no cops patrolling the border. They've hardly got enough police to man the traffic boxes around Vientiane. We've got it made here."

"That's why we've upgraded and called in you people," said the headman. "The Thais we worked with before were small fry. Ten years and we barely made enough to run even. When we heard about you we knew you were pros. Knew you'd have an eye on the authorities."

"We haven't been busted in all the time we've been operating," said Beung, who seemed angrier at the dust on his shoes than the sheerness of the climb.

They arrived at a windowless hut with a corrugated metal roof. A man slept under a handmade shelter of banana leaves by the door. The headman woke him up by kicking him in the head. The guard staggered to his feet and made a meal of opening the padlock.

"Once I'm satisfied with the merchandise I give you half your fee," said Beung, wiping his shoes with a large cloth from his briefcase. "You take them down to the river to your raft and carry them over at night. Our people meet you on the far bank and hand over the other half."

"Sounds good enough to me," said the headman.

The drowsy guard finally got the door open and Beung stepped into the doorway. The first thing to hit him was the stench. The only light came from behind him and a few gaps in the roofing but it was enough. There were some fifteen children inside. Beung judged them to be somewhere between five and twelve years of age. They all lay on the dirt floor. Some had the strength to look up but there was no vitality in their eyes.

"They're all alive, are they?" said Beung.

"Sure they are," said the headman. "We give 'em poppy tea to keep 'em drowsy. Easier to look after. You want to check 'em?"

"No," said the visitor. "If they're breathing I'm satisfied. Excellent work. This is a very professional unit you're running here. How many kids do you think you've shipped over the border in the past ten years?"

"Must be over a thousand by now."

"All down for adoption in Malaysia?"

"Most of. Then the older ones . . . Well, there are enough perverts to keep us all busy. Know what I mean, Bangkok?"

"I certainly do," said Beung. "Well, look, this has been a lot of fun, but I'm afraid I have to shoot you now."

"Yeah, right," the headman laughed.

Beung unfurled the cloth he'd been using to clean his shoes to reveal a small handgun. He aimed it at the headman who seemed confused, not sure whether this was still some sort of joke. But from the surrounding vegetation there appeared half a dozen armed male and female officers including Hok, the motorcycle taxi driver. There was a brief gunfight during which one of the lowlifes was killed but the others gave up their weapons and put up their hands. All, that is, apart from the headman who stood smiling at the man he'd called Bangkok. The team had been secreted around the village since before the sun rose. They knew of the trafficking operation but not where the children were being kept. So everything hung on Wee's ability to convince the gang he was a Thai trafficker and be shown the hidden trail. Without Hok on his motorcycle, Wee had been on his own and, once again, he proved his worth to the team.

The men were handcuffed and the children were carried outside and laid in the warming sun. They'd be taken to a hospital and treated for their sores and diseases, and an effort would be made to reunite them with their families. But not all of the kids would have been kidnapped. There were parents who saw the act of selling a child as a necessary evil in order to feed the other siblings. In that case, history would no doubt repeat itself. There were no protection agencies to judge the suitability of a family to raise children.

The traffickers were led back down the trail in a human chain at gunpoint. In the village, an armored truck was waiting for them. As he was being loaded on board, the headman stopped and leaned toward Wee. His breath stank.

"I guess these kids are yours now, Bangkok," he said. "Did you notice the little hotty in the man's khaki shirt? If you're going to keep one, I highly recommend her, if you know what I mean."

Wee smiled, took the headman's arm and guided him up the steps of the truck.

"Let me help you up there, old fellow," he said.

Vientiane had its hue moods. Some days the colors were so vivid it was as if a team of landscape painters had worked through the night to give the place some character. On others, one might be hard pressed to tell yellow from brown. On this evening, even with the aid of a setting sun, the riverbank in front of Madam Daeng's shop was a print setter's rag of greys and blacks.

"Where is he?" asked Madam Daeng.

"I've got him somewhere safe," said Phosy.

"And what are you planning to do with him?" asked Civilai.

Phosy looked into the faces he'd learned to respect, trust and love over the past few years.

"I'm considering sending him back to work," he said.

He'd expected a barrage of "What?" and "Are you mad?" but instead he saw the tilting of heads as his friends considered the consequences of such an act.

"That might work," said Daeng.

"I don't know," said Nurse Dtui.

"If we make a song and dance of arresting him, Director Maysuk will know that whatever scheme he'd been planning was foiled," said the policeman. "Like this, it's business as usual at Judge Haeng's office until we know how the girl was killed and what the director's role was."

"You think the judge will go along with this?" asked Dtui.

"I think he'd grasp any chance at redemption," said Daeng. "At the very least he'll be in favor of getting revenge on his so-called friend."

"What if he makes a run for it?" asked Civilai.

"Haeng? At least that wouldn't be out of character," said Siri. "But, honestly, where would he go? I don't see him swimming the Mekhong and making a new start in Wisconsin. He's sampled power and that's a hard act to follow."

"It's worth a chance," said Daeng. "Phosy announces that he's leaving for his seminar in Houay Xai, which shows that Haeng got him out of the way as he'd promised. Then perhaps we find out what this is all about."

"Couldn't you just arrest Maysuk and beat him up a bit?" asked Dtui.

They all looked at her.

"Dtui!" said Daeng. "I'm surprised at you." She stared at the blushing nurse then turned to Phosy. "But you could, couldn't you?" she asked.

"I thought about it," said Phosy, "and it's not out of the question some way down the track. But there's a lot to be said for letting him make his own mistakes first."

"But you aren't going to the seminar, are you?" said Civilai.

"No," said the chief inspector, "Dtui and I will be taking a little trip along the river. Our super spies here, Mr. Geung and Tukta, have identified the middleman who's buying and selling the animals."

Geung and Tukta high-fived.

"It's the only link we have to the origin of the skeleton. We need to find out where she came from."

"You're taking your wife on a case?" said Civilai.

"We're a team," said Dtui. "Country people are much more open about telling secrets to a couple than to a single man."

"You want us t-t-t-to look after Malee?" Geung asked.

"She's okay with the neighbors for a day," said Dtui. "In fact, she's got a crush on their son."

"And what do you want us to do?" asked Siri.

"I was wondering if you'd like a trip to the zoo," said Phosy. "You can take your wife too."

"And what is our motivation apart from a feeling of superiority over the lower species?" asked Daeng.

"There's a keeper there named Chong," said Dtui. "He's been there for a while. Everyone tells us the animal trade has been cleaned up since the old regime. Director Maysuk told Phosy a trip around the world is every bear's dream."

"I hear they get to watch a movie on the flight," said Civilai.

"I'd be interested to hear just how clean the business really is," said Phosy. "I'm wondering if our skeleton girl might have learned some truths about the trade and upset the wrong people."

"You think she was some kind of animal rights advocate?" said Daeng.

"It's not impossible, given what we've seen so far," said Siri.

"And us?" said Geung.

"Someone has to keep the noodles flowing," said Daeng. "And I've been told by a lot of customers that there's no difference between a Mr. Geung spicy number three and a Madame Daeng spicy number three. There is nothing more I can teach you."

Geung and Tukta hugged with broad smiles on their wide faces.

The meeting disbanded, but before everyone went their separate ways, Tukta broke away from her fiancé and whispered to Dtui.

"Can I see you privately?" she said.

"Of course, love," said Dtui.

She followed the girl to Mr. Geung's private quarters.

Civilai was the only one with no role in this—in his opinion—rather dull investigation. They threaten the judge who implicates the airport director who confesses to the murder of the girl. It was a script even Hollywood would yawn at. So instead, Civilai responded to the note he'd received from Dr. Porn.

"You wanted me?" he asked, leaning against her office door frame. There was no actual door.

"Ah, Civilai," she said, looking up from her files. "Nice of you to come. Sit."

Civilai sat.

"We are being attacked," she said.

"By whom?" he asked.

"Ministry of Culture."

"For what?"

"Breach of contract," said Porn.

"What contract?" said Civilai. "We have no contract, no agreement, no copyright. Nobody's signed anything."

"They say you engaged in an oral contract with the vice minister."

"Well," said Civilai, smiling, "as some Hollywood producer once famously said, 'An oral contract isn't worth the paper it's written on.' And, Porn, it has nothing to do with them at all. It's our damned film that they hijacked. And we, in turn, decided to share it with the Lao Women's Union."

"Which is also an oral contract."

"It's different," said Civilai. "We're friends. Comrades. We rely on trust."

Dr. Porn swiveled in her chair and took down a wad of papers from the shelf beside her.

"Here's a transcript of our oral contract," she said, "just in case you plan to dump us as well. Please take a look at it and sign it."

"It's long."

"Twenty-two pages."

"Can't you just pick out the highlights for me?"

"If you insist. We have final say on the script. We approve the actors. We have no obligation to provide funding but it's not out of the question and we get forty percent of profits derived from the completed film."

"That's quite some oral contract," said Civilai. "Have you rewritten the script already?"

"Certainly not. In fact, we liked it very much. Your Dr. Siri has a knack. I loved the way he wove in the ghosts for a little comedy. We might up the female roles a little, absolutely enhance the Madame Daeng part. But, besides that, I'd say it pretty much stands as it is."

"You do realize that even a written contract has no legal status here?"

"Of course," said Porn. "But we'll send a copy to our sister organization in Hanoi. You wouldn't want to mess with them."

"Where do I sign?"

She handed him a pen and pushed the oral contract across the desk. He signed, *Dr. Siri Paiboun.* That was good enough for her.

"When do we start?" said Civilai.

"We've taken the liberty of running auditions already," said Porn. "There's been a lot of interest."

"Is that so?" said Civilai. "And how many roles have you filled?"

"All but one," said Dr. Porn. "Actually, we've been debating whether to make your character female."

Civilai's mouth opened but nothing came out. He reached for the contract but Porn beat him to it.

"Well, it seems to be baking just fine in that oven of yours," said Nurse Dtui.

Tukta giggled. She lay on Mr. Geung's cot with her legs akimbo.

"It's not indigestion?" asked Tukta.

"No," said Dtui, "you really are pregnant. Your body seems in a hurry to announce it."

"I knew two days after we danced," said Tukta.

Dtui had spent much of her career in the gynecology ward and she'd learned to read the signs. There were the mood swings, the bloating, the light bleeding, the sore breasts, the nausea, the lethargy. It was all there and more. But the main test was that a woman knows her own body. Tukta could feel the changes. There was no doubt in her mind. Usually Dtui was delighted to pass on such news to her young ladies but there was something uncomfortable about this. Tukta had a life inside her but the baby had a pentathlon ahead of it to make it into the world. It would have to combat disease and sickness and all the odds that nature stacked up against a Down syndrome mother just to make it to the ninth month. Then the serious problems would begin.

"I'm happy," said Tukta.

"Me too," said Dtui.

CHAPTER TWELVE
All about Yves

"You can sit at your desk," said Phosy.

"I don't understand," said Judge Haeng.

"We're putting you back in the game for a while," said Phosy.

The two men were in the judge's office. Despite all the drama Haeng had only been absent for forty-eight hours. In Laos that wasn't even cause for a search party for a public official. They disappeared all the time. Haeng sat and rested his hands on his desktop as if he'd never expected to be sitting there again. He seemed meek and confused.

"Why?" he asked.

"This is your chance to apologize," said Phosy.

"How?"

"By solving the case for us."

"What . . . what do I have to do?"

"Just be your normal, obnoxious self," said Phosy. "You pretend you got away with the Zil thing and you ordered me out of the city. You work through your in-tray as if nothing had happened."

"What do I do if Maysuk gets in touch?"

"That would be perfect. That's what we're hoping will happen. We want to know why he set you up and who the girl is."

"You expect me to act as if nothing's happened?"

"Is that a problem?"

"Of course it is," said Haeng. "Everything's different. I'm nothing now, nobody. A little play acting for you and your team isn't going to change my future. No matter the result this isn't going to get me out of the gutter."

"No, but you can make it your starting point. As long as you're aware you're in the gutter you only have one direction to go. This way you can start your new life by doing something selfless, something positive. The alternative is that you stay in the cell I just pulled you out of and you start to rot there. This is a second chance."

Haeng looked at his hands and sighed. "What's to stop me from leaving?" he said.

"Your conscience, if you have one." Phosy shrugged and headed for the door.

"Chief Inspector," said Haeng.

"What?"

"I understand I'm not in a position to ask a favor."

"Then don't ask," said Phosy.

Haeng stood and walked to the front of his desk. "And I would completely understand if you said no, but this isn't for me. It's for my family."

"Well?"

"My career's over, probably my life is in the balance. The shame is already eating me. I deserve everything I'll get for abusing my position. But, there's my father."

"What about him?" said Phosy.

"He loves this country. He sent me to study in the USSR,

and I promised to return and dedicate my life to Laos. It will be hard enough for him to learn of my stupidity over the skeleton affair. But if he ever thought I'd betrayed my country it would kill him."

Phosy turned to face him. "Are you talking about the letter?" he asked.

"Yes."

"You offered to hand over state secrets to the Americans in return for a green card. That's treason, boy."

"I know," said Haeng staring at the ground like a school-boy in front of his headmaster, "and not a day goes by that I don't wish I could unwrite that letter. It was totally imbecilic of me. I was going through a bad period in my life. Look, Phosy, I'm already finished. You have me cold. I deserve no favors, but disclosing the contents of that letter to my family, that would be cruelty. You'd be stabbing a corpse."

"I thought Dr. Siri gave that letter back to you."

"Phosy, you know very well that wasn't the original. It was a very good Xerox copy but the signature was not written by pen. Another one of the doctor's little jokes. He still has the original."

"You deserve nothing."

"I know. But, please. Please let me see that letter turned to ash before I'm stood in front of a firing squad."

"I don't know."

Judge Haeng, as if felled by a bullet, dropped to his knees and groveled. "I beg you," he said.

Phosy looked away embarrassed. "I'll talk to Siri about it."

"That's all I can ask. Thank you. Thank you so much."

◙ ◙ ◙

They were sitting in a bamboo hut out of the sun and Chong brought them coconuts with straws sticking out of them. The coconut water was sweet and warm.

"Do you mind if we ask you a few questions?" said Siri.

"It's one of my jobs to answer questions, Your Lordship," said the old man.

"Right, but this isn't specifically about the zoo," said Daeng.

"It's sort of connected to the civet incident," said Siri. "Nurse Dtui got the feeling there was more you'd like to have told her, but you weren't so comfortable with your boss around."

"She's a smart lady," said Chong.

"You said civets don't attack people," said Daeng.

"Only to defend their young they might. Unlike people, they know their limitations."

"But you saw the bone," said Siri. "You knew it was civets that chewed on it. It isn't impossible that the girl was killed by them."

"You don't know for sure, do you?" said Chong.

"No," said Daeng, "but the corpse wasn't so old when it was found. Our fear is that she might have been eaten alive."

"Oh no," said the old keeper, "they'd have to be starving to death themselves to resort to that."

"Any idea why there might have been a crate of starving civets with a dead girl inside?" asked Siri.

The keeper chewed on imaginary buffalo skin with his imaginary teeth. It made him appear to be smiling but his eyes said otherwise.

"Was this at the airport?" he asked.

"It might have been," said Siri.

"Then the question as to why there'd be a crate of starving animals is easy enough to answer. There's hardly a day goes by when a box of hungry this or that doesn't arrive at Wattay."

"They don't get fed?" asked Daeng.

"They're cargo," said Chong. "Once they arrive at the airport they're packed in the hold like the parcels and the bundles. You'd like to think they had a good meal before the trip but the only responsibility the agent has is to get them on the right flight. They sedate them and ship them. There's only a few species that hibernate naturally. Civets aren't one of them. You can't sedate an animal for as long as it takes to get them to the other side of the world. And even when they're asleep they relieve themselves on whoever's in the crate below. Can you imagine the state of them when they arrive? And transit's even worse. Do you see some overworked Russian airport worker breaking open the crates and giving the inmates a bunch of fresh fruit to sustain them for the rest of the journey? There's no clean up. There's no temperature control. You have to be some tough critter to survive an air trip."

"We were told the business had been regulated," said Daeng. "Conditions were better."

"That's true," said Chong. "So, you can imagine how nasty it used to be."

"Any idea how a human body might have found its way into one of those crates?" asked Siri.

"The dealers are a mean bunch," said the keeper. "They're not really that fond of newcomers to the business. It could have been someone who tried to muscle in. Someone being taught a lesson."

"It was a young girl," said Daeng.

"Is that so? I'm sorry about that."

"Who does the packing?" Siri asked.

"Depends," said Chong. "There used to be a lot of collection points, including this place. They'd pack and ship their own animals. But as our new rulers aren't so fond of private enterprise I hear there's a big clearing house somewhere out east now. Most of the agents send their stock there. They get a lot of stuff from Vietnam and Thailand."

"Does this zoo still send animals?" asked Daeng.

"What?" The old man blushed through his dark skin.

"I'm sure locals bring you animals they've caught," said Daeng. "What do you do when you're overstocked?"

The old keeper sighed. "We get more sent here than we can take," he said. "There are costs. We can't survive just on the entry ticket money. We get no funding from the government. Selling animals is the only way to hang on to the ones we put on display."

"You don't like this trade, do you?"

"Why do you say that?"

"Because you aren't under any pressure. You don't know who we are but you're spilling a lot of beans."

"Who am I to do anything?" said Chong. "Be nice to think there was somebody who cared enough to, you know, get involved and do something about it."

"Why do the Thais and Vietnamese send their animals here?" asked Daeng.

"That's a long story," said the keeper, "and I don't think I'm the man to tell it. I was just a worker all through the trade agreements. I think you should talk to the man who was running it in the sixties."

"I thought he was French," said Siri.

"Yeah, that's right. Monsieur Yves. Before the PL moved in he was the biggest dealer in Southeast Asia."

"He's still alive?" asked Daeng.

"His mind's going a bit but he still has all the stories."

"We don't actually have a budget for long distance phone conversations," said Daeng.

"How did you get here today?" asked Chong.

"Motorcycle," said Siri.

"Then that and a bottle of cognac's all you'll need."

Phosy and Nurse Dtui were sitting in the same coffee hut that had launched Mr. Geung and Tukta on their careers as freak show celebrities. The owner was chatty and, as Geung had said, shifty. Phosy had managed to stall the Vespa just past her place and spent twenty minutes trying to restart it. While doing so he pocketed the live spark plug and replaced it with a dead one. Dtui had walked back to ask the woman where the nearest mechanic could be found and the owner's son had run off to fetch him. The mechanic, a middle-aged man who looked as if his grease stains had been applied strategically like stage makeup, arrived ten minutes later. He seemed overwhelmed by the 1960 collector's item and the task of getting it back on the road.

In that first half hour, at least a dozen hunters had arrived at the wildlife agency opposite. Some had rifles slung over their shoulders, others had machetes hanging from their belts. They'd come in pairs with fruit bats or giant squirrels suspended by the feet from a bamboo pole or individually with heavy burlap sacks on their backs. A group of happy children arrived with a cane cage full of box turtles, and an old man staggered up with an elderly macaque lashed to the crossbar of his bicycle. But the market could absorb it all. Nobody was turned away.

"Is that a food market over there?" Dtui asked the coffee shop owner.

"Sort of," she said.

"I was thinking we might get some meat to take home with us," said Dtui.

"It's not that sort of market," said the woman. "They won't sell you meat."

"What else would they do with all those animals?" Dtui asked.

"Sell 'em of course," said the woman. "Live, most of 'em. Make a nice little income, they do. One of these country boys comes in with a mongoose and they give him fifty kip and he's happy. Then they up and sell the same thing for eighty thousand. I wish my husband had got us into that business, I tell you. No getting rich selling coffee and biscuits."

"Might as well take a look anyway," said Dtui.

And with the bemused mechanic still tinkering, Dtui and Phosy strolled across the wide dirt street. With every step the stink grew more overwhelming. It looked at first appearance like a regular market with a corrugated tin roof and aisles but no walls. It was an annex to a sturdy two-story house with a fine metal gate. It was the only non-wooden building in the village. But there were no tables in this market. Instead the aisles were lined with cages and boxes. A squat man with Chinese features sat behind a desk cooling himself with a rattan fan. He wore a damp white singlet and football shorts. A pair of dark glasses hung on a string around his neck although it was clear from his chalk white skin that he'd never been in the sun. He looked up from a pile of money when the couple walked in.

"What?" he said.

"I'm Chom," said Phosy, "and this is my wife, Pun."

"I didn't ask for a roll call," said the man.

Phosy was sure the pasty man was nicknamed Whitey when he was a kid.

"No, that's true," said Phosy. "My wife and I have a little export business, nothing spectacular, mind. We just send Lao goods to my wife's family in Udon."

"And what's that got to do with me?"

"Well, my bike just broke down," said Phosy, "and we've been waiting for the mechanic to fix it. And we noticed the impressive volume of trade you've been doing here. I think we could probably be of service to one another."

Whitey looked them up and down. "Not interested," he said.

"I haven't made my offer yet," said Phosy.

"You don't need to. I've got a regular customer. He'll take everything I've got."

"What if I took everything you've got for a better price?" said Phosy.

"Let's just say I'm a faithful dealer," said Whitey. "Now leave me alone."

Dtui had veered away from the conversation and was walking the aisles heading for a yard at the back. She couldn't bear to look into the overcrowded cages: clawless otters crammed together, young komodo dragons piled one atop the other like bags of rice, turtles in dry buckets. She leaned over an unplugged ice chest, lifted the lid and recoiled at the sight. Inside was what looked like oversized spaghetti, but it was moving, packed to the rim with all varieties of snakes.

"Oi, what are you doing there?" shouted Whitey.

He reached under the desk in front of him but Phosy was on him before he could pull the revolver from its hidden shelf. The policeman had the gun out of Whitey's hand and was holding it by the barrel before he could say anything. He smashed it down onto Whitey's fingers, but the yell was muffled by the animal cries from behind the market.

"Sorry," said Phosy, "hope I didn't break your trigger finger."

"Who do you think you are?" said Whitey, wringing his injured hand. "You can't just walk in here and hit people with no reason."

"You were just about to shoot my wife," said Phosy. "That's reason enough, don't you think?" He called to Dtui. "What do you see back there?"

"A lot of miserable animals," she said. "Those that aren't being crushed to death hardly have voice left to cry. There are bigger cages out back. Bears and wild cats as far as I can see. They don't look any happier. I smell disease and death everywhere."

"And there's another good reason to break your hand," said Phosy. "I'm on the animals' side."

"You won't get away with this," said Whitey.

"Why, what are you going to do?"

"I don't need to do anything," said the man. "My customer looks after his people. You've made a serious mistake here, pal. He'll find you and he'll make you very sorry. You won't be able to hide."

"I have no intention of hiding," said Phosy, "in fact I'd

be delighted to meet him. It's the least I can do considering I'll be taking over his business."

The man laughed. "What happened to the little family exports to Udon?" he asked.

"I lied."

"You have no idea who you're dealing with," said Whitey.

"I don't really care," said Phosy, "and you know why? Because you'll all be working for me soon enough."

Dtui was unlatching cages but few of the inmates had the energy to take their chance for freedom.

"Oi, stop that," shouted Whitey. "Tell her to stop."

Phosy raised the pistol and scratched his nose with the barrel.

"She's a free spirit," he said. "No controlling her."

"That's my livelihood, that is. I'm just working to feed my family like all of us."

"A friend of mine in Vientiane—a very wise man— once told me some famous philosopher whose name I can't recall said there are some occupations that make it impossible for a man to be virtuous. This is one of them."

"You're mad," said the man. "You'd need an army to take over this business."

"I've got one," said Phosy, reaching inside his back pocket. "You probably heard there have been some changes at police headquarters. I'm the man now."

Phosy held up his ID long enough for Whitey to see the photo and read the line, Chief Inspector of Police, but not long enough to read the name.

"It seems such a shame to shut down all these profitable enterprises along the border," said Phosy, "especially as our budget's so modest. So we're nationalizing them, starting with you and your boss. You want to give me an address so I can pop in and say hello?"

The man was confused. The freed animals, those that could walk, were staggering around the market dumbfounded. Dtui, quite wisely, only released the ones she knew were more afraid of her than she was of them.

"Just stop her, will you?" said Whitey. "I don't know where he lives."

"Bull dung."

"No, really. I've never been there. I've heard it's out east somewhere, but we've done all our business here. The truck drivers won't say. It's some secret compound."

"You got a name for him?"

"I can't . . ."

"Believe me," said Phosy, "you should worry more about what I'll do to you than what he will."

They were on their way back to Vientiane on the Vespa. Dtui had to shout into the back of her husband's head. Even without helmets it was hard to be heard above the growl of the bike on the gravel.

"Are you sure that was wise?" said Dtui.

"What's that?" said Phosy.

"Declaring war on a trafficker."

"They're cowards, Dtui. They make their living out of cruelty. I'm not worried about some businessman who has no respect for life."

"I told you you'd make a good Buddhist."

"Can't be a good Communist and a good Buddhist at the same time."

"What worries me is that you're staging a turf war in the name of the police force."

"We got a name, didn't we? Comrade Vilai."

"Whitey's going to tell him what happened. They'll know it was you that threatened him."

"What are they going to do? Call the police?"

"I thought you were just going there to ask about the girl in the crate."

"The truck driver delivers the crates to the airport then stops off at the agents to pay them off and load up new stock. You saw the condition of his cages. There was nothing there they'd allow on a plane. No, our new friend Comrade Vilai does all the export packing at his secret location. That's where we ask our question."

"We still don't have an address."

"I'm a detective. I can find it. Then we can go over there and have a little chat."

"Phosy, you don't have to do all these excursions yourself. You're the chief inspector. You have men and women who work for you. Siri was right. You have to start delegating responsibility."

"I will, but not for this case. Since my appointment, I haven't exactly achieved much."

"It's not something you can hurry," said Dtui. "You have to rebuild the team from the bottom up. Bring in new blood that hasn't learned the art of corruption from their corrupt superiors. Train the right sort of people. It takes time."

"The republic needs results, Dtui, not hope for the future. We need a victory to start the right sort of momentum. Make people proud of us. High-profile arrests early on will win us the time to build. Right now, we're an unknown quantity but we're about to bring down a judge. We're a short hop from naming the killer of our crate girl.

Shutting down a sleazy businessman who thinks he's above the law will be the icing on the cake."

"You don't think you're taking on too much?"

"Relax. I'm in control."

Dtui couldn't relax and it wasn't only because of the insects battering her face and the lousy Vespa shocks. She had one of her feelings. They were wrong sometimes, which was why she didn't always share them. She loved and trusted her husband, but she was worried that he, in turn, trusted too few of his officers. A thousand ants could move a tree branch but none would attempt it alone.

It wasn't the grand colonial home one might expect of the continent's most notorious trafficker of wildlife. In fact, the little house was dowdy and lacking both character and maintenance. It was a bungalow with an uncared-for front yard. There were chickens pecking at the dirt and a characterless dog on a leash that was in turn looped around a length of rope stretching from one side of the yard to the other. If the dog ever felt so inclined he might run to ward off visitors, but he'd long since learned there was nothing to be gained from it.

From Siri's point of view there was much more to the house than just the flaky stucco walls and the flowers dead in their pots. The place was ghostly. It was as if the building were wrapped in pelts, layer upon layer rotting slowly but constantly replenished with more pelts. The outer layer dripped with blood. Madam Daeng could not see this but she could sense her husband's apprehension. She knew there was a presence.

On the front porch was a sturdy rocking chair

surrounded by a halo of empty beer bottles. The front door was open but there were no sounds from inside.

"Monsieur Yves?" Siri shouted.

A wall lizard tutted. The dog didn't stir.

"Monsieur Yves?" Siri tried again. "We've brought you a bottle of cognac."

"Good luck," came a voice from the depths of the house. It was a common Lao toast. "I'm coming."

The zoo keeper had described Monsieur Yves as a magnificent human specimen with a body to make women melt and men feel threatened.

"He's tall with a sea of blond hair," Chong had said, "and could wrestle a bear to the ground."

The Monsieur Yves twenty years on who staggered out to the balcony could barely have overwhelmed an elderly chicken. His blond hair was white and oily and the seas had parted to reveal a passage of liver spots. He was as rotund as a planet but still wore a Diana Ross and the Supremes T-shirt that was several sizes too small. His Lao fisherman's pants clung to the outer limit of his girth. It was midday but he was clearly out of his head.

"Ah, my friend," he said in a slurry version of French.

He charged toward Siri like a musk elephant.

"It is such a long time since I saw you."

Madam Daeng's French wasn't nearly as accomplished as that of her husband, but it seemed to her the Frenchman was struggling to remember a language he hadn't used for many years.

"How have you been?" he said, kissing the doctor's cheeks repeatedly but ignoring Daeng.

They might have mentioned that Monsieur Yves was mistaken, that he and Siri had never met, that perhaps he bore a resemblance to someone from the trafficker's past. But Siri decided to canoe the rapids and see where they ended up.

"So, my friend," he said, "what have you been doing since last we met?"

Thence began a disoriented account of the Frenchman's adventures in Africa and his fiancée back in France and hemorrhoids and Charles de Gaulle. Daeng took the opportunity whilst being invisible to enter the house where, in the unsanitary kitchen, she came upon a woman of perhaps her own age. She was the type of Lao who'd advanced from her teenage dawn to her current dusk without fundamentally changing shape. Along the way, she had not learned to dress appropriately for her advanced years. She wore a black halter neck top and red hot pants. She stood several centimeters above Daeng on what they called platform heels. Given the state of the floor Daeng regretted having left her own shoes outside.

The woman turned to face Daeng, not at all surprised to see her standing there, and smiled. Her lips were rouged, her eyelashes mascaraed and her skin crumpled. She'd been dicing tomatoes so her fingers were damp and pink but Daeng accepted a limp handshake. And with no introductions, the two women sat at the kitchen table chatting as if it were the most natural thing. They talked about the change in temperature and the dearth of food at the market, and Daeng listened to a short list of medical conditions her Frenchman was currently struggling through.

"I'm surprised your husband's still here," said Daeng.

"Why?" the woman asked. Her voice was a cigarette growl from deep in her throat.

"He's French."

"They're not all the enemy," said the wife. "There are others allowed to stay. Men with families who are still in a position to support them. They're dotted around. Tolerated. Forgiven. We don't socialize with them much."

"Children?" asked Daeng.

"Grown and gone."

"I heard your husband dealt in animals."

"Loved them, he did. We have so many stories from the good old days."

"And he sent them overseas?"

"Wanted the world's children to learn to love exotic animals as much as he did."

"Why did he stop?"

"Ah, look at me," said the wife, "where are my manners?"

She stood, hobbled to the sink on her platforms and opened the cupboard. Inside, Daeng could see an armory of spirit bottles on a rack. The wife pulled out a half-full gin bottle.

"You must be parched after your long journey," she said.

Monsieur Yves had dragged a second rocking chair to the balcony and he and the doctor were swigging cognac from the new bottle. It took some time for Siri to maneuver the Frenchman's mind around to the sixties and his trade in wildlife but once there it wallowed and dwelled.

"Oh, brother," said Yves, "I was rolling in money. Didn't know what to do with it all. I had eighty regular customers in zoos around Europe and no end of pet shops and private individuals with enough money to set up their own menageries. I couldn't keep up with the demand."

"Then we took over and spoiled it all for you," said Siri.

"I gave it up long before that," said Yves.

"Why?"

The Frenchman looked around the yard to be sure they were alone, and he leaned closely into the doctor's ear. Siri could smell a cocktail of drinks and drugs and body odor.

"You ever have a nightmare?" Yves asked.

"Too often," said Siri.

"Then you'll know, brother. They never go away. They're always there watching you, the dead ones. You'd think having sent them so far off that the spirits wouldn't be bothered to find their way back, but they come. They're all here."

"Your house is wrapped in their skins," said Siri.

Yves leapt frantically from his chair and dropped the bottle. "That's right! That's right!" he shouted. "You can see them, right? Most people can't. Some nights it's so stifling we can't breathe. We have to camp out here under the tree. One day they'll suffocate us in our bed."

Monsieur Yves was pacing back and forth. The dog moved way to the end of its rope.

"I thought I was a good one," said the Frenchman. "The Thai dealers, the Chinese, they were heartless. They didn't cull out the sick and dying animals. They sent everything and claimed they'd got their diseases in transit. Blamed the airlines for the deaths. I fed mine. Gave shots to the sick ones. Nursed them back to health. If I didn't think they'd make the journey alive I held them back. I used to think I loved animals. I had pets. I set up the zoo so the locals could understand nature. But you know? In my soul, I knew what suffering I was inflicting on the beasts. I ignored my soul. Now my soul is repaying me. The trade has quadrupled since I gave it up but they haven't learned from my experiences—from my mistakes. I know the dealers will see out their lives in purgatory, but there's no convincing them now. They see only profit. This trade will only cease when there are no more animals to torture."

Monsieur Yves wheezed from the effort of ranting. He held his heart, waiting for the beat to slow. He leaned down to rescue the cognac bottle and took a long swig as if it were medicine.

"How do we stop it?" said Siri.

"The trade? You can't. There are laws, international agreements, but there will always be countries like Laos that don't recognize animals have rights. This country is the center of regional trade because, unlike Thailand and Vietnam, they're not even pretending to introduce regulations. They're proud of what they do. I made my fortune because I could slip a few dollars into pockets here and there, and the officials didn't even think they were doing anything immoral."

"Isn't the new regime clamping down on trafficking?"

Yves laughed. The bottle was his now and he wasn't sharing it. He took another swig and swayed left and right.

"You know what clamping down means?" he asked. "You tax the trade. You charge for veterinarian certificates guaranteeing the animals left Laos in good health. Those documents are printed in the Ministry of Agriculture for twenty dollars each. You just fill in the gaps. You have a spokesman who tells foreign governments that Laos is at the forefront of animal protection and you gladly accept their grants. Do you see the government allowing any of those do-gooder animal rights NGOs to set up in Vientiane? Not on your life. The country's got such a reputation we import illegal animal parts from fucking Africa. You get hundreds of kilos of tusks and horns and skins every week.

It's all shipped up to China and over to Vietnam for the witchdoctors to mix with whisky and convince all those impotent old bastards that they'll be stallions."

"And yet there you were fine-tuning the trade," said Siri. "A lot of what's happening now is down to you."

Monsieur Yves flopped down onto his chair which over-rocked so violently it threw him against the wall. Only Siri's swift hands prevented the Frenchman from hitting the deck. This time he held on to the bottle. Once the chair was still and Monsieur Yves calm, he began to cry.

"Brother, look at me," he said through the tears. "Do I look like someone who's found peace on his planet? I don't get any forgiveness nor do I deserve it. I've dedicated my old age to righting the wrongs I've committed. I've produced articles. I wrote a book. I've given most of my money away to organizations fighting the trade. But still I'm deteriorating. Some things are not repairable. I won't be around much longer. I certainly won't be here long enough to make amends."

"Who took over your business?" Siri asked.

"They were like cockroaches," said Yves. "I announced I was stepping out and there they were. Everyone wanted a piece of it. The Commies shut down a lot of them or sort of amalgamated them into bigger units."

"Who's the biggest?" Daeng asked, stepping out from the house. She had pink cheeks so Siri knew she'd been tippling.

"Who are you?" said Monsieur Yves.

"Friend of your wife," said Daeng. "So? Who's the biggest dealer in wildlife at the moment?"

"His name's Vilai Savangkeo," said Yves. "Biggest by far. He made his money during the war exchanging wildlife from the PL soldiers for contraband arms. He's got a big complex over in Hong Tong. Right on the river. Really convenient for bringing in stock from Thailand. He's started breeding tigers too. Hundreds of them out at Thakhek. Nobody's ever going to make a dent in that empire. The place is guarded like the mint, and he has some very influential friends. He's the only one with a license to fly wildlife out of Wattay these days."

"Then he sounds like our man," said Siri.

CHAPTER THIRTEEN
Polar Opposites

Two odd things happened as Siri and Daeng walked back to their motorcycle from Monsieur Yves' house. First, they passed an elderly Lao couple coming the other way. The man carried a bottle wrapped in paper. He looked nothing like Siri and the woman bore no similarity to Daeng. They nodded as did Siri and his wife. When they were out of earshot Daeng asked, "Do you think . . . ?"

"I guess all old people look the same to an alcoholic," said Siri. "Let that be a lesson to you not to drink in dark kitchens at lunchtime. I bet . . ."

Daeng looked back to see why her husband had stopped talking but Siri wasn't there.

"All right, I get it," said Siri.

He was walking on the lane from Monsieur Yves's house, but there was now a layer of crunchy snow on the ground. He looked back over his shoulder and saw that the bunga-low had become an igloo. The figure walking ahead was no longer Madam Daeng. It was Auntie Bpoo in her polar bear skin coat.

"And what is it you think you've got?" she asked without bothering to turn around.

"I should be talking to the bear," he said.

That was clearly the abracadabra she'd been waiting for. The bear's head, which until that moment had hung loose like a hood, began to lift. The neck cricked left and right, the eyes opened, and there before Siri a miraculous transition took place. Auntie Bpoo was no longer wearing the bear skin. A magnificent polar bear was wearing the skin of a transvestite fortune teller. The hairy arms were pulled around the bear's neck like a scarf. It was not a pretty sight.

"About bloody time," said the bear.

"Sorry," said the doctor. "I'm still quite new at all this symbolism malarkey. I'd prefer something a little bit more—you know—simple."

"You should have chosen a different spirit guide," said the bear.

"I didn't actually choose . . . oh, never mind. What's next?"

"You tell me what you think this is all about, and if you're right I give you your badge and you move on to the next test."

"I get a badge?"

"It's a figurative badge."

"How many other tests are there?" Siri asked.

"Depends on what path you choose," said the bear. "Path one has twelve-thousand and eleven. Path two has six."

"What do you get at the end of path two?"

"It's a sort of laissez-passer to the other world."

"And path one?"

"Same thing."

"Then, why . . . ?"

"Some people like puzzles," said the bear. "Look, can we get on with it? It's freezing out here."

"All right," said Siri. "Here we go. There I was talking to Auntie Bpoo and although I might have thought to myself what an attractive bear skin she was wearing, I didn't give a thought as to how or why you became a coat."

"And the connection to your other world is . . . ?"

"We're trying to solve a mystery of a dead woman," said Siri. "But we aren't seeing the bigger picture. She was in a crate of civets but we didn't give a thought as to how they got there or where they were going. I know now. The death of one woman shouldn't be our main concern. Humans will be around forever. You and your pals won't. Message: If you can't see us, how can you feel compassion for us?"

They stared at each other.

"How's that?" asked Siri.

"Yeah, good enough," said the bear.

Siri was momentarily distracted by a wall of day fireworks that whizzed and banged black against the blue sky to celebrate the passing of his second test. And when he looked down, there was Madam Daeng sitting on the motorcycle in a snowless landscape.

"Been anywhere nice?" she said.

"I passed my second test," said Siri.

"Good boy," said Daeng.

When Phosy walked along the corridor of the Ministry of Justice he couldn't help but notice the expressions on the faces of the people he passed. Some looked away; others appeared embarrassed. He'd not leaked the results of his investigation of Judge Haeng but clearly someone had.

In Laos, holding on to a secret was like trying to keep a length of greasy noodle on a spoon. One of the most senior officials at the ministry had been involved in, at the very least, covering up a murder. Once a story like that got around it broke the faces of everyone who worked under the perpetrator. In some ways, a policeman could be considered their enemy too.

The chief inspector had wondered whether the judge might have indeed taken his chance on an inner tube across the Mekhong, but, to his credit, when Phosy pushed open the door without knocking, Haeng was deep in the paperwork on his desk.

"You got anything for me?" Phosy asked.

Haeng jumped nervously. "Yes," he said, "I believe I do. Maysuk contacted me."

"And you said what I told you to?"

"Yes, I said you have some credible leads in the girl's murder. I was thinking about that. It does seem ridiculous that he'd go to so much trouble just to avoid paperwork. I think he must have known where the girl came from, and it's possible he was responsible for her death."

"The great mind of a judge at work," said Phosy, rolling his eyes.

"I know," said Haeng. "I've been very naïve through this whole thing. I regret that."

"But you led him to believe that my investigations have gone nowhere, you're still in your job and he's not a suspect."

"That's correct," said the judge. "But there's something you should know. I believe he's planning to leave the country."

"What makes you think that?"

"He suggested it in our last telephone conversation."

"What did he say, exactly?"

"He said in a couple of days he wouldn't have to worry about Laos and its arbitrary legal system. He said he wanted to see me before he goes."

"What about?"

"He didn't say," said Haeng, "but I'm afraid."

"Did you make an appointment?"

"I said I'd meet him at the airport this evening."

"Today?" said Phosy.

"I could try to put him off for a day," said Haeng.

"No, he'd get suspicious."

"What if you go?" said the judge.

"Me? He thinks I'm at a seminar up north."

Haeng put down his pen and laced his fingers under his chin. "You could tell him you didn't really go," he said. "Tell him I ordered you to leave the capital, but you disobeyed me because you're investigating me. That you believe I'm responsible for the body in the crate. You have compelling evidence against me. Get him to make a statement that he knows nothing of the incident you're investigating."

Phosy was surprised at the judge's acumen.

"That won't stop him from leaving," he said.

"It'll let him know you're in town and your men will be watching the airport and land borders to make sure I don't leave the country. That might slow him down."

Phosy stared at the judge and considered the plan.

"There's something else," said Haeng.

"What?"

"If I go, I'm afraid of what he might do to me. He's threatened me before."

Phosy chewed his lip. "I'll go see him this evening," he said.

"There's a flight to Hanoi at five," said Haeng.

"I'll be there earlier."

The policeman walked to the door then turned back. He reached into his briefcase and pulled out a manila envelope. He came back and handed it to Haeng. "I tried to talk the doctor out of this," said Phosy, "but he said there's no point in turning the screw more."

Haeng reached into the envelope and pulled out a sheet of paper he remembered very well. He checked the signature at the bottom of the letter and smiled. "My letter," he said. "Thank you. Thank you so much."

"Think yourself very lucky."

"Phosy?"

"What?"

"Do you think . . . as I'm cooperating . . . do you think this period of helping you might count in my favor if there's some kind of review. You have to agree there was no malice in what I did."

"Let me ask you," said Phosy, once again heading to the door, "would you want to live in a country where the senior judge has no spine and no scruples? I'm not Dr. Siri. I don't see the good side of bad people. The only thing cooperation will get you is a warm bowl of rice porridge on the morning of your execution. People like you disgust me."

He slammed the door behind him.

Phosy had been telling the team about his visit to Judge Haeng.

"I'm surprised he's stayed put," said Daeng.

"Running away would be a confession of guilt," said Phosy.

"And Siri was right, where would he go?" said Civilai.

"He's got the taste of power and privilege. I don't think his vanity would allow him to start again from the bottom in Bulgaria or Havana. He'd just be a little Asian clerk over there. And given the enemies he's made at justice I don't see him surviving long in a refugee camp. No, we're the best deal he has."

"But it wouldn't surprise me if he was hoping Director Maysuk would put a bullet in our dear chief inspector when he had him alone in his office," said Siri.

"Didn't even get a whiff of his aftershave," said Phosy.

"You think he might have taken that flight to Hanoi?" Daeng asked.

"I got there before the flight, checked at admin and stuck around the airport for a while," said Phosy. "No sign of him. His name wasn't on the flight manifest. I waited in his office for half an hour. Walked around a little bit. Didn't see anyone. It felt like a national holiday. Couldn't even find a secretary to ask where he'd gone."

"Didn't it occur to you he might have wanted to harm you?" said Nurse Dtui. "He'd told the judge to get you off the case any way he could."

"No, Dtui," said Phosy. "He wasn't expecting me to turn up there. His appointment was with the judge. But I did have a gun, just in case. No bullets mind."

"They still rationed?" Daeng asked.

"It's astounding," said Civilai. "They drop two million tons of ordnance on us in the war, and we can't even squeeze a bullet out of the system."

"It's not a joke," said Dtui. "By insisting on doing everything yourself you put us all in danger."

"I suppose there's a chance Haeng was lying about the appointment," said Daeng. "He might have even warned

Maysuk off. Encouraged him to get out of town. That might explain why Haeng stuck around. He thinks he's got the upper hand."

"All possible," said Phosy. "I've alerted all the border crossings to look out for the director. His official vehicle and the airport trucks were all accounted for."

The team was back in Daeng's noodle shop and had spent the past hour putting together a plan for their visit to Vilai Savangkeo's animal clearing center at Hong Tong. They didn't have the administration on their side. The business that Vilai ran—the trade in animal parts and bi-products, the tiger farm, the export trade to zoos, the cross-border trafficking—it was all licensed. Everything he did was perfectly legal as far as the government was concerned. His was a company the Ministry of Trade was delighted to have on its books. Phosy had no legal right to break in and arrest the owner and his workers. They couldn't even take out a warrant to search the premises. So they needed their utmost guile to get into the compound and gain access to Vilai's files. They were all sure the businessman was connected to the body in the crate, and even though killing animals was not against the law, killing people was not acceptable.

"Okay, team," said Daeng. "Enough talk. We need an early night. Busy day ahead."

"Up at dawn's crack," said Civilai, with a smile.

"Our first movie," said Siri. "How proud I am."

CHAPTER FOURTEEN
A Highly Respected Animal Torturer

The rented bus left the morning market motor vehicle parking lot at 5:20 A.M. It was more full than a pre-war bus with rusting shocks ought to be. But passengers kept arriving even after there were no seats available and people had to sit in the aisle.

Thanks to the Lao Women's Union, actors had arrived from near and far hoping for their big break. They were Ramayana dancers and puppeteers from the old regime. They were comics from wandering wagon shows. They were unknowns who'd done well in productions at school. But none of them had been in a movie. So the adrenaline on that journey, fifty-five kilometers east of the capital, would have been enough to fill the fuel tank three times over. Just looking at the elegant Panasonic camera on its tripod at the rear of the bus convinced everyone they were about to make history.

The scene supposedly being shot that day was a classically rural pastiche set on the banks of the Mekhong River in the year 1828 of the Western calendar. King Anouvong of Laos had attempted to make inroads into the Siamese empire but was beaten back across the river. There followed a brave attempt by the Lao to defend Vientiane from the invading Siamese forces. In Siri's version the Lao were successful in turning back the technically superior Thais. In reality, as Civilai reminded him, the Lao got their backsides kicked and lost their lowland city.

The scene they claimed to be shooting this day showed the locals being recruited to boost the Lao army. Most of the actors were to play villagers, which dispensed with the need for elaborate costumes. Everyone brought along loin cloths and grimy underwear to pass as pauper fashion of 150 years ago. Civilai did not tire of telling them that these were the days before the priggish missionaries brought their tiresome morals to the region. Village women of 1828 wore their hair short and their breasts exposed. The female actors were surprisingly willing to whip off their tops. This naturally led to a substantial turnout of local men, many of whom had not seen a shapely breast since their suckling days.

The big-movie atmosphere permeated every hut, every household all the way east along the riverbank to the vast compound of Comrade Vilai. It was a sprawling estate with a white, three-meter concrete wall topped with barbed wire. There was a metal gate with a guard post in front. Its similarity to the US embassy in Vientiane was no coincidence. Comrade Vilai was obsessed with security but he too was affected by the buzz that day. He had joined some of his workers and passersby on the street in front of his compound, looking back along the river to the large crowd gathered there. He was a vain seventy-year-old with dyed charcoal-black hair and false teeth that were a touch too large for his mouth. He refused to dress in anything but brushed silk, the most expensive from Bangkok, and ordered everything in the size he'd been thirty years before. He'd shrunk a good deal since then.

Madame Daeng, wearing a tracksuit, a baseball hat and dark glasses, walked at speed toward the group.

"What are you doing back there, sister?" Vilai asked.

"We're making a movie for the Ministry of Culture," she said. She showed him the letter stamped by the vice minister. "But we've come to a bit of a standstill."

"What's wrong?" he asked.

"Do you work here?"

"I own the place," he said.

"We'd sent a dozen buffalo and some goats from Vientiane to be here when we arrived," said Daeng. "But they seem to have been rerouted somewhere along the line. So apart from one old buffalo and some stray dogs we don't have any animals in our village scene. The village headman said you had some sort of zoo and might be able to lend us some animals."

Vilai laughed. "We certainly don't have any buffalos or goats," he said. "This is an exotic animal farm. But we do have one or two serows and a tapir or two that might fool the average cinemagoer."

"Of course we'll pay you," said Daeng.

"No need for that," said Vilai, "happy to help out the ministry. I'm a close friend of the minister, you know."

"You don't say?" Daeng lowered her sunglasses and studied the face of the old man.

"What?" he said. "Never seen anyone as good looking as me?"

"In a way," said Daeng. "You know, it's rather uncanny."

"What is?"

She reached into her shoulder bag and pulled out a sheet of paper with a sketch on one side.

"Has anyone ever told you how similar you look to King Anouvong?" She held up the pencil drawing.

"I can't say anyone has," said Vilai.

"Isn't it remarkable?" she said.

Some of the workers gathered around to see and they agreed Vilai looked a great deal like the old king. This was not a coincidence as Daeng had commissioned a budding artist from the lycée to copy Vilai's face from an old newspaper feature photograph. She'd added a war helmet and a chainmail necklace and made him a little younger. Not even Vilai could deny the likeness.

"You know . . . I hope you don't mind me asking," said Daeng.

"What?" said Vilai.

"Could I make a suggestion," she went on. "Later in the movie there's a scene where King Anouvong rides through the village on an elephant recruiting soldiers. It would be such a great help if we could shoot that scene today rather than wait for an actor. We have the costume already."

"You want me to be in a movie?" said Vilai, slicking down his hair.

"It's a two minute scene, maximum."

"I can't act."

"No need. Just sit on the elephant and look down at the villagers."

"I don't know," said Vilai.

"The president's really excited about this project. I'm sure he'd be delighted if you agreed to help us."

"The president?"

"Yes."

"Well . . ."

"Please."

"I suppose I could help out," said Vilai. His workers whooped.

"Excellent. Excellent," said Daeng. "I . . . ?"

"Yes?"

"I don't suppose you have an elephant, by any chance?"

As it happened, Vilai did have an elephant although it no longer had tusks. He also allowed twelve of his workers to appear in the scene as bearers and footmen. His animal handlers led an assortment of drugged mammals and placed them strategically around the village. Civilai had borrowed a royal costume from the currently closed royal history wing of the revolutionary museum. There was also an assortment of antique trousers and sandals. The museum curator seemed glad to be rid of them. So the kingly procession was in place. The director, Dr. Siri, spent most of the morning shouting directions through a large cone. Civilai was in charge of the camera complaining about the light and the heat and the lack of color. The director told the actors not to worry if they heard what sounded like explosions in the distance. These, he said, were merely charges being detonated for atmospheric purposes. Scenes were shot and reshot, all with the benefit of a camera that didn't work. And it wasn't until around 2 P.M. that anyone first noticed something was amiss back at the animal compound.

A chevrotain, drowsy and disoriented, had ignored its instinct to return to the jungle and instead came to see what all the excitement was about on the river. The clumsy mouse deer lacked agility and was tasty enough to have been hunted out of existence in war-torn Laos. There was only one place it could have come from. Vilai sent one of his handlers to recapture it and another to go to the compound to see how it could have escaped. Meanwhile he sat atop his elephant beneath a tiered umbrella hamming it up for the camera. That was until he was made aware of the smoke billowing from his compound. He dismounted and headed back along the river. His workers raced ahead. He was the slowest of the group, and when he entered the open gates of his empire, the scene in front of him was far from the order he'd come to demand. To one side, all of his men including the movie extras, had been rounded up and were being held at gun point against one wall. Across the compound his house was burning and all around, cages had been opened, and, bemused by their freedom, animals were searching for an exit.

The last thing Vilai noticed was a pinprick on the back of his neck.

He came around in a deckchair on the balcony of his house. Behind him the wood beams cracked and the heat of the flames singed the back of his neck. From the concrete balcony he could see the rear wall of the compound and the gaping hole that had been blasted in it. The hill beyond was visible through the smoke and he could see two black leopards and a reunited family of gibbons and a wild elephant heading for the jungle beyond. Tapirs grazed hungrily on the sienna and two injured langur limped to a point beyond the tree line. All he could smell was the scent of burning house: plastic and wool and foam and electronics. Sitting on the balcony railing was a peculiar-looking man with a quiff. He was wearing crocodile skin boots.

"Here we are then," said Wee. "I estimate you have about thirty minutes of house left. You'll be pleased to hear we evacuated your cook and your minor wife before we started the fire. We left the safe in there because the label claims it's fireproof. We'll see, eh?"

"Who the hell are you?" said Vilai.

"We're from the World Animal Protection League," said Wee. "As you can see, we set a lot of your animals free. Probably a waste of time. We warned the villagers to stay indoors. But most of your residents were too sick to move. The worst ones we've put down. We also set fire to your little warehouse of skins and tusks and the like. We gave their previous owners a nice sending off. Had a monk in here and everything, paving their path to nirvana. Your workers tell us you have a tiger farm in Thakhek. Not sure what we'll do there. Probably not a wise idea to release a dozen tigers into the wild at the same time. Know what I mean?"

"No," said Vilai. "I mean what is your name?"

"Why would you want to know that?" said Wee.

"Because if you make the mistake of leaving me alive after this, I'll hunt you and tie you upside down to a tree, and I'll gut you."

"And why would knowing my name assist you in that endeavor?"

"Because once you're dead I'll track down everyone with the same surname, and I'll skin them and rip their hearts out too."

"I must say you have a lot of bold and unkind ambitions for a man tied to a chair on a burning balcony," laughed Wee.

"Try me," said Vilai.

"If I gave you my surname you'd find yourself skinning at least two Party members," said Wee.

"Don't give me that, boy. You aren't connected. I know all of them. I have ministers down here for hunting weekends. Two politburo members attended my daughter's wedding."

"I bet you don't know the chief of police," said Wee.

"Comrade Oudomxai," said Vilai. "We play petong together when I'm in the capital."

"Must have been a while ago," said Wee. "Oudomxai is rotting in jail somewhere up country."

"Ah, so that's what this is all about," said Vilai. "I heard about you lot from one of our dealers. The mysterious new chief who's planning to take over my business. Better men have tried and failed."

"You aren't so special," said Wee. "You're scum."

"You'll regret talking to me like that. I'm a respected member of the business community."

"Respected? You call this business respectable? Too bad your victims don't get a say in that. But we got lucky. You crossed the line from killing animals to killing people. We found your girl in the crate. That's serious. My boss is going through your files as I speak. Won't be long before we find a certain invoice for a box of civets dated around August fifteenth. That would be a potent piece of evidence in a murder inquiry. Or you could just confess right now."

"Listen, you freak," Vilai shouted above the hiss of burning synthetics, "I have no idea what you're talking about. And whoever you lot are, I'll get you for harassment and vandalism. I promise you I'll not only have your boss's job but I'll have his balls too. Then I'll hang his corpse from that banyan tree beside yours."

"I'm not an expert but I'd say that was a threat," came a voice.

Phosy had arrived on the balcony from the outside stair-
case. He held a box file and nodded at Wee.

"Ooh, it's hot up here," he said. "You know, these brick
places build up a lot of heat, but I prefer a good, old-fash-
ioned wood-house fire. Can't beat organic smells."

"Who are you?" Vilai asked.

"He's big on names," said Wee.

"Well, if you survive this accidental fire, here's a name
you'll be hearing a lot of," said Phosy. "I'm Chief Inspector Phosy Vongvichai, the man whose balls you'd like to
be juggling. Threatening to hang my dead body from a
banyan tree isn't the best way to get on my good side."

"I don't have to get on the good side of a tyke like you,"
said Vilai. "What are you? Twenty?"

"Yes, flattery might work," said Phosy. "But a confession would make me happier. You see? I found this file
in your cabinet downstairs. It says you shipped a crate
of civets to Wattay on the fifteenth of August. The shipping number matches the one in my case report. What
we don't know is why it was stuck at Wattay for four days.
Nor do we know why there was more than just civets in
the crate."

Phosy cast a look at Wee. They'd decided earlier that
the chief inspector would play the evil-bordering-on-psy-
chotic cop. When he was younger he could have carried
it off with more aplomb and less conscience, but with promotion came responsibility. He had to consider justice and
political correctness. Burning down the house hadn't been
intended, but he had to admit it felt damned fine and it
played into the drama of the raid. Without a confession,
the actions of that day would have been hard to condone.
But the decision had been his.

"And, if you're worried about my qualifications for this job, you're asking the wrong question," he said. "My age isn't important. What you should wonder is how did I get to this position so early in life? How many people did I have to kill to get here? And I'll tell you—a lot. And do I regret it? Not at all. My personal favorite is death by torture. I've had a lot of accolades for my torture over the years. When I look around your compound I can see you're a fan of that too."

Vilai's shirt was drenched with sweat, but still he held up his chin.

"You don't scare me, boy," he said. "You won't lay a finger on me. As soon as my friends in Vientiane hear what you're doing here they'll have you shot."

Phosy knelt beside the old man and pushed his face up close. "But that's just the loveliest part of all this," he said. "Your dear friends in Vientiane won't ever get to hear your version of events. I was down here observing a movie production. We noticed a fire along the river road and we ran to help. But the gates were locked and we didn't have a key. I ordered villagers to bring sledgehammers and we broke in through the wall. But, sadly, it was too late. The fire had already caught the dry hay and the house had been consumed. We recovered the body of brave Comrade Vilai who'd died trying to rescue his beloved animals. You'll probably get a posthumous medal, but would it make up for the agony you'd suffered before you were consumed by the flames?"

Phosy and Wee had turned the deckchair around to face the conflagration. Shards of fire were rising from the ground floor. Phosy noticed a moment—a look of recognition on the old man's face that marked his transition from valiant invincible to probable fricassee. No number of influential friends would help him now.

"What have I done wrong exactly?" he asked.

The two policemen continued to push the chair toward the sliding doors. The glass leaned outward precariously as the frames began to melt. Phosy said nothing.

"For god's sake," said Vilai. "If the point of this is to torture a confession out of me, at least give me something to deny."

"You've had the question," said Wee. "You chose to lie about it. End of story."

"What question?" asked Vilai. "The crate? Is that what this is all about? I told you, you moron. We dispatch crates of animals. We don't put bodies in our shipments. It's bad for business."

"Don't believe you," said Phosy.

The chair continued its slide toward oblivion.

"I swear," said Vilai. "Look. I check every shipment that leaves here personally. We weigh them. They weigh them again at the airport. We sell by the kilo. The shipping clerks are pedantic up there. They have to answer to European standards. They watch every bit of cargo get loaded onto the plane. They have to get the figures right or they lose their percentage. They know how much a crate of civets should weigh. If there was a body in there, they'd know. When it left here it contained nothing but civets. If you found the invoice downstairs, check the weights for yourself."

"Still the wrong answer," said Wee, but Phosy had stopped pushing.

CHAPTER FIFTEEN
Rajhid, the Grim Reaper

The following day, Crazy Rajhid was feeling hungry. He could have walked along the empty street, but he preferred to fight his way through the vegetation that clogged the riverbank. He arrived at Madam Daeng's noodle shop mid-morning, usually a good time to find Daeng less stressed than during the breakfast and lunchtime rushes. But the shop was shuttered and there was no sign out front to explain what had happened. He sensed calamity. He climbed the back wall and entered the building through the upstairs window. There was nobody there. The bed was made, but Mr. Geung's room on the ground floor was disheveled as if there had been a skirmish. Nobody had made noodles that day.

On this day, Rajhid was conservatively dressed in shorts and a red T-shirt. His father, Mr. Tickoo, the cook at the Happy Dine Indian restaurant, always left a set of clean clothes on the back fence in an attempt to preserve what little dignity the boy had left. Rajhid rarely took them and, if he did, never gave them back. But on this day, wearing clothes seemed more appropriate. He had a mission. He set off in the direction of the That Luang Monument, marched across the parade ground and arrived at Siri's official house. The front door was open as usual but there wasn't a soul inside. There were clothes strewn around and evidence of a struggle. In the kitchen, chairs lay on the ground, the table was set and there were seven bowls laid out for rice but the steamer was full. Two spoons lay on the floor. In the sink lay a plate that had broken neatly in half, and the tap water was running. There was no blood nor were there signs of life.

For a young man whose mind was already muddled, this conundrum made his head throb. He went to the police dormitory where Phosy and Dtui lived, but all of the rooms were padlocked. There was no guard at the entry post. At the nurse's college where Dtui taught, a woman he didn't know was in her classroom. He was ready to explode from the incongruities. His last resort was police headquarters. He'd only ever been there once, under duress, but he knew where Phosy's office was. That's what he needed: a logical policeman to explain away all the weirdness. But on the door was a name other than Chief Inspector Phosy's. And before he was shooed away by a frightening man with a pistol in his holster, Rajhid caught a glimpse of a fat man sitting at Phosy's desk, comfortable, as if he'd been there for a long time.

Rajhid sat naked in the Mekhong up to his waist in cool muddy water. His clothes were laid flat on the bank like a steamroller victim. He was surrounded by an enormous new reality. All the things he thought he knew were wrong. All the people he loved and admired, but to whom he had never spoken, were gone. And one thing dawned on him. What if people only existed if you completed the cycle of communication? By not speaking to them he had failed to anchor them to the earth. Because of his selfishness, he had exterminated an entire tribe of good people. It was all his fault. He, Rajhid, was the grim reaper. He had no choice but to undo the damage he had done. To bring everyone back to life.

He went off in search of paper.

CHAPTER SIXTEEN
From Pig to Man and From Man to Pig

Chief Inspector Phosy awoke from a troubled nightmare with a head like a lead block. He'd been in enough fights in his life to recognize bruised ribs and the smart of cuts and wounds about his face. There was congealed blood on his shirt. It was obvious what had happened, but for the life of him he couldn't remember who'd beaten him up. Whoever it was, he or she had done a pretty thorough job.

He tried to sit up and it was only then that he realized he was lying on concrete. He was in a cell with no furniture. The only door was barred. He used those bars to pull himself to his feet. He identified two, possibly three broken toes, perhaps a broken rib. There was one slit of a window high on the back wall, but all he could see was blue sky and cobwebs. It was daytime. It was hot. He was wearing soiled civilian clothes and he was sweating. Through the door, he could see that his was the last cell in a block of eight but all the other doors were ajar. He was alone. He had no idea where he was.

"All right, I'm up," he shouted. "Let's get this over with. Whatever this is."

But nobody came. The only sound he could hear was

the throb of a generator somewhere outside the building. He leaned against the wall and forced his mind to recall what had happened. He remembered their good day: the fake movie, breaking into the unmanned compound, the monster Vilai. Phosy could still feel how the disgust had seeped through his skin. Even now, the bile rose in his throat. He'd seen the tiger and bear skins piled high, one atop the other. There were bins of pangolin scales. He'd been unable to count the jars and bottles of bear gall bladder remedies and tiger aphrodisiacs, the animal parts in alcohol, the vials of powdered tusk, the ivory chunks cleaned and ready for carving.

The walls of Vilai's house had been decorated with the types of animal heads you'd expect to find on the walls of cowardly hunters. But the old man had done nothing to deserve the trophies other than wait for the enslaved beasts to die slowly in captivity. Some minion would skin them and sever their heads. It probably wasn't the wisest decision to set fire to the house. Before setting light to the cellophane-covered sofa, Phosy had had the foresight to take out the metal filing cabinets from the home office along with any other papers that might have been of value. Even so, he'd not really intended to burn the place down. He'd just wanted to vent his anger on the ugly vinyl couch. He'd been surprised how rapidly the flames spread. It was significant that none of the members of Wee's anti-trafficking team stepped in to take the burning torch from his hand or rushed for buckets of water.

Phosy had found the invoice in the files. He could prove that the crate of civets originated from that compound. But even with the threat of a premature cremation, Vilai had refused to admit to killing the girl. Phosy had no choice other than to bring the old man back to Vientiane, handcuffed inside their bus. The bus—that was it. Something had happened on the bus. The mood had been light. The banter was chirpy. They all had their own reasons for being pleased. The movie extras were excited about their first day on the set and confident they'd be picked for additional roles. Wee's team members were all running on adrenaline. They knew the animals they rescued had little hope of survival but, given the option, wouldn't they sooner take their chances in the jungle than behind bars? And the police were certain this high-profile intervention would yell out a warning to other traffickers. To their minds it was a success.

Siri and Civilai had been particularly bubbly on the journey home as they'd argued camera angles and lighting. Both imagined what the day's film might have looked like if only the camera had rolled rather than sat idly. Daeng, following her cameo as production manager and her role in convincing Vilai to be in their film, was wagging her tail for the entire trip.

Phosy could visualize every facet of that journey home in his mind. Only he had considered their day a failure. The skeleton that haunted his days still had no identity. He was no closer to working out where and when she was put in the crate. As a decent human being he might have joined the others in the celebrations, but as a policeman he'd overstepped the mark with his actions and he was embarrassed. He knew when he returned to the dormitory and told his wife, she'd shake her head and tell him she didn't want their daughter to grow up in a lawless society. That he was the chief guardian of what was right in their country. And she would be correct.

Except, he didn't see her. He didn't make it home and he didn't know why. He could remember the bus slowing down, a roadblock perhaps. Roadblocks were common enough. But that was the last clear memory in his head.

He had no idea how long he'd been sitting, leaning against the wall beneath the window coaxing memories from his battered head. But he was pulled from his thoughts by the sound from afar of a lock sliding open. This was followed by footsteps and another lock. The door at the far end of Phosy's block opened on rusty hinges and three burly middle-aged men walked in. He recognized them. They were men he'd fired from the police force for various reasons. Things immediately became clear. This was some sort of vengeance. One of the men was holding a fold-up chair. He marched to Phosy's cell and spent some time working out how to open it. Phosy laughed.

"I see being a civilian hasn't pumped up your IQ any," he said.

The man set down the chair and spit in Phosy's direction. "You want another beating?" he asked.

"I doubt you'd manage it if I'm conscious," said Phosy.

The man went back to join his colleagues at the door. They seemed to be waiting for something. All the activity had triggered one more memory in Phosy's head. A roadblock. The bus stopped. He was about to leave his seat when he felt a sharp pain in his neck. Not a knife. A needle. He'd been given a shot of something that knocked him out. It was obviously injected by somebody on the bus. Perhaps the same sedative they'd given Vilai. There was only one possible reason for all this. Men who should have been in jail were now his jailers. There had been a mutiny. His head swam. Who in this disorganized community could have orchestrated such a coup? He looked up. The men at the far door took a step back to let someone through. As he passed they saluted. He walked confidently up to Phosy's cell and smiled.

"I can't tell you how long I've yearned for this moment," he said.

CHAPTER SEVENTEEN
A Haeng Jury

The judge sat on the fold-up chair with his legs crossed and his arms folded. Phosy remained leaning against the back wall shaking his head slowly, a wry smile at the corner of his mouth. It didn't take a genius to work out that something serious had happened in his brief absence. He didn't speak, so he and Judge Haeng merely stared at each other from a distance. At last the judge chuckled.

"I am enjoying this too much to spoil it with conversation," he said.

Phosy remained silent.

"Did you honestly believe I'd sit back forever and allow you and your group of mutants to walk all over me? To humiliate me?"

Phosy continued to smile.

"You don't reach the position of authority as a judge if you don't have a logical mind."

"Or a wealthy father," said Phosy.

"Yes, keep it up with the smartarsed comments, mister policeman. You can joke your way to hell for all I care. I don't mind anymore. Because now I have you exactly where I want you."

"Illegally locked away?"

"In this country the term 'legal' is amorphous. You are about to feel what it's like to be humiliated. To be convicted of more crimes than you can talk your way out of in a hundred years."

"Is that right? And what is it I'm accused of?"

Phosy got painfully to his feet and staggered across to the door. Despite the thick bars between them, the judge leaned backward as if expecting an attack.

"Oh, I'll save that little surprise for your hearing tomorrow," he said.

"Well, that's nice," said Phosy, his face through the bars. "I'll have a hearing. Wouldn't it have been easier just to have me shot?"

"Easier, yes," said the judge, "but not nearly as much fun. This way you die with a shameful reputation. Your name will be pig shit for eternity. Your daughter will grow up pretending she's never heard of you. You and your cronies will be buried in unmarked graves beside the bodies of other traitors and despots. Oh, this is such bliss."

"Haeng, you do realize that once I get out of here, the first thing I'll do is cut off your feet and shove them down your throat?"

"Beautiful," said Haeng. "One never has a tape recorder when one needs one. No, wait, perhaps I do." He lifted his baggy shirt to show the Walkman attached to his belt. "The wonders of technology," he said. "That and exhaustive paperwork, the two pillars of authority. Of course, you've never been a slave to paperwork, have you? Another failing. Another nail in your coffin."

"You think people won't hear of your bogus court?"

"I think everyone will hear of it." The judge smiled.

"I've certainly advertised it far and wide. We even put an announcement in the Pasason newsletter. Came out today. And it's hardly bogus. Your case is scheduled to be read in the center courtroom starting tomorrow morning. The Minister of Justice will be conducting the tribunal."

"You're mad."

"Brilliantly mad. And you'll learn just how seriously you've underrated this mad man all these years." He stood, attempted to re-fold the chair, gave up and left it crippled in front of the cell. He walked away.

"Who's representing me?" Phosy called after him.

The judge stopped. "Given the dearth of qualified lawyers in this country, I thought you might prefer to represent yourself," he said.

"I have a right to representation. I want Civilai Songsawat to speak for me."

Haeng laughed. "Oh, I'm so sorry," he said. "Didn't I tell you? It would appear your friend Civilai has been sent away for reeducation. So too have Dr. Siri and Madam Daeng and most of your top aids and allies. I doubt whether the old folks will survive the harsh conditions in the north."

"I don't believe you."

"I don't care."

"How could you swing all this so fast?"

The judge walked back to the cell with a spring in his step. "Methodical planning over a long period," he said. "Nothing fast. Patience. A brilliant mind. Cold revenge in the heart. While you were busy underestimating me, I was equally busy plotting your downfall. Everyone you ever trusted has been arrested for subversive activities and relocated."

"Where's my wife?"

"She's in the women's prison on Don Nang Island. Horrible place. Dirt and disease everywhere."

"You have no right."

"I have every right. Her husband is on trial for acts of treason against the republic. Once we've convicted you, she'll be up next as an accomplice. Then all your other accomplices and—"

"Where's my daughter?"

"No need to worry about her."

"If she's in any danger I swear I'll kill you."

The judge lifted his shirt and grinned. "Still rolling here," he said.

The man's sudden vein of confidence and poise was more worrying than his words.

"This is all bull," said Phosy. "There's no way you can pull any of this off. You're a moron and a loner. Something like this needs a team—an army."

"That's true," said the judge. "And I do have my army. I've been collecting my soldiers since the first day your Dr. Siri showed me disrespect. Since you all began to mock me and doubt my ability. I have been mopping up the dregs you discarded and turning them into a force against you. The men you dismissed from the force are working for a department I established. You never followed up. You can't just discard men and show no interest in their careers. They hate you almost as much as I do."

"Was it these brave soldiers of yours who beat me when I was unconscious?" Phosy asked.

"You were an uncooperative prisoner."

"I hope you got a few kicks in yourself because that was the last chance you'll get."

"You'll be feeling a few more blows before this is all over, I assure you."

"I think you overvalue your abilities," said Phosy.

"And I think you ignore your gullibility," said Haeng. "You placed the final span in my cantilever bridge when you gave me back my letter to the American Embassy. That was the last piece of physical evidence you had against me. Now it's your word against mine. And I have the law on my side."

He laughed all the way to the main door, leaving Phosy to chew things over. The last time he'd seen Haeng, the idiot judge was at his desk begging for forgiveness. Was it possible the little man really had the savvy to put together some sort of legal case against him? Against all of them? With no constitution, the state of the law had reverted to village wisdom. Everything had been left to the decisions of committees of elders. His fate clearly depended on who the judge had on his side and how much common sense prevailed during the trial.

He sat on the floor and considered all he'd heard, and for the first time in years he was truly afraid. He'd seen communities swayed by liars. The world's history was garnished with mass misunderstandings. Presidents had risen to power on the back of false propaganda. If Haeng was as smart as he now claimed to be, Phosy was in the sewage overflow pipe and on his way to the depths of the Mekhong current.

After a nutritious breakfast of one baguette and a bottle of water, Phosy was led to the courtroom the next morning. His guards were men he'd kicked out of office and thrown into jail for graft. The handcuffs were too tight. The handling was unnecessarily rough. Neither man spoke. Phosy had expected a closed-door trial with just a committee and one or two witnesses, so he was taken aback by the number of people crammed into a courtroom the size of a tennis court. He recognized a lot of those in attendance: Party members, military personnel and ex-senior police officers, all of whom he'd worked alongside, been dissatisfied with and eventually fired. Perhaps it shouldn't have occurred to him this late but Phosy realized just how many enemies he'd made during his tenure in Vientiane. Diplomacy hadn't been his forte.

The district administrator and his staff were there, writers for the two unpopular, unread newsletters and at least four Vietnamese advisors and their interpreters. At the rear of the room was a large professional-looking video camera whose operator was in military uniform, scowling. The committee sat in a line in the front row with their backs to the audience like judges at a rural beauty pageant. The head of the group was the Minister of Justice, a man with whom Phosy had clashed a number of times. Seated on either side of him were the vice minister, two generals, the governor of a distant province and the director of Mahosot Hospital. Phosy understood too well that the composition of committees only made sense if you knew of alliances. And the last man seated in the front row left him in no doubt. He was wearing the uniform of a senior police officer. His name was Oudomxai. Until three months earlier, when Phosy had found him guilty of mass corruption, he'd been the chief of police. He had no right to be out of jail. Even less right to be wearing his uniform and sitting on a tribunal—especially this tribunal.

Phosy had decided that whatever the outcome of this

ridiculous trial, he would maintain his dignity and cooperate. He'd be polite and answer accusations against him with only the truth. He knew there was no protocol for anything like this. There were no rules of engagement. He took his seat behind a table covered in what looked like billiard table baize. He looked around the room. There were people he knew, helped, had done favors for, lent money to. But on this somber first morning there was no eye contact, not one friendly face daring to look back at him.

Judge Haeng made his entrance dramatically through the other door. He was wearing a navy-blue suit that made him look like an old regime undertaker and accompanied by three assistants carrying large files and notebooks. They all sat together at a table opposite Phosy. As there was no stage, all anyone had to look at was a pale-blue wall hung with black-and-white photographs of the politburo members. Not one of those faces cracked a smile.

As was the norm, the Minister of Justice gave an overly long speech about justice and corruption and the law. It ate a large chunk of the morning session. Everyone was relieved when he handed it over to his deputy.

The Vice Minister of Justice, a sinewy khaki-colored man, stood and looked in Phosy's direction. "Are you Phosy Vongvichai?" he said. "Until recently the chief of police?"

"No," said Phosy.

So much for cooperation. The vice minister looked embarrassed. "Did you not understand the question?" he asked.

"I understood the question, comrade," said Phosy, "but until I am officially relieved of my position, I am still the chief of police."

Oudomxai, too big for his police uniform, turned to his left and raised his substantial eyebrows.

"Consider yourself relieved," said the minister.

"Much appreciated, sir," said Phosy.

The vice minister continued with a little less bluster. "You are at this tribunal facing the following charges," he said, "the establishment of vigilante murder squads, the abuse of state funds, harassment, the destruction of property, dereliction of duty, colluding with known anti-government agents, and two counts of premeditated murder. How do you plead?"

Phosy had gone deaf after "establishment of vigilante murder squads." Any one of those charges, were they to be proven, would warrant execution. The odds were stacked against him. He stood.

"Not guilty to any and all of them," he said. "And as this is the first time I've heard the charges against me, I have had no time to put together an argument. So, I'd like to request a week to answer the accusations and solicit the assistance of an attorney."

"Any thoughts on that, Judge Haeng?" asked the minister. He was a lean man with scaly skin and a scar on his chin. Like all the ministers he'd been a warrior with the Pathet Lao and had a number of war wounds and little patience.

Judge Haeng got to his feet and grabbed the lapel of his jacket.

"Given the seriousness of the charges and the duplicity of Comrade Phosy's connections in the outside world," he said, "we would not recommend the temporary release of the accused to collect evidence. The ex-chief inspector did request the assistance of one Comrade Civilai Sonsawat, who is currently undergoing reeducation in the north and, together with his coconspirators, also faces forty-nine charges of sedition. The accused did not name an alternate. It is therefore our decision that we should proceed with this case in its agreed format as a presentation of the overwhelming evidence against Comrade Phosy and leave it to the wisdom of the court to assess its veracity."

"Well, that's fair," said Phosy. "Can I at least request the removal of one of the members of your tribunal committee?"

"Absolutely not," said the vice minister. "In your position, you hardly have the right to request anything."

Phosy remained standing. "I'm just curious as to how impartial Comrade Oudomxai can be given that he was convicted of corruption and thrown in jail largely as a result of evidence I gathered against him."

Judge Haeng was also on his feet. "Given that Comrade Phosy's fitness and legal standing as a policeman are at the heart of this trial, any arrests credited to him must also be considered questionable," he said. "Therefore, Comrade Oudomxai must be presumed innocent and his position as chief of police is still tenable."

Phosy laughed out loud.

"I suggest you take this tribunal more seriously," said the minister.

"I suggest you . . ." Phosy remembered his manners just in time.

"What was that?" said the vice minister.

"I'm just saying that I should like to request copies of the transcript of the hearing each day," said Phosy.

The minister looked at Judge Haeng who shrugged. It was clear who was running the show.

"That is permissible," said the minister.

Phosy looked around for a court stenographer and finally located a small woman impeccably dressed in a *phasin* skirt and vintage pink top. She seemed to be struggling to get ink out of her Bic pen.

"Then, if everyone is satisfied, let us go ahead with the proceedings," said the vice minister. "I call on Judge Haeng Somboun to begin his reading of the charges."

The judge walked from behind his table with a set of prompt cards in his hand. He stood between the committee and the politburo'd wall.

"Respected gentlemen," he said, "I appreciate you taking time out from your valuable work to be here with us. I must begin by telling you that one of my duties as head of the public prosecution department is to assess the suitability of those who enforce our laws at all levels. If there are complaints we take them very seriously. If those complaints persist over a period of time, we compile a file."

He walked to his table where one of the assistants handed him a thick folder.

"My department has been maintaining a file on the misdemeanors of then Inspector Phosy since 1976. It is not our intention to enter all of the complaints into evidence here—merely to point out their existence and to cite one or two that are relevant to this hearing."

"Let's see it," said Phosy.

"Comrade Phosy, you will have a chance to comment on charges at a later stage," said the vice minister. "This isn't your time to speak."

"Why not?" said Phosy. He stood. "Why not pass the notes around to the committee and show them what terrible things I'm accused of doing? Surely it can only help the judge's case."

"Phosy, if you don't wish to be restrained I suggest you sit down and control your outbursts," said the minister.

Phosy, recognizing the hopelessness of the situation, retained his seat and folded his arms. The judge continued:

"As I said, my point is not to list all the accusations we received—and there are many—but to bring your attention to one particular chain of events. Its relevance will become clear as the trial continues. In June of this year, Comrade Phosy paid a deposit on a small house at Nong Tewada. There, he set up a prostitute by the name of Vatsana as his second wife."

Phosy's eyes rolled inside his head like slot machine tiles.

"He made regular visits to Miss Vatsana," Haeng continued, "and, amongst other things, they partook of various stimulants and drugs. It was as a result of his introduction of hallucinogens that Miss Vatsana became an addict."

"You have evidence of this?" asked one of the generals.

"I have the lease agreement signed by then Inspector Phosy," said Haeng. "I have photographs of them together. I have signed statements from witnesses who saw the inspector make his regular nighttime visits to the house on his police-issue motor scooter. I also have transcripts from neighbors describing the abusive relationship. Evidently, Comrade Phosy threatened the girl with violence many times and told her that if she informed anyone of their relationship, especially his wife, who was out of the country at the time, that he would kill her. All this is in the file labeled B."

Phosy was mystified. He'd never been the philandering

type. He could barely hang on to one wife, let alone two. But the judge's report left him with too many questions. None of it made sense. The judge had obviously gone to a great deal of trouble to fabricate this lie but what was the point of it? Most of the married men Phosy knew had affairs. A number of the wealthier ones kept women. He was sure everyone on the committee was, at that moment, blushing with memories of their own philandering. But, given the wreckage of the other charges he faced, setting up a house for a mistress barely made a dent. So . . . ? This had to be a prelude to something far more serious. He bit his tongue and waited for the crash.

"On the night of August ninteenth," Haeng continued, "Comrade Phosy took his whore to a drug party at a shed behind Wattay Airport. His old friend, Maysuk, the director of the airport, had keys to all the buildings on airport grounds. He also had a minor wife of his own, Miss Soukjanda. He'd given her a job as his secretary. He often invited Phosy there to drink, take drugs and, when they were suitably intoxicated, to exchange partners."

Phosy was astounded how much more fun his secret life was compared to his mundane, more public one. But he'd stopped seeing the funny side of it. He looked at the faces of the onlookers. They were buying the whole sack of shit.

"Supporting evidence?" said one of the generals.

Haeng was given a wad of papers by his assistant.

"I have here a signed statement from Miss Soukjanda dated August twelfth, made in front of a witness, describing the usual goings on at the airport," said Haeng. "This statement was collected a week prior to the events of the nineteenth as part of our ongoing investigation of Comrade Phosy. At the time, we had no way of knowing what was about to unfold at the party. Miss Soukjanda cannot be called here as a witness as she subsequently fled as a result of the tragic events of the nineteenth. My people are searching for her."

Phosy's heart dropped to his stomach like a turd into a toilet bowl. At last, he knew where Haeng was leading.

"On the evening of the nineteenth—the night of the party," the judge continued, "Miss Vatsana became hysterical as a result of drugs. She was threatening to expose her relationship with Comrade Phosy. As the mood of the party had fallen into decline, Director Maysuk drove his lover back to her apartment. When he returned to the shed, Comrade Phosy was standing over the naked body of Miss Vatsana who was bruised and bloody. Comrade Phosy told Director Maysuk that she had overdosed and fallen to the ground. They could feel no pulse. They began in a panic to think of a way to dispose of the body. Phosy knew that if she were to be identified, the trail would eventually lead to him. He knew that there were two competent forensic pathologists in the country, one of whom was his wife. He was aware that merely dumping the body would not hide Miss Vatsana's identity.

"Director Maysuk told him of a controversy at the airport. A shipment of animals scheduled to be dispatched to Europe had been bumped from its cargo flight for a more important shipment. There would be no space available for a week. The animals had not been fed and nobody was prepared to accept responsibility for them. So the crate had sat there under a tarpaulin, the animals, in this case wild civets, slowly starving to death. That was when Phosy hatched his evil plan. He knew that the animals would strip Miss Vatsana's body of its flesh and internal organs, thus removing any evidence that would lead to her identification. I will not speculate as to whether Comrade Phosy had been aware that Miss Vatsana was not in fact dead when they put her in the crate, but the evidence suggests that she was eaten alive."

The onlookers let out a gasp. The video operator looked up from his viewfinder and sneered. Phosy, who was no great fan of American culture, could think of nothing better to say than, "Wow." Were he sitting in the audience he would be rooting for the prosecutor. Even though there was no truth in the judge's allegation of Phosy's involvement, the possibility was high that his anonymous skeleton now had a name and an identity. And he was equally certain that the judge had been responsible for her death. Yet there was much more to it than Haeng merely covering up a crime of his own. This had been part of a vast, carefully planned and orchestrated scheme to incriminate Phosy and his friends. Instinctively, Phosy knew the worst was yet to come. As he was not able to cross-examine, he started to argue his case in his mind and work out how the magician Haeng had accomplished his tricks. The little man was still in stride.

"On the morning of the twenty-second," he said, "three days after the murder, Comrade Phosy put in a request for a vehicle to go to the airport. He asked for a car rather than a readily available jeep. As usual, he refused to have a driver. On his requisition form, which I have here, he claimed to be meeting the Cambodian chief of police. There was, in fact, no flight from Phnom Penh, and the Cambodians have yet to nominate a chief of police as they are still under an interim Vietnamese administration. The requisition was merely an excuse to go to the airport, where he drove to the shed and loaded Miss Vat-sana's skeleton—picked clean now apart from tendon and sinew—into the trunk of his car."

"Witnesses?" said the same general who'd spoken earlier.

Phosy had had dealings with the military. Most were convivial and mutually beneficial. The soldiers were the only tribunal members even remotely likely to be open-minded at this hearing.

"There was nobody there," said the judge. "Director Maysuk had ordered all the airport ground crew to attend an impromptu political seminar. This left Comrade Phosy free to destroy the surviving civets and burn the crate to remove any trace evidence. When the crew returned, they found the ashes of the crate."

Phosy willed the general to object, to say that without witnesses, this account was merely conjecture. But the soldier kept quiet and Haeng charged ahead uninterrupted.

"I too was at the airport on the morning of the twenty-second to meet a dignitary from Hanoi. I'd seen the official police vehicle and noticed that Comrade Phosy was driving. We exchanged eye contact. He looked extremely guilty."

"Objection," said Phosy to himself.

"On later reflection, it may have been that chance meeting which led to Phosy's outrageous plan to incriminate me," said Haeng. "Once the body had been discovered on the twenty-third, Comrade Phosy abandoned all his official duties and took the unprecedented step of investigating the case personally, despite having a team of qualified detectives at his disposal. Do not forget that my department had been conducting an investigation for a number of years on the conduct of this man who had, somehow, elevated himself to the position of chief inspector. It's conceivable he found out about our work. If so, he had even more reason to silence me and my team. We decided to follow up on the case of the skeleton ourselves."

He had the committee and the onlookers at his feet. They listened silently, rapt.

"In the beginning," he said, "we didn't know the identity of the skeleton. But we heard from one of Miss Vatsana's neighbors, one who had given us witness testimony earlier, that the young woman hadn't been seen for several days. We immediately considered whether the skeleton discovered at the Anusawari Arch might be that of Miss Vatsana. We too believed that only an official vehicle would have been able to deposit the body during the curfew. But, whereas the chief inspector dismissed out of hand that a police automobile might have been involved, we included all government department vehicles in our inquiry.

"At that time, I had in my department a Vietnamese pathologist who had trained in evidence collection in the Soviet Union."

"Convenient," muttered Phosy.

"I took him to the police vehicle compound and, on a hunch, I had him look at the vehicle used by Comrade Phosy the previous morning at the airport. It had been cleaned quite meticulously but in the trunk my expert found a tiny sliver of bone and a human hair. We collected those and a hair from the skeleton at the morgue and another from the shower recess at Miss Vatsana's house, and with the use of microscopic analysis the expert proved beyond a doubt that they belonged to the same person."

"Is your Vietnamese expert here to give evidence?" asked the minister.

"He is," said the judge, pointing to the third row of the gallery where a nondescript, grey-haired man nodded drowsily. His official interpreter seated beside him translated Haeng's words and the expert waved, which seemed an inappropriate gesture at such a gathering.

"We will hear from him later should the need arise," said Haeng. "I do have a copy of his detailed report here in File C."

Phosy was wondering whether the witnesses would ever be heard.

"That brings us to why Comrade Phosy would wait until that night to leave the skeleton at the arch," said the judge, "but as our esteemed committee will only convene for half-days, that question and its answer will have to wait until tomorrow."

He may have bowed respectfully to the gathering at that point and there may have been a ripple of applause from the onlookers. But Phosy stood and looked toward the minister who ignored him. The vice minister began to thank the committee and announce the time for the next day's proceedings and the audience started to leave.

"When do I speak?" Phosy shouted above the throng. His guards were already stepping forward to move him back to the cell. The vice minister ignored him too. Before the guards were on him, Phosy put two fingers in his mouth and shrilled out a whistle that could shatter glass. The room quieted.

"When do I speak?" he said again.

"You'll have your chance when all the charges have been put on record," said the vice minister.

"Will I at least get a copy of today's evidence?"

The vice minister looked toward the judge who was already exiting through the far door. The minister had also left in a hurry to get his lunch.

"I don't have the authority to permit that," said the vice minister.

Then, to Phosy's surprise, the chattier of the two generals took a step back into the room and said, "Give him access."

"I can't . . ." the vice minister began.

"I said give him a copy," said the general. "This isn't North Korea. He has a right."

There was no leeway for negotiation. The vice minister nodded and raised his eyebrows to one of Haeng's assistants. The general gave Phosy a fleeting glance as he left the room. The two guards grabbed Phosy by the armpits and marched him out. It was perhaps just as well the court hadn't given him time to speak because he didn't know what the hell he could have said. "It's all a lie" isn't likely to sway a jury. The only truth of the hearing was that he had, in fact, driven to the airport on the morning of the 22nd. He'd gone in response to a memo from the ministry telling him to meet his counterpart from Cambodia. The origin of that memo was now pretty damned obvious, and they would have trashed all the screwed-up messages from his litter basket long ago. His word against Haeng's.

His cell now had a straw mat and a bucket. He felt like he'd been upgraded to business class. But he didn't mind concrete. It was good for his crooked disc. He lay down on the floor to rest his aches and woke up three hours later. The notes from the morning session and a Xerox of the evidence were wedged between the bars of his door.

He doubted Judge Haeng had been consulted on that. The judge would have preferred Phosy to remain shackled and blindfolded. Phosy wondered whether the general could be an ally. He needed one.

He sat on the mat and went through the documents. The supposed witness statements from the neighbors were all matter-of-fact, probably written by some clerk in Haeng's office. They spoke of seeing Phosy riding his lilac Vespa to and from the house at Nong Tewada and of hearing the couple fighting often. There was no mention of how they had been able to identify Phosy. The Xeroxes of the photographs were confusing. They showed a young, pretty, dark-haired girl beside a casual-looking Phosy, sharing a secret? Telling a joke? Looking into each other's eyes. He had no recollection of the meeting. But there was no end of weddings and birthdays at which to get drunk and laugh with strangers. In one of the photos there was someone to the other side of him cut off at the shoulder. He recognized the flab under the arm. It was his wife. They'd taken candid shots of him at some social event and cropped them to delete Nurse Dtui. Clever.

The photos depressed him. He looked again at the pretty girl he'd only known as a skeleton. What had she done to deserve such cruelty? She'd been lied to and manipulated and thrown alive into a crate of wild animals. Her last memory of her life had been the horror of realizing it was soon to end. Nobody deserved such a fate. Nobody could forgive a man who would do such a thing.

He ran his index finger over the image of Dtui's arm. It hurt not knowing where she was, what discomfort and sadness she must be feeling. And where was their daughter? Haeng's plan was working. Phosy had been isolated from his loved ones and his closest supporters. He had no way of knowing whether they were dead or alive. Haeng had purged the police Phosy trusted and replaced them with men who hated him. Siri, Daeng and Civilai were in camps from which many did not return. In a perverted way, he admired the judge for the thoroughness of his attack. Civilai had been right. It was a mistake to under-estimate your enemies. Phosy had seen the little judge as nothing more than incompetent and corrupt. He'd never considered him capable of a master battle plan. Phosy was already defeated without firing a single shot in retaliation. Brilliant.

CHAPTER EIGHTEEN
Skin Only

On the second day of the tribunal there were two more surprises awaiting Phosy. Firstly, the sympathetic general was no longer on the committee. They said it was due to illness, but Phosy had a feeling Judge Haeng had objected to his being a thinker. He had been replaced by an elder-statesman type in a crumpled uniform, a man Phosy had once ridiculed. It was true that a man's past sins eventually catch up with him.

Secondly, he recognized men in the audience whom he'd spoken to during his inquiries about the judge. Sitting in a row behind Haeng's table were the judge's old Zil driver, the night watchman at the Zil parking lot, the guard Sihot had spoken to at the salt farm, and one Westerner who seemed very uncomfortable being in an exclusively Asian room. Phosy had never seen him before. But he had seen Comrade Vilai, the owner of the animal compound, who should have been securely locked away but now sat one row behind the committee grinning at Phosy.

The vice minister stood and re-introduced everyone for the benefit of the transcript. He surprised Phosy by asking him if he had anything to say. Phosy stood.

"There are no laws that I can refer to," he began, "and, so far, we haven't signed any international agreements on human rights, so I know the committee isn't answerable for what's happening here. But there are inalienable rights that every man and woman should be granted. I have not been allowed to answer my case. I have been deprived contact with my wife and child and medical care for the beating I received after my arrest. I am underfed and—"

"Very well," said the minister, "if all you can do is use your time to complain we should press on with the tribunal. We have a lot to get through."

Phosy sat and raised his hands to the heavens.

"That's correct," said the vice minister. "Judge Haeng, could you continue with the charges?"

The judge rose and took center stage with even more bounce in his step. "The next charge is that of false accusation and slander," he said. "I have placed this item before that of a second murder charge because it allows us to see chronologically the events that transpired up to and including September first. It will also serve to demonstrate how the accused's mind was working over that period. We have already shown his lust for power by illegally ousting his predecessor and stepping into the role himself. Almost immediately after his appointment he set up his first death squad on the Lao/Thai border to distribute his own version of justice. We shall be presenting that evidence at a later stage, but it does illustrate the temperament of a man who considers himself above the law. It also explains why he set out to falsify a case against the man who posed the greatest challenge to his aspirations—myself."

Phosy snorted and was met with sneers from the committee.

"Sorry," he said. "Mucous."

"Once Comrade Phosy attained the position of chief inspector he had access to certain confidential files," continued the judge without missing a beat. "He learned about me and my team's investigation into his activities. I should at this stage like to enter into evidence two cassette tape recordings. The first was made at my office a few weeks after his appointment as chief inspector. If I may I would like to play you a short extract."

One of the assistants pressed play on a recorder before realizing it wasn't plugged in. The young woman hurried to the wall socket and righted her mistake. She pressed play once more and turned up the volume. The recording was surprisingly clear. Phosy heard the voice of the judge followed by his own voice:

"I may remind you that I am a judge and the director of public prosecution, which means I am your superior."

"Yet I was recruited and promoted by the Ministry of Interior, which puts us on different tracks. You aren't my boss, and if I have my way you won't be anybody's boss by the end of the week."

Phosy thought back to the day in his office when the judge admitted to his crime. He'd been carrying a copy of the manifesto, or at least a hollow version of it. They'd considered it another of the judge's quirks but, in fact, the cunning little bastard had recorded the meeting, selected that one passage from the tape. That same tape had once contained enough of a confession that would have ended this farce once and for all.

"Can we hear all of it?" he shouted.

"Phosy, you've been warned about speaking out of turn," said the vice minister.

"The tape will be admitted as evidence," said Haeng.

"Everyone on the committee is welcome to listen to the entire recording."

"Yeah, I bet," said Phosy to himself.

The assistant took out the cassette and inserted another.

"And just in case that first recording failed to make Comrade Phosy's intentions perfectly clear," said the judge, "I have a second tape recorded just two days ago."

He pressed play.

"Haeng, you do realize that once I get out of here, the first thing I'll do is cut off your feet and shove them down your throat?"

"Hardly the words of a responsible police inspector," said Haeng. He went once more to his table and took another file.

"I have here Comrade Phosy's report of my supposed involvement in the death of his lover, Miss Vatsana," he said. "As is his style, it is a slapdash, badly written account with no corroborating evidence whatsoever. It was a rather pathetic attempt to besmirch my name. It clearly shows how Comrade Phosy set about framing me for the murder of his whore lover. I have highlighted one or two points."

He read from the report:

"Although I have yet to find witnesses to this effect, it is my belief that the judge used the excuse of going to the airport to meet a foreign expert in order to collect the body and hide it in the trunk of his vehicle.

"You will notice the remarkable similarities between the accusations against me and the events that actually took place. I have to admit Comrade Phosy is a very clever man. But the cleverest men are the most dangerous. The report continues:

"The judge removed the key from the Zil key ring so his driver would not discover the body. That night, the judge feigned

drunkenness in order to hijack his own vehicle and take the skeleton to the Anusawari Arch."

"Why I should choose to put a skeleton in a public place is not explained although I am convinced he heard about my attendance at the Soviet compound and decided that would be a perfect opportunity to connect me to the skeleton. After this meaningless charade, I supposedly drove my limousine back to the Zil parking lot and presumably walked home three kilometers to my house without being seen."

The judge performed a staged face to face with each member of the committee and smiled at the audience.

"Really?" he said. "Honorable gentlemen, you all know me and of my unerring devotion both to the Party and to the process of the law. I'm certain you would not expect me to dignify such a wishy-washy accusation with an argument. But, for my own peace of mind I should like to call on witnesses to describe my actions on the night of the twenty-second and twenty-third of August."

The live witness statements and interviews dragged on through the morning. There was to be a football match—the Lao national team against an amateur club from Cuba in the afternoon, so the hearing adjourned at eleven.

Phosy sat cross-legged on his straw mat and meditated. He hadn't meditated since his childhood back in the village. In those days he didn't have so much on his mind and meditation had been an annoying waste of his time. But now, alone, without even the company of a god or a buddha or a fairy godmother, he tried to find some inner peace. He controlled his breathing, searched for truth. Truth was hard to come by. It had been all but absent over the past two days. He doubted they'd ever give him a chance to rebut—to tell his version of the truth.

At around three, a grumpy woman in an ugly jacket came by the cell to drop off the day's transcript and copies of evidence. Phosy was surprised to get them. His sympathetic general was no longer around to force the issue. He thought of the tiny scribe in her neat clothes throwing down her shorthand, rushing off to the typing pool where she and her colleagues would hammer the keys of heavy metal typewriters to get the documents together as quickly as possible. And nobody would read them but Phosy. Nobody on the committee would bother. They'd decided long ago he was guilty so what was the point?

With no team on his side, Phosy had to put together some sort of plan. He had to analyze, to theorize, to search for a way to scuttle Haeng's meticulous plot. The documents he held were his only weapon. There had to be an Achilles' heel. He read:

> *WITNESS ONE, Phoukon Bounsak: Zil limousine driver on night of August 22nd and the early morning of August 23rd*
>
> *STATEMENT: On the morning of August 22nd I drove Judge Haeng to Wattay airport at 7 a.m. We were there for two hours waiting for a foreign dignitary to arrive. He did not arrive. At no stage did the judge ask for the key to the Zil, which was with me the entire time. I returned the judge to the ministry at around 9:30 a.m. At around 8 p.m. I collected the judge from his house in Sikhotabong and drove him to the Soviet Residence on Dorn Pa Mie near the Ammone Temple. At around*

*2:50 a.m. on the morning of the 23rd I started
to drive the judge back to his house, but he was
extremely drunk and insisted I get out of the Zil
and allow him to drive home alone. I reluctantly
agreed to this and walked back to my residence.
I did not see the limousine again until 7 a.m.
when I discovered it in the Zil parking lot
behind the national assembly. It was in good
condition. I checked the trunk and nothing was
out of place.*

*(Note: Judge Haeng admitted his drunken-
ness, apologized to the driver and thanked him
for his honesty.)*

Phosy smiled, had a bite of his stale baguette and washed
it down with warm water. He turned to the next statement.

*WITNESS TWO, Kiengkhum Wunphen: night
watchman at the Zil parking lot two blocks
behind the national assembly building*

*STATEMENT: At around 3:45 a.m. I heard
the voice of Judge Haeng calling me from the
road outside the parking lot. I went to investi-
gate and found Zil number 17—the car allotted
to Judge Haeng—parked about twenty meters
from the entrance with the key in the ignition.
It was undamaged. I drove it into the lot and
logged its return.*

Phosy wondered why Haeng didn't drive the limousine
into the lot and stick around to make certain he'd been

seen, as that was the point. But the only person who could answer that question was Haeng himself. Of course, it didn't escape Phosy's attention that the statements had already been written. The witnesses had signed the sheets after giving practical evidence. The script was already there in black and white. All that was needed was the pretense of a fair trial.

> *WITNESS THREE, Sergei Lavlov: third secretary of the embassy of the USSR (evidence given through Lao/Russian interpreter)*
>
> *STATEMENT: I had met Judge Haeng on a number of occasions at various functions of our respective governments. On the evening of the 22nd there was a function at our residence on Dorn Pa Mie in the Sok Paluang area. Haeng and I drank a good deal and lamented the shortage of good wine from Europe since the Thais shut down the border. At one point, he told me that he had some excellent wine in his car and would like to share it with me. His limousine was parked in an empty lot along the road. Judge Haeng was angry because the keys were left in the ignition. He opened the trunk and there was a crate of cabernet sauvignon. He gave me three bottles, locked the trunk, put the keys back in the ignition and we returned to the function. There had been nothing in the trunk but the wine.*

Phosy recalled the laughter in the room when the judge asked his Soviet pal whether, given the amount of alcohol he'd consumed, he might have overlooked a skeleton in the trunk. The judge was confident enough to mock. He'd laid his traps and Phosy had stepped into every one. He turned to the next.

> *WITNESS FOUR, Nor Sanavong: night guard at Wattay airport*
>
> *STATEMENT: I did not see a Zil limousine drive into the airport grounds on the morning of August 23rd.*

There! Nice. Short and sweet and a total lie. But why not? There were any number of ways to coerce a witness, especially a man in such dire straits he needed to take on two jobs. He'd looked uncomfortable even before the short interview. Phosy forgave him.

The night took a long time in coming, but when it arrived it was as black as any night he could remember. He lay back on the straw mat and thought back to a tiger he'd seen at Vilai's compound. She paced confidently in her two-meter cage. She was an old girl, magnificent and proud despite having no kingdom other than the concrete and the bars. Zoos wanted them young, mate-able. The card on front of her cage read: SKIN ONLY. Expert hide workers could skin a tiger without damaging the valuable pelt. No amount of prancing and posing would alter her fate yet the tiger ruled its domain. She would never renounce her vital role in the universe. She would never go peacefully.

Phosy was sure he had a similar card in front of his own cage. He could feel the knife cuts on his hide. He'd already lost a lot of blood, but he was damned if he'd go quietly.

CHAPTER NINETEEN
The Tiger's Final Roar

Day three, and every day had a new revelation. It was the day of the introduction of the second charge of premeditated murder. The mood was cheery in the courtroom because Laos had beaten the Cubans by two goals to one. It was the only known victory for the Socialist Lao team since records were first kept. The committee members were discussing the winning goal when Phosy arrived in the courtroom. On the far side of the room Judge Haeng was reprimanding his assistants for something that had gone missing.

"Do you know how much those things cost?" he shouted. "It's from Japan. I want it found."

Phosy didn't know what they'd lost but he was glad something had gone wrong on the prosecution bench. It was a good omen. The vice minister, who was not a football fan, quickly called the assembly to order and recapped the previous day's proceedings. He named those present for the benefit of the stenographer and thanked the respected guests. On this occasion, he didn't ask Phosy if he had anything to say. Even though he still had a point to make, Phosy would have passed on the offer. He'd decided he would be making his point without the benefit of words. He'd gone through the files and statements and found no magic key to escape his destiny. On their march into the courtroom, one of the guards had mocked him for sending out police officers with empty guns. He'd mentioned that with Judge Haeng running the show there would be bullets for everyone. He told Phosy that he had a loaded gun in his belt and that his dream was to be allowed onto the chief inspector's firing squad. The guards sat behind and to one side of him during the hearing, and the gun was within reach. This would be his tiger's final roar.

With his acne still enraged, Judge Haeng returned to his pitcher's mound.

"On the evening of September first," he said, "my team was scheduled to conduct an interview with airport director Maysuk. Our net was tightening and we were one or two interviews short of putting together an airtight case against Comrade Phosy. Maysuk's testimony was crucial as his own minor wife had fled and only he was an eyewitness to the proceedings on the night of the nineteenth. Maysuk had talked to me over the phone, told me what had transpired, and agreed to give evidence for this tribunal. One of my assistants and I arrived at his office at six P.M. only to find him stabbed to death and stuffed into a cupboard. According to eyewitnesses, he had been visited an hour earlier by Comrade Phosy. We found the murder weapon hidden down the back of the air conditioner. Obviously, Phosy had used gloves as there were no prints."

"Clever of me," said Phosy.

"What was that?" said the minister.

"Nothing, boss," said Phosy.

The judge continued, "We were fortunate to find

a signed statement in Director Maysuk's desk drawer. I submit that document in File D. In it, the director confessed that he had fallen into what he called a criminal abyss. He'd been dragged there by his supposed friend, Phosy, and forced to cover up a murder. The policeman had threatened him to keep the events of the night of the nineteenth and all of the subsequent subterfuge a secret, but remorse is stronger than fear. Maysuk decided to tell all. Comrade Phosy, by this stage, had no choice but to silence his friend the only way he knew how. We have two eyewitnesses who saw him park in front of the office just before five P.M. and return hurriedly to his jeep thirty minutes later. Nobody else went into the office until we arrived for the interview. I regret that we turned up too late to save the life of the airport director."

There, thought Phosy, *time to do away with the only witness who could substantiate all this bullshit.* The judge had sent Phosy to the airport that night knowing full well he wouldn't meet Director Maysuk. Come to think of it, the poor man was probably bleeding to death in the cupboard as Phosy sat there at his desk.

"I have here an airplane booking to Houay Xai in Comrade Phosy's name," said Haeng. "The date is not fixed. I can only assume he was keeping the option open for an escape from the capital if his plans fell through."

And naturally I'd flee to a province in the middle of nowhere rather than leave the country, thought Phosy.

Haeng began to read through a number of minor charges that seemed to have no purpose other than to sully Phosy's reputation even further; ignoring regulations, recruiting unqualified personnel to assist in criminal cases, perverting justice, and what he called "the trumped-up charges that put an honest, hard-working police chief inspector in a cell." Some thirty men had signed a petition objecting to their unlawful dismissal from the police force without a hearing. Phosy was surprised they could write.

That took matters to lunchtime and Phosy had yet to go on a blind rampage with a stolen handgun. For some reason he wanted to hear all of the charges against him first. Perhaps a massacre a few seconds before the committee's findings would be dramatic enough.

The judge announced that the following morning's session would be the last. It would be spent looking at Phosy's involvement in the setting up of a private vigilante death squad responsible for the murders of over ten people. The committee would be hearing evidence from Comrade Vilai Savangkeo, a respected businessman and close friend of the minister who had been lucky to escape the talons of Phosy and his hired killers even though his house and belongings were destroyed and his livelihood threatened. It was a spicy premise to guarantee the onlookers would arrive early for a good seat.

That evening, hungry and unwashed, Phosy looked through the new transcripts until it was almost too dark to read. As the letters faded before his eyes he thought again of the sweet old stenographer. As he expected, he hadn't yet been given a chance to answer the charges against him. Once again, they said there would be ample time to state his case once all the evidence had been presented. He doubted that.

Again, he wondered about his life and his death. He'd never really experienced defeat. He'd lost a few smaller conflicts perhaps but had always come out on top in the larger battles. He'd taken on challenges that everyone considered to be beyond him but always found something that worked. And now he had to consider life after Phosy. What would his legacy be? Would they see him as an architect of the new regime? Would they ignore his lifetime as a warrior and only remember him as a murderer, a liar, and a traitor? At least, in his few seconds with a gun in his hand, he'd be able to dispense his own justice. Rid the world of Haeng. Perhaps take out his predecessor, Oudomxai. It was all he had to look forward to. He'd have no chance to kiss his wife and child goodbye. No hugs or handshakes. No time for thanks.

His eyes were tired. His vision was playing tricks. The words on the grey pages were blurring together. But three of those words stood out in bold text, highlighted with a pen. They were out of place in their sentences but he was sure nobody but him would notice the incongruity.

"Malee . . . . is . . . . fine."

CHAPTER TWENTY
Not Over Till the Minor Wife Sings

Whilst waiting for Judge Haeng to arrive for the final morning of the trial, Phosy had time to look around the room. The video cameraman was new. Vilai the trafficker still sat behind the committee awaiting his chance for revenge. There was one Vietnamese expert with an interpreter who looked too young to be taken seriously. Phosy made brief eye contact with the stenographer. She'd changed her blouse. Today's was darker, more somber, like one might wear on the morning of a funeral. He smiled at her. She blinked and immediately looked down at her pad. He wanted to tell her what joy she'd given him. How he'd actually found sleep thanks to her. It wasn't just the knowledge that his daughter was safe, it was the fact that amidst all this loathing he'd found one friend. One person who cared. A little bit of faith to hang on to.

Haeng, flushed red, arrived through the far door with his team. He seemed elated. He spared a glance at Phosy and the look said, "Farewell." Phosy instinctively knew the last log had been placed on the pyre. Something had happened. There was no way out now. However brilliant his closing remarks, there'd be nobody listening. He glanced over his shoulder at the pistol in its unfastened holster.

The vice minister did his maître d' duties and finally asked Phosy if he had anything to say. The policeman shook his head.

"And, Judge Haeng, what insights do you have for us today?" asked the minister.

"Thank you, comrade," said Haeng. "I am delighted to say that the last spade-full of dirt has just been shoveled into our defendant's grave."

"Go ahead," said the minister.

"The case has become more airtight than I . . . than we could have expected."

He walked to the front of the room. His smile was like a zipper halfway around his head.

"On this final day of the hearing," he began, "my original plan had been to present witness statements to support my belief that Comrade Phosy had established a death squad to mete out his form of justice along our southern border. Despite the fact that most of the witnesses are either dead or fearful for their lives, we had damning evidence to support my theory. But the reason I was late this morning is I had some good news to attend to. Thanks to the diligence of the ex-police officers I recruited in the wake of Comrade Phosy's cull, we were able to capture five members of the death squad. They had fled during his arrest. They are ashamed of their association with Comrade Phosy and have agreed to speak publicly about their missions. Their statements directly implicate the defendant who undoubtedly advocated their violent behavior."

"Where are they?" the minister asked.

"Outside in the reception area," said the judge.

"Well, don't keep them waiting," said the minister. "Show them in."

When they were led into the courtroom, the five death-squad members clearly disappointed the onlookers. There were hushed comments and snickers as they shuffled down the aisle in their leg irons and handcuffs. Everyone had expected thugs. What they got was a motley crew comprising four less-than frightening men and, heaven forbid, a woman. She wore thick-lens spectacles and had obviously never exercised a day in her life. They were accompanied by four armed military escorts who forced them to stand before the committee. They all avoided eye contact with Phosy, who assumed they too had turned on him. One of the escorts was a man he'd once trusted.

Judge Haeng, who would never be accused of having a sense of humor, couldn't keep the smile from his lips. He addressed the court. "What you see here is the hard core of Comrade Phosy's death squad."

There was laughter.

"They look like people who have lived on the streets for a long time, but do not underestimate them. Under orders from Comrade Phosy they have killed." He turned to the newcomers. "Which one of you should I consider to be the leader of this rabid pack?" he asked.

The death squad members exchanged confused glances. Finally, one gangly character with a gravity-defying hairstyle and crocodile boots raised his shackled hands.

"That might be me," he said.

"Very decisive," said Haeng. "What's your name?"

"Wee."

"And, Comrade Wee, who is it that brought your fearsome group together?"

"Chief Inspector Phosy," said Wee without hesitation.

Phosy studied the faces of the group but saw nothing legible.

"And what was your mission?" asked Haeng.

"To clean up illegal trafficking traders along the Thai border."

"By whichever means," said Haeng.

"By whatever skills we could employ," said Wee.

"Perhaps you could give us an example," said Haeng. "Were you, or were you not involved in a project in Kham-mouan?"

"I was, sir."

"And what was the point of that project?"

"To shut down a human-trafficking gang."

"And did you not achieve your ends by killing the leader of the gang before he was brought to trial?"

"No, sir, he died of a heart attack."

"Most convenient," said Haeng, playing to the crowd.

"And did the village headman in Ban Mapao also have a heart attack?"

"No, sir, he committed suicide."

"Right. I'm sure we all believe that. (More laughter.) Now, look there. Have you ever seen our good friend Comrade Vilai who is sitting in the second row?"

"I have, sir."

"On the second of September, were you instructed by Comrade Phosy to raid Comrade Vilai's compound?"

"Yes, sir."

"And during the course of the raid did you threaten his men, release a number of his legally registered animals, and set fire to his house?"

"We did, sir."

"And was Comrade Phosy there with you at the time?"

"He was."

"And did he torture Comrade Vilai and threaten to burn him alive?"

"No, sir. He threatened to torture him and burn him alive."

"What exactly is the difference?" asked the judge.

"If Comrade Phosy had actually tortured him, Vilai wouldn't be sitting there in the second row with that smug look on his face."

There were some giggles from the audience. Phosy raised his eyebrows.

"Hey, you," said the minister. "Show some respect."

"What sort of respect am I supposed to show to a man who massacres animals for a living?" said Wee.

Phosy allowed himself an ironic smile as he remembered one of Dr. Siri's famous lines, "There's no such thing as *more dead.*" Wee was driving in the final nail for both of them. Phosy looked to his left where the guard was distracted by the proceedings. It would have been easy enough to overpower him were it not for one of the armed military escorts, who'd taken up a position behind them all.

"I was all for throwing him into the burning house," said Wee. "Chief Inspector Phosy talked me out of it."

"All right," said the judge, "I think we've heard enough."

The vice minister pointed at Wee. "You're in enough trouble as it is," he said.

"Oh, I think I can get in much worse trouble," said Wee. "Especially considering what just happened in the back room."

"Guard, take this man to the cell," said Haeng.

"There you were, little judge, telling us what to say," said

Wee. "How you'd go easy on sentencing us if we blamed everything on Comrade Phosy. Shame on you."

"Guards!" shouted the vice minister.

Phosy's minders got to their feet, then, mysteriously, sat down again with their weapons still holstered. Phosy couldn't see why. The armed escorts who'd accompanied the new witnesses didn't move. The committee members seemed uneasy. There was a buzz of anticipation from the audience.

"Guards, are you deaf?" shouted Haeng. "I want all of these mutants out of this courtroom."

The guards were not deaf, neither were they guards. Only the two policemen on either side of Phosy could claim that role, but they had been silenced by the escort behind them, who was holding a gun to their heads. One other escort drew the pistol from his holster and trained it on the committee. Its members clucked like worried fowl. The other escorts also drew their weapons, took up positions at the corners of the room and told everyone to remain calm. After a lifetime of war, the Lao were not given to mass panic so the counter-mutiny proceeded in a rather orderly fashion. The five accused death squad members shook off their unlocked shackles, reached into their belts and produced handguns of their own. The new video operator did the same, as did the interpreter and the Vietnamese advisor, who, it turned out, wasn't.

"You'll all lose your heads for this," said the minister.

Phosy thought that was quite brave under the circumstances. Like most of the people in the room, he was seeing the action disconnected from any reality.

Wee nodded to the escort nearest the door who went outside.

The minister got to his feet. "I promise you this coup will not change the outcome of this hearing," he said, "nor the steadfast progress of socialism."

"Oh, Uncle," said Wee, "sit down and don't get your underwear twisted. This isn't a coup. This is a . . . What did we decide to call it?"

The female member of the squad removed her glasses. "An intervention," she said.

"That's right," said Wee. "This is an intervention. We have no intention of overthrowing the government. In fact we're all very fond of it. We're all committed socialists. I'm a paid up member of the Communist Party. I'd show you my card, but they took it off me when I got arrested this morning."

Judge Haeng had fallen silent since the overthrow. There was an escort with a Luger at his back. The judge was clearly disoriented. None of this was in his script, but he did manage one cliché question.

"What is it you hope to gain by all this?"

"Be patient, little spotty man," said Wee. "All will be revealed soon enough."

At that moment the escort returned and threw open the double doors. And in walked every friendly face Phosy had missed these past three days. Leading the parade were the president's personal secretary and his chief of staff. These were followed by officials of the Ministry of the Armed Forces including the quite healthy general who had been removed from the panel after the first day. Then came Phosy's Captain Sihot with a group of police officers Phosy trusted and respected. Then came Dr. Siri, Madame Daeng, and then Comrade Civilai who walked to the front of the room and commandeered the table of one shell-shocked judge.

Bringing up the rear was Nurse Dtui with her daughter Malee in her arms. They made their way directly to Phosy who scooted over the table and looped his shackles around his loved ones. They cried, the three of them, although Malee probably didn't understand what she was crying for. All she could say was:

"Daddy smell bad."

The guard closed the doors even though there were clearly a lot of people outside in the reception area. The newcomers took up places around the room, many sitting cross-legged on the floor. Members of the original audience attempted to give up their seats to the elder statesmen but were waved away. Siri and Daeng raised their thumbs to the chief inspector who sat impertinently on his table with his girls beside him.

He watched Civilai who had obviously been nominated as spokesman for the invading forces. He was both a lawyer by training and a diplomat. There were those who wondered how these two conflicting demons could occupy his soul, but somehow the old man had achieved a balance. Phosy knew his friend needed to recruit both for the task ahead of him. He had to use guile to defuse what promised to be a keg of gunpowder.

It was astounding what influence a brief bronchial cough could have over a room full of noisy people. Yet everyone seemed to hear Civilai's throat-clearing and shushed. Within seconds he was presiding over a deathly silence.

"My name is Civilai Songsawat," he said. "You may remember me from my years on the politburo. Six days ago my comrades and I were dragged from a bus, locked in a cell and told that we would be sent north for reeducation.

We heard no charges and were not allowed to make contact with the outside world. But, thanks to a remarkable, some might say magical, chain of events, one that I shall not describe here, we were released along with a number of others who had been rounded up and incarcerated. We heard of the arrest of our Chief Inspector Phosy. Thanks to friends on the inside—"

"Traitors," said the judge.

". . . we were able to learn of the charges against him and the location of this tribunal. We could probably have disrupted these proceedings at an earlier juncture, but we decided to follow the process of law and refute all of the accusations made here. I apologize to Phosy for leaving him rotting in jail for so long, but I'm sure he'll forgive us when he learns of the results."

Phosy was so chuffed he would have forgiven dismemberment.

Civilai continued. "We have all had dealings with Judge Haeng, so we know how devious he can be."

"That," shouted Haeng, "is slanderous. I demand an end to this circus."

"As the panel is still seated I suggest we let them decide who in this room is guilty," said Civilai.

"The charges have already been read," said Haeng. "All we expect from the committee now is a judgment."

"Then consider this a last-minute introduction of new evidence," said Civilai.

"Respected committee members," said the judge. "I had the resources of the Ministry of Justice at my disposal. I had a professional team of investigators. Our minister signed off on all the charges. The evidence we have presented is irrefutable."

"If that were true I would hesitate to refute it," said Civilai. "But given the background of your investigators and your own biased motives, I feel it within my right to question every piece of flawed evidence you've submitted."

"You couldn't possibly know what evidence I have," said the judge.

"I have copies of everything," said Civilai.

"That you couldn't possibly have obtained legitimately."

"They arrived on my desk from an anonymous source," said Civilai. "It would appear you don't have the staff loyalty you think you do." He turned to the Minister of Justice. "With your permission, comrade," he said, "I should like to demonstrate the inaccuracies in the judge's case."

The minister looked over his shoulder at the representatives from the office of the president and at the military officers.

"Did you think to ask my permission to overrun my courtroom and point weapons at our heads?" he asked angrily.

"No, comrade, and for that I'm truly sorry," said Civilai. "I hope, as the morning progresses, you'll see why it was necessary to intervene."

"I went through every item of Judge Haeng's files," said the minister. "I was, and still am convinced that your Comrade Phosy is guilty of the crimes he's accused of committing."

"Then, if I'm unable to change your conviction by lunchtime I shall yield to your superior judgment," said Civilai. "All I ask is to be able to present my evidence to the panel."

The minister shook his head and glared at Phosy. "You can have an hour," he said at last.

"That should be more than enough," said Civilai.

"Minister!" said Judge Haeng. "You can't side with these insurgents."

"Don't tell me what I can't do," said the minister. "I'm prepared to listen, but as far as I'm concerned your case still stands."

"It's not—" the judge began.

"Enough," said the minister.

"Thank you, comrade," said Civilai. "I shall begin with the most fundamental question, 'Did Comrade Phosy have any sort of relationship with the deceased, Miss Vatsana?'"

"Minister," said the judge, "I think we've proven beyond a doubt that Comrade Phosy was having an affair with her."

"Comrade Civilai?" said the minister.

"All that's been proven is that Miss Vatsana had regular visits from a man in a full face mask helmet riding a lilac Vespa."

"The only one of its type in Vientiane," said Haeng.

"That used to be true," said Civilai, "until one of our investigators found a second Vespa in a lockup some two kilometers from Judge Haeng's house. The scooter had been spray painted lilac. I have here a photograph of the machine and the garage." He handed the photo to the minister.

"What's that supposed to prove?" asked Haeng.

"Prove?" said Civilai. "Perhaps nothing. But it does beg the question, why would Chief Inspector Phosy drive some other vehicle to the lockup and ride the lilac scooter to his lover's house? And why would he wear a helmet that covered his face?"

"Why not?" said Haeng.

"This is Laos," said Civilai. "Nobody wears a full helmet

here. In fact, nobody wears any type of helmet anymore, especially when pottering along on an old scooter that barely hits thirty kilometers per hour."

"Then it was clearly to hide his face from the neighbors," said the judge.

"Odd then that he'd ride a scooter that immediately identifies him."

"Are you suggesting someone other than Phosy was Miss Vatsana's lover?" asked the vice minister.

"So far, all I'm suggesting is that there's no proof that Chief Inspector Phosy went to her house or that they had any kind of relationship at all. We showed his photograph to all of the neighbors and none of them could identify him."

"Then what about the intimate photographs from the party?" said Haeng. "Are you saying they lie?"

"They don't lie exactly," said Civilai. "They just withhold the truth from time to time."

He pulled some prints from his briefcase.

"These," he said, "are the photographs exhibited to the tribunal on the first day. They purportedly show Chief Inspector Phosy talking to Miss Vatsana at a social gathering. In fact you attended that function with Miss Vatsana and positioned her beside the chief inspector. These (he took out three larger prints) are the original, uncropped photographs from that day. The clerk you had dispose of them hadn't got around to it when we visited your office. As you can see, Comrade Phosy is sitting beside his wife and talking to someone behind the deceased. I doubt the chief inspector would remember very much about that day as he looks exceedingly drunk."

"As a cane toad in a bucket of fermented rice," shouted Phosy.

The audience laughed. The minister called for order.

"And it most certainly does not prove that Comrade Phosy knew the deceased," said Civilai. "Neither does it prove that Miss Vatsana knew the identity of the man sitting beside her at the party."

"Nonsense," said the judge.

"Which brings us to the supposed relationship between Chief Inspector Phosy and airport director Maysuk," said Civilai. "As far as we could ascertain, there was none. It would appear they met for the first time when Phosy went to the airport on August twenty-fifth. But we did find an interesting link between Maysuk and our own Judge Haeng. According to records at the Soviet Embassy, they studied in Moscow at the same time. They attended all the fundamental courses together. Other students who were there at the time say that Haeng and Maysuk socialized together. When they returned to Laos they continued that relationship. Maysuk married to please his family, then quickly took on a mistress named Soukjanda, who he put up in a residence. On occasions, they would have drink and drug parties at—"

"I object to this pack of lies," said Haeng.

". . . at an outbuilding at Wattay airport," Civilai continued. "We have signed statements from a number of the women Judge Haeng brought along to these parties. It upsets my stomach too much to describe what took place there, so I shall leave it to your imagination. These 'girlfriends' were all paid for their services and none were regular. Not until recently. Two months ago, Judge Haeng brought along a woman he referred to as his lover. It appears he had set her up in a house out at Nong Tewada. He brought her to the parties on three occasions riding pillion on the back of his lilac Vespa."

"I will not stand here and listen to this drivel," shouted Haeng. "Can't you see what they're doing? The only way they can get their man off the charges is to dirty my name. It's an old trick. I hope we're mature enough not to fall for it. Where are these supposed witnesses?"

Civilai smiled and called to the escort at the door.

"Would you call in Miss Soukjanda, please?"

The escort went out of the room and returned a few seconds later with Maysuk's minor wife, Soukjanda. The video operator gave up his seat for her. The judge's brow collapsed.

"We found Miss Soukjanda in Bolikhamxay," said Civilai. "It was nice to see that she hadn't been disposed of as we'd feared. She had, however, been threatened not to speak to anyone about the parties and had been given a wad of cash by one of the judge's assistants to stay away from Vientiane. She was disturbed but perhaps not heartbroken to hear of the death of Comrade Maysuk. She is prepared to give evidence about the parties. In spite of what you've heard at this hearing, Chief Inspector Phosy was not one of the participants. But there is one odd connection. According to Miss Soukjanda, when the judge started to bring his lover, Miss Vatsana, to the parties, he had her believe he was a policeman. Miss Soukjanda was paid a little extra to sustain this charade. As far as Miss Vatsana knew, her lover's name was not Haeng, but Phosy."

Gasps bubbled around the room.

"This sounds like a lot of he said, she said to me," said the vice minister.

"At last," shouted Haeng, "someone who understands the law. Of course, this is all one huge fairytale. Who's going to believe the word of a slut from the rice fields against a respected member of the government?"

Miss Soukjanda smiled at him.

"Me for one," said Civilai, which elicited a brief ripple of applause from the audience. He pointed at Phosy. "Miss Soukjanda," he called, "have you ever seen the man sitting there on his table before?"

Miss Soukjanda stood and smiled beautifully.

"Yes, Uncle," she said.

"Where?"

"He came to the office at the airport one afternoon to talk to my . . . my boss."

"Had you seen him before that?"

"Never, Uncle," she said.

"Liar!" shouted Haeng.

She poked her tongue out at him and sat down.

"And let's suppose Miss Soukjanda is telling the truth and she and Miss Vatsana were there at the airport shed on the night of the nineteenth," said Civilai. "And let us suppose one of the two men in attendance was Judge Haeng. It's conceivable that Miss Vatsana did overdose and that the two men believed she was dead. I hope, for her sake that she was. As I have no evidence to support the alternative, I will also assume that the overdose was an accident and not premeditated."

"Oh, so I am a suspect in a murder trial now, am I?" said Haeng.

Civilai ignored him. "But either way," he continued, "the judge had spent over two months establishing a false relationship between Miss Vatsana and Chief Inspector Phosy. The girl's death gave Haeng the launch pad for an all-out assault. When the body had been eaten to the bone, he and Maysuk disposed of the civets. It was possible they were afraid an autopsy of the bodies might reveal the drugs they gave Miss Vatsana that night. They buried the animals at the back of the airport grounds and burned the crate to destroy any trace evidence that might prove Miss Vatsana had been killed there."

"I want it on record that I am deeply offended by these allegations," shouted the judge. "I demand that this man be silenced."

"Noted," said the minister.

CHAPTER TWENTY-ONE
Pop Goes the Weasel

One of the air conditioners had stopped working so there was a lot of impromptu flip-flop fanning going on in courtroom one. But nobody would have dreamed of walking out. People outside had come to the nailed-shut windows and were struggling to hear the proceedings through the glass. There was no television station to cover the event but Laos had its own oral communication network that stretched back hundreds of years. Quite soon, even before it was concluded, those at the market would be gossiping about the trial of Chief Inspector Phosy.

"This brings me to events of August twenty-second and Judge Haeng's elaborate plot to frame the chief inspector," said Civilai. "Phosy was at the airport that morning to meet a VIP under instructions from the Ministry of Justice. We have the carbon copy of the memo sent from Judge Haeng's office. Phosy did request a car from the police pool but only because he had to deliver a stash of war weapons confiscated during police raids. When his meeting at Wattay did not materialize he took the weapons to the national armory where they were signed in by the clerk. That document is also submitted here as evidence."

"Then how did the hair and bone samples get into the trunk of that car?" asked the old general. It was his first question of the tribunal.

"We can only assume they were planted there," said Civilai. "As the war booty contained a leaky canister, the staff at the armory sprayed the trunk with a fire extinguisher and hosed it clean. It's unlikely any human evidence could have survived that."

"Pure garbage conjecture," said the judge. The remaining air conditioners were no longer keeping him cool. He took off his jacket.

"On that evening, Judge Haeng went to the Soviet residence and established through a witness that there was no body in the trunk of the Zil. We can only assume that this trickery was designed to mislead the chief inspector and cause him to make false assumptions. There was a period of fifty minutes between the judge leaving the party in the limousine and finally logging it in at the Zil lot. We wondered why he decided to leave the vehicle in the street rather than drive it inside. It was badly parked so one might guess that he was still drunk at that stage. But what if there was another reason? What if the person who dropped off the limousine was not Judge Haeng?"

The judge laughed shrilly. He seemed to have lost some of that early bristle. "Rot," he said, "rot, rot, rot."

But the audience was gripped.

"We checked the statements of the curfew guards," said Civilai. "They'd seen several Zils after twelve-thirty on the morning of the twenty-third: three Soviet Embassy vehicles and a private car that we confirmed was that of the Swedish ambassador who had attended the reception. Two of the patrols also noted having seen an old military truck with a faulty cam shaft belt. Our friends from the armed forces ministry checked their transportation data but could find no trace of our noisy truck. We had better luck with the air force. It's still a very small air force so it didn't take them long to recognize one of their three vehicles. This truck, it turns out, was an old Kaiser left over from the US occupation. The fliers used it for carrying engine parts over short distances. And it was usually parked behind the maintenance shed at Wattay airport. They confirmed that the airport director had a spare key."

"What's wrong with you people?" said Haeng, addressing the committee. "Why are you taking all this in so intently? Why aren't you questioning the lack of witness statements? The flawed evidence? The . . . the total bull of it all? Come to your senses, why don't you? You've already heard what happened that night. Whose side are you on?"

The minister scowled at the judge. "Haeng," he said, "why don't you take a seat and loosen your collar?"

"My . . . ?"

"Sit!" said the vice minister.

The judge reluctantly ambled to his table and flopped down onto his chair.

"So," said Civilai, "what was a truck from the airport doing in the middle of Vientiane on the morning a skeleton was discovered? Could it have been that Maysuk, the airport director, was delivering the skeleton to the arch while Haeng laid a false trail to distract the chief inspector? That in itself would have been enough to establish an alibi for the judge because around the time the skeleton was deposited, the judge's Zil was seen at a number of locations down by the river. But that leaves two questions unanswered. If Judge Haeng was driving the Zil, why didn't he show his face to the attendant at the limousine lot to leave no doubt as to his identity? And why was the Zil seen entering Wattay airport forty minutes before it was logged in at the lot? By then all the other Zils had been signed in. Only the judge's car remained on the road."

"Ah, I think if Comrade Civilai had bothered to check the records he'd see that the airport watchman lied about seeing a Zil that night," said the judge.

"And I think if we ask him to step back into the courtroom we'll hear how his statement was coerced under threats to his family," said Civilai.

"Who made those threats?" asked the minister.

"One of the ex-policemen hired by Judge Haeng," said Civilai. "He too has confessed."

"Again, my word against that of an ignoramus," said Haeng.

"But you have to admit these ignoramus words are piling up," said Civilai. "Once we assured the watchman you'd be in no position to follow through on those threats to his family he was only too pleased to affirm his original statement that he'd seen a Zil arrive at the airport shortly after three-fifteen. We timed the journey. With no traffic it was possible to get from Wattay to the Zil parking lot in fifteen minutes."

The judge got to his feet again. This time he ignored the committee and addressed the audience. "What we have here is very simple," he said. "It is the trial of a corrupt police officer. A man who has abused his position and lied and cheated and killed innocent people. But suddenly our official court hearing is invaded by his cronies and the whole proceedings are suddenly about me. Do you see how devious they are? This is our chance, brothers and sisters, to be rid of their type once and for all. If we don't, they will continue to make a mockery of the system. To make fun of those of us in authority. They are like naughty children with no respect for their parents. A good socialist . . . (Phosy knew the judge only resorted to maxims when he was on the back foot.) . . . is like a bird in flight. He approaches the tree and instinctively he knows what branch he belongs on. He does not attempt to land immediately on the top branches because that is—"

"We only have the room for another hour!" shouted Dr. Siri to a gale of laughter. There was nobody to call, "order."

"See?" said Haeng. "See? This is exactly my point. Immature people like this can only bring down the system."

His voice had become whiny.

"Again, noted," said the minister who was clearly losing patience with the judge.

"Where was I?" said Civilai. "Ah, yes. The strange decision to park the Zil outside the lot. One possible reason for this dichotomy arrived in our interview with Maysuk's minor wife, Miss Soukjanda. When describing her lover she often cited his fear of ghosts. He was a most superstitious man, which perhaps explains how the judge had been able to manipulate him so easily. The director believed in the oddest things. For example, he was certain that merely shaking hands with an insane person would transfer the insanity. In the same light, it was beyond question that handling a corpse would open a channel for the spirits to enter one's soul. So, with such beliefs, Maysuk was the most unlikely person to be entrusted with the delivery of a dead body. To him, the skeleton was the portal for everything evil. Miss Soukjanda believed that her lover would sooner die than come in contact with a corpse."

"I see," said Haeng. "Now we're calling in ghosts to give evidence?"

The demeanor of authority he'd worn so splendidly on the first three days was looking threadbare and ill-fitting. Phosy recognized a man in sharp decline.

"So," said Civilai, "we considered another scenario to explain the events of that morning. Haeng, having convinced Maysuk that he was party to a murder and, at the very least, would be jailed for covering it up, now found himself with an accomplice. The judge's plan was complex. He explained to Maysuk how it would lead the police in a merry dance and all eyes in a subsequent investigation would be on Haeng. Maysuk would take the military truck with the skeleton aboard into Vientiane. At a prescribed juncture, Maysuk would offload the body at the arch. Nobody would even remember the old truck.

"But, of course, Haeng's accomplice would have nothing to do with such a plan. He refused to handle the skeleton. The judge had to rethink his subterfuge. What he came up with was equally clever. Haeng loaded the skeleton into the truck and convinced Maysuk that merely driving with a dead body did not constitute handling. There would be no vengeance from the other side. Somewhere at the start of Haeng's drunken Zil ride, at some unlit spot, they arranged to meet. There, they exchanged vehicles. Maysuk would continue to drive the Zil erratically around the town to be seen by the curfew units as often as possible. Haeng would wait in the shadows in the army truck until the curfew team passed the arch and then sit the skeleton under the light. The decision to display the corpse at the arch was undoubtedly made because the act would be seen as a political statement. Chief Inspector Phosy was responsible for all crimes aimed at the government. Haeng knew Phosy would take a personal interest in such an event. It took the judge no time at all to drag the skeleton to the arch and be on his way. After the limousine was signed in, he would pick up Maysuk a few blocks away, drive to his apartment and send Maysuk back to the airport with the truck. It was an operation of spider web precision.

"What Haeng didn't know at the time was that Maysuk, sitting in the truck waiting in the dark, half a bottle of gin in his gut, a dead body behind him wrapped in a plastic sheet, started to panic. And with panic came some sort of paranoid clarity. He could see how Haeng's plan served mostly to provide the judge with an alibi whereas Maysuk would have no alibi at all. Nobody but Haeng had seen him that morning. If the body was discovered and the truth of Miss Vatsana's death came out, Maysuk would be the chief suspect. So he laid out a plan of his own.

Once he and Haeng had exchanged vehicles, Maysuk abandoned his instructions to drive aimlessly around for half an hour and headed directly to the airport in the limousine. He went to his office, turned on all the lights and made sure the guards knew he was there. There weren't that many private phones but his was a priority position so he called his major wife. Woke her up. We've spoken to her. She remembered some garbled nervous stream of consciousness. She assumed he was drunk which, after throwing down the rest of the gin, he was. She wasn't surprised. He drank a lot. He told her if anyone asked, that he'd phoned her at 3 A.M. and they'd talked for half an hour. She could tell the time. It was actually 3:22 A.M. and in the two years they'd been married they'd never spoken for longer than five minutes at a time. The call that morning lasted no more than two minutes. She wasn't fond of her husband and, yes, she knew he had a girlfriend. But that didn't worry her because she had one too. Theirs was a marriage of family lineage with no love lost or gained. She drew the line at lying at his say-so."

Phosy looked across the room to the prosecution table where Judge Haeng had put on headphones and was listening to a cassette recorder that wasn't plugged in. He seemed to be twitching.

"As far as we know," said Civilai, "beyond traditional graft, Maysuk had never been involved in criminal activities. He'd certainly never been party to a killing. He had no idea what length of time constituted an alibi, so with the soul of the dead woman leaning over his shoulder and a second bottle of gin open on his desk, he wrote a brief confession."

Civilai removed a sheet of paper from his file.

"'If things go badly,'" he wrote, "'this is my apology to the girl we killed.'" The note is signed, dated and stamped. He was a most thorough public official. He filed the letter under *C* for confession in his cabinet, left on all the lights and went back to the Zil. He drove into town and arrived at the lot at exactly 3:50 A.M. He shouted for the attendant to come and get the car and walked west two blocks, where he met the judge in the now-empty truck. Haeng had no idea that Maysuk had driven to the airport that morning. He still believed the director had been driving around as instructed. He didn't learn the truth until later. Once he realized Maysuk was a threat to their plan he had no choice but to be rid of him."

The minister tilted his head to one side.

"Judge Haeng," he shouted.

The judge pretended to be listening to something else. The minister shouted again and Haeng removed the headphones.

"Yes?" he said.

"What do you have to say to this new version of events?"

"It seems you'll believe whatever you choose to believe," said the judge. "Goodness knows I've put in enough hours at your flaky, badly run ministry to earn at least an iota of respect for my work. Some trust. Some support. I cannot begin to tell you how hurt I am that you should side with this rabble."

Malee, ever fatigued by the constant babble of adults was already asleep in her father's arms. He rocked her gently, thrilled beyond words to be reunited with the simplest of pleasures. Not only was he loved and respected again, he was exonerated. Against the far wall, Daeng held Siri's hand, not so much as a show of love, more to keep him anchored there. This would be a bad time to be floating off to some other dimension. Siri himself was staring with admiration at his old friend Civilai. He looked a lot like an overgrown cricket but Civilai, the lawyer and the diplomat, was a class act. Siri saluted him.

"And so, to pad out the files, you invite complaints," said Civilai, addressing the judge. "You collect comments from remote villages concerning Chief Inspector Phosy's anti-trafficking units. They're reports from local cadres and they aren't complaining about the results of the missions, merely inappropriate paperwork. The units have, in reality, been a tremendous success. But one man dies of a heart attack and another kills himself and suddenly this elite police force is labeled a death squad. You have gathered every negative opinion and collated them over there in that fat file. And they're all meaningless."

Civilai walked to Haeng's table and made a show of lifting the file of complaints. "Five years of obsessive stalking," he said. "This isn't an investigation into the behavior of a flawed police officer. It's an album of lies. But it's an impressive file. The collection of witness statements alone is most convincing even though most of them are forged. Our Judge Haeng has everything dated, as well as signed affidavits and discrete photographs. I'd say it's the most comprehensive paperwork I've seen in all my years of administration. If I were the judge's employer I would have found every page credible. It's Haeng's *pièce de résistance.* His life's work. His *Das Kapital.*"

Civilai paused for effect and looked into the faces of the audience.

"But it's all fiction," he said. "Every word. The witness statements were not written by the witnesses. The tape recordings were selectively chosen. The evidence was planted. But the report came from a credible source: the head of the Public Prosecution Department. It was convincing. Nobody would blame you, minister, for—"

"Don't even start with the condescension," said the minister. He slouched forward onto the table in front of him and looked at his thumbs. "I get it," he said. "I'm ashamed. I authorized warrants and arrests and detentions based on the pile of buffalo dung you're holding there. I didn't call for independent assessments. I was bamboozled by a man whose enthusiasm overwhelmed me and for that I am most sorry. I trusted this weasel and that makes me every bit as guilty as he is."

Judge Haeng, clearly overwhelmed by events, paced to the front wall and stood beneath the gallery of old soldiers. He looked up at them.

"Marvelous, old comrades," he said. "Marvelous. Two weeks ago you tell me what a credit I am to the development of a just legal system in the republic. Now you unilaterally decide I'm a weasel. Shouldn't we have a vet here to test the veracity of such a claim? Perhaps have the great Dr. Siri test my stomach contents for insects and small game? Must be a few snakes in there, right?"

In an odd way, Phosy felt sorry for the ranting judge. He'd been forced into a career that was too big for him. He'd begun to see respect as a perk of the job rather than a reward to be earned. If anyone failed to kowtow to him they became the enemy. He'd declared war on his doubters and his mockers and all those who'd shown contempt to him. This was his Waterloo and he'd been routed.

"What about the death of Maysuk?" asked the vice minister, hungry for more blood.

"The judge arranged a meeting between Comrade Phosy and Maysuk on the evening of the first," said Civilai. "Phosy went to the airport but could not find the director. Nor could he find any office workers to ask about the director's whereabouts because they were tending to their vegetable allotments. Phosy assumed the director had fled and he returned to police headquarters. Meanwhile, Judge Haeng, who had lied about Maysuk's intentions to fly to Hanoi, had instead arranged to meet him for coffee in town. They sat at the back of a small café near the black stupa. The owner was able to identify the guests from photographs. He came forward when he heard about our enquiry. Maysuk and Haeng had a coffee each and remained in the coffee shop until around four fifty-five.

"Judge Haeng then drove Maysuk back to the airport on his motorcycle. The Hanoi flight had left and the well-wishers and relatives had gone home. There were only one or two ground crew members and security staff still there. Some noticed a motorcycle arrive at around five-fifteen. Phosy had already left. The driver and passenger were wearing full face helmets. I assume the judge insisted on Maysuk doing so. The motorcycle drove directly to the administrative offices. Twenty minutes later, the motorcyclist drove out of the airport alone. Forty minutes passed. The night watchmen had locked up the buildings. A car arrived. The driver announced that he was from the Ministry of Justice and that Judge Haeng was in the back seat. The judge lowered his window and told the guard they had an appointment to see Director Maysuk and that he wanted the guard to come with them. He didn't give a reason. They parked and walked to Maysuk's office where Judge Haeng went immediately to the cupboard and discovered the director's dead body. Unless the judge confesses there is no way of knowing what happened when he went with Maysuk to his office earlier."

"Nor will there ever be!" shouted Haeng.

"All we can say is that at five-ten P.M. Director Maysuk was alive," said Civilai. "At six P.M. he was dead. In his handwritten confession, Maysuk confirmed that he was afraid of what Judge Haeng might do to him. He went on to describe the events of both the night of the nineteenth, when Miss Vatsana overdosed, and the judge's plan to incriminate Chief Inspector Phosy. If you look at the judge's version of that confession you'll see that the signature was forged."

Judge Haeng had begun to sing the national anthem as he rocked back and forth on his chair.

"Could you stop that?" said the minister. But Haeng ignored him.

"I'm a free man," said Haeng. "This is all unsupported conjecture. I'll be out of here in a few hours." And he continued to hum the anthem because he'd forgotten the words.

"In a way, the judge is correct," said Civilai. "A lot of the evidence is circumstantial. As I say, in order to confirm many of these points we would need a confession from Judge Haeng himself."

"Why would an innocent man make a confession?" sang the judge.

"Well, in fact, you did," said Civilai.

He went to the table and from a manila envelope he produced a small cassette player.

"It was you," said Haeng. "Arrest this man. He stole that."

"It was on my front porch one morning when I woke up," said Civilai. "The fairies must have brought it. It contains the tape that the judge played a selective part of during Chief Inspector Phosy's hearing. It was recorded on the day he confessed to his crimes at police headquarters. He had it running inside his hollowed-out copy of the manifesto. Now, if the judge had been a little more technically savvy he would probably have edited the tape to contain only the segment of the conversation he wished the committee to hear. But it appears he was so confident nobody would take the time to play the entire cassette, he failed to delete everything else that was on it. With the committee's permission I should like to play the tape of Judge Haeng's confession in its entirety."

"Oh, hell," said the judge.

CHAPTER TWENTY-TWO
Man Steak

Had the coup at the Ministry of Justice not been successful, the wedding would never have taken place. In fact, the bride and groom in their respective work camps may never have seen one another again. As part of his grand sweep up of undesirables, Judge Haeng had separated Mr. Geung and Tukta and sent them north. The morons, as he liked to call them, had been a pain in his backside ever since Siri had insisted on giving Geung equal pay for his work in the morgue.

"There's a place for these people," Haeng had said, "and it's not in the public eye." He had tried to remove the couple without success on a number of occasions. Siri had reminded him that the only public eyes in the morgue could no longer see and that equality was the fundamental tenet of the Communist movement. But as part of his purge, one of Judge Haeng's first actions was to send the couple to cooperatives.

Now they were back and amid the pandemonium that followed the reshuffle of personnel at the Ministry of Justice, they had been granted permission to wed. It helped that Tukta was pregnant. The Party had initiated a fast-track marriage program to decrease the number of babies born out of wedlock. Mr. Geung's entourage had overwhelmed the desk clerk at the Civil Partnerships Department and left her office with an official stamp.

A registrar had come to Madame Daeng's noodle shop mid-morning on Friday for the official ceremony. This amounted to the couple signing a register and listening to a litany of highly recommended traits for a good socialist couple to adhere to. The elderly man performed his task with no enthusiasm. He shook the hands of the newlyweds and wished them luck. If he noticed they had Down syndrome he certainly didn't show it. In fact, he exhibited no emotions at all.

But, as everyone knew, signing a name in a ledger had nothing to do with being married. Without a blessing from the monks and a *basee* ceremony with its cone of flowers and its boiled eggs and strings to join the wrists of the participants, and without Madam Daeng's special rice whisky shared with loved and respected guests, no couple could seriously consider themselves wed. The actual nuptials were to take place at Dr. Siri's official Party residence in the evening.

As many wrongs had been righted that week, the mood was vibrant. The Minister and Vice Minister of Justice had stepped down. Judge Haeng was headed for a firing squad even without having the charges against him trumped up. The famous letter from the judge to the US consulate had resurfaced. The document had been too valuable to give up. The version Chief Inspector Phosy had handed to Judge Haeng was a retyped copy with the signature carefully inked by Madam Daeng. That letter alone would have been enough to condemn the man to a chest full of holes. Adding the falsification of evidence, unlawful imprisonment, and the murder of two citizens would not have made the holes any deeper or the judge any deader. All Phosy had to do was make sure the guns were loaded.

There remained only one more delicate matter to take care of before the wedding. When Sergeant Wee arrived at Phosy's office, the chief was already in his dress uniform. Captain Sihot was seated at the second desk. They both shook Wee's hand before he sat down.

"Nicely done," said Phosy.

He hadn't seen Wee and his unit since they raided the tribunal. Everyone had been too busy going over old evidence and documenting the charges against the judge. Ex-Chief Inspector Oudomxai and his gang of crooked police were all back behind bars where they belonged.

"Thank you, sir," said Wee. "Me and the team had a lot of fun that day. You wouldn't believe how hard it was to get ourselves arrested."

"If it weren't for you and your team I'd probably still be back there behind bars," said Phosy.

"You know that's not true, sir. You had an army of fans out there. We were just the front line. Once the president's office and the military had seen the evidence it was just a matter of time before they shut down the hearing."

"Either way I'm grateful for the . . . what did you call it?"

"The intervention."

"That's it," said Phosy, "the intervention."

"Any luck with the zoo out at Dong Paina?" Sihot asked.

"We detained the zoo director, Sisouk, on some fictitious charge," said Wee. "Nothing that'll stick. He was a government appointee. It seems everyone knew the zoo was a front. Everything found its way to the hub in Hong

Tong eventually. All they did was take over the French-man's franchise. All the bullshit about showing respect to the animals, that was just for the benefit of the UN and any foreign dignitaries wanting to see what Laos is doing to stop the trade."

"Which brings me to Comrade Vilai and his Hong Tong operation," said Phosy.

"He was the sleaziest of the lot," said Wee. "What we did there was beautiful. I'm so proud we were a part of that. To think he had the gall to sit there and give evidence against you. He had nothing to be innocent about. He was a millionaire ten times over—money earned from suffering."

"He was?"

"What?"

"You said he was a millionaire—past tense."

"Yeah, well I'm hoping he lost all his money after we busted him."

"It wouldn't be because he's dead, would it?"

"He's dead?" said Wee.

"The local cadre in Hong Tong found what was left of him yesterday morning in one of the cages. Someone had thrown him in there with a half-starved clouded leopard," Phosy told him.

"Really?" said Wee. "I hope it was slow and excruciating."

"You don't know anything about it?"

"How could I?"

"Right," said Sihot, "you know, your team said they haven't seen you for a couple of days. You told them you were doing some secret work for the chief inspector here. What secret work would that be, Sergeant Wee?"

"All right, you got me there," said Wee, tapping the cigarette pack in his top pocket. "You know, I'd been working straight through since the day you were nabbed by the judge's men. I decided I deserved a bit of R and R. Have a little bit of fun with a certain young lady friend."

"That sounds fair enough," said Phosy. "If you'd put in for a few days of leave I'm pretty sure I'd have approved the request."

"Yeah, sorry about that, brother," said Wee. "Old habits die hard, you know?"

"Where did you take your young lady?"

"Not far. Just out to the ferry at Tha Ngon. They've got chalets up there. I'm sure you don't want a blow by blow account of what we got up to."

"Not at all," said Sihot.

He nodded when a balding man in peasant's clothes entered the room without knocking. The man stood inside the door and returned the nod.

"Wee, this is Captain Lai," said Phosy. "Do you recognize him?"

Wee turned in his seat and studied the old man. "No," he said.

"That's not very observant of you," said Sihot. "I thought you were more aware than that. He was on the same bus as you on Thursday. But the bus wasn't on its way to Tha Ngon. In fact, it was headed in the opposite direction, east along the river road."

"Then he obviously wasn't on the same bus as me, was he?" said Wee, removing the pack of cigarettes from his pocket.

"Have you looked at yourself lately?" said Sihot. "If you ask me, you aren't really the mistakable type."

"Well, who asked you, you fat fart?" said Wee.

Captain Sihot smiled and patted his paunch. "The

sergeant's been watching you since you announced to the team you'd be working with me," said Phosy.

"You had me followed?" said Wee. He tapped a cigarette from the pack, put it between his lips and felt around for a lighter.

"Yes," said Phosy.

"Because some rat on my team didn't like the idea of me taking time off?"

"Because we were concerned," said Phosy.

"What about?"

"About Judge Haeng's assertion that your team was a death squad," said Sihot.

"Now you're trying to tell me the judge isn't a lying little turd?" said Wee.

Two more officers entered the room.

"No, he's certainly a lying little turd," said Phosy, "but we were wondering whether he'd got this one right. You see? The three missions you worked on before you joined me on the raid of Vilai's compound all had something in common. They all ended with the chief perpetrators being involved in fatal . . . incidents."

"What's that got to do with me?" said Wee. His search for a cigarette lighter in his pockets had come up empty and he was looking around the room either for a light or an escape route.

Phosy was thumbing through the notes in front of him.

"The child trafficking gang in Ban Mapao," he said. "The report stated that the village headman wrestled your weapon from you and shot himself. The nearest member of your team was thirty meters away. He couldn't see clearly so he took your word for it."

"And my word's suddenly worth shit?" said Wee.

"In the circumstances, I would probably have been keen to believe you too," said Phosy. "The headman was scum. Nobody was that concerned that he might want to shoot himself rather than rot in jail. But then came your next mission: another trafficking gang in Ban Siphon. Your unit had laid out a plan similar to the one in Ban Mapao. But, as it turned out, the brothers that led the gang drowned the night before your team got there. Their boat capsized. Two girls on the boat on their way to a whorehouse in Thailand were rescued by some unknown stranger but the brothers didn't make it. The peculiar thing was the girls couldn't swim but the brothers were strong swimmers. What are the odds against the girls surviving and the brothers not?"

"The Lord Buddha moves in mysterious ways," said Wee. "Any of you fellows got a light?"

They ignored the request. Sihot took over the report. "That brings us to what happened in Khammouan, your own hometown," he said.

"Oh, right," said Wee, "now you're suggesting I gave a man a heart attack?"

"In fact, yes," said Phosy. "We have two excellent coroners available here in Vientiane. They just got back from the south. It seems your uncle was buried rather than cremated. Lucky for us. Dr. Siri had the fellow dug up. I imagine you know what they found in his stomach lining."

Siri hadn't been to the south and after such a long time underground, the body wasn't likely to give up too many secrets. But Phosy's little off-white lies often saved him a great deal of trouble. Wee sighed and turned up one corner of his mouth.

"Cobra venom, I guess," said Wee.

He gave up both the pretense and the smoke and forced the cigarette back into the pack. "I was going to give up smoking anyway," he said.

"When did you decide your uncle wouldn't be making the trip to Vientiane?" Sihot asked.

"Probably the moment we talked about it here," said Wee. "My uncle was rolling in money. Whatever shit charge we brought him in on he'd get out of it. Rich guys always do. I knew he'd be back in business within the week."

"And you got away with it so why not kill off all of them?" said Phosy.

"Come on," said Wee. "Don't pretend this isn't what you wanted. There's only one way to wipe the arrogance off their faces. I'm sure every man and woman in my unit wanted it done. You and your boys wanted it done. What was the alternative? Smack a heavy fine on 'em and tell them to be good? Give me a break."

"And it was only natural you'd take the next step: torture," said Sihot.

"I don't see putting a man in a cage as torture," said Wee. "I gave him a fifty-fifty chance. The leopard might have taken pity on him. If the beast had been well fed and healthy it might have even decided to pass up on man steak and wait for dinner. Couple of chicken carcasses. Much tastier than a greasy old bag of bones like Vilai. Those were better odds than he'd given the leopard until then. Right?"

"And you sat there and watched him get eaten alive?" said Phosy.

"Oh, don't pretend you weren't as delighted as me when we stormed their nasty little meat market and burned the place down. What's the difference between what you threatened and what I did? If it was such a terrible thing why didn't your skinny old Captain what's-his-face here stop me, eh?" said Wee. "If he followed me all the way to Hong Tong he must have known what I was up to. He could have put a bullet in me and ended it all."

Wee turned to the old man by the door.

"Isn't that right, grandpa?" said Wee. "You didn't do anything because you knew it was right. It's no less than he deserved. His men had already fixed the wall and rounded up what animals they could find. It was business as usual. But once they saw what was left of their boss in the cage, once they'd witnessed what Lao justice had lined up for them all, there wasn't a man in that compound who'd dare stick around in that profession. That's what it should be about, Phosy. They were petrified. They'd do right because they were too afraid to do wrong. You hurt another living being, we hurt you."

He looked around at the silent police officers and shrugged.

"I won't be getting a medal then?" he said.

CHAPTER TWENTY-THREE
Noodle Power

The wedding was a beautiful affair. Siri's official residence looked like a Chinese brothel. They'd left the decorating to Crazy Rajhid and the children, and they'd spent the day cutting and pasting paper chains. They'd rescued the paper from the vacated Chinese bazaar. Its owners had left the place in a hurry. Most of the Chinese businesses were closed in the wake of China's threats of invasion and retribution. Laos had sided with Vietnam in the Asian cold war and Vientiane was looking ever more like a commercial wasteland. Along with the crimson crepe paper, Rajhid had borrowed a hundred red foldable tasseled lanterns and fifty embroidered candle holders. The chances of a cataclysmic house fire were high.

A number of uninvited cadres had turned up at the party. It was as if the news of Chief Inspector Phosy's victory over the justice ministry had sounded out a warning to all the other ministries. Corruption was no longer a right. The Deputy Minister of Trade was one of the gate-crashers, but he'd brought along a crate of Glenfiddich so nobody turned him away. Siri cornered him in the kitchen of the residence and asked him directly about the import and export of wildlife. He'd expected the man to be defensive and apologetic, but the deputy seemed proud of their record.

"It was disorganized and fragmented before we got to work on it," slurred the man. He'd clearly been sampling the scotch before turning up at the party.

"So, you turned it into a fruitful trade?" Siri asked.

"Too right we did, comrade."

"And what would it take to shut it down?"

"Shut it down? Are you mad? It's our fourth biggest income earner. Why would we want to shut it down?"

Siri frowned and let out an ironic laugh. "Oh, I don't know," he said, "because it's cruel and inhumane?"

"Nothing cruel about it, comrade," said the deputy. "Your type would have us give names to pigs and chickens and let them live a long and happy life while we all starved to death."

Siri immediately conjured up the image of the chickens in the yard behind the noodle shop to whom Mr. Geung had bequeathed names and decorated with neck ribbons.

"My type?" he said. "What is my type?"

"The bleeding hearts," said the deputy. "The do-gooders who'd have us all living on yams and coconut meat."

"Does it not worry you what the civilized world thinks of us?"

"The civilized world?" said the deputy. "You mean places like Australia? They exported six million sheep to Europe for slaughter last year. What does the civilized world think of them? I'll tell you. The civilized world wished it had half their business acumen. What's a few tigers compared to that?"

The deputy trade minister was thrown out of the party

without his crate of booze, but he'd left a question in Siri's mind. Why was a tiger worth more than a sheep? Perhaps it was because nobody humiliated the sheep before killing it. Perhaps it was because the death was sudden and clinical, not stretched over months. Perhaps it was because the sheep was sacrificed as part of the chain of survival not for vanity, tradition, some mythical unfounded belief, or for sport. Perhaps it was because the sheep had not known freedom or been given time to build up a bond with its environment and qualify for the right to live out its life as a part of a natural habitat.

Or perhaps there was just an arbitrary man-decided cut-off line, and the creatures beneath it were not afforded any respect or admiration. He had no definitive answer to the question, but in his gut he knew he was right.

He walked out to the backyard where the pumpkin was rotating on a spit. Mr. Geung and Tukta had gone to the market early that morning to select a fine fat pig for the wedding roast. They'd chosen a live porker that weighed in at 120 kilograms and were about to pay for it when the pig called Mr. Geung over and whispered so low that the others couldn't hear her:

"Don't   eat   me."

So, Geung and Tukta had paid for the pig, loaded her in a *samlor* and driven her to the edge of the forest. There, they'd said goodbye to her, wished her a long and happy life, and let her go. They'd returned to the house with a pumpkin because, fortunately, the pumpkin hadn't said anything in its own defense. And, for whatever reason, that was the day that Dr. Siri Paiboun stopped eating meat.

The bride and groom, as far as anyone knew, the first ever Down syndrome couple joined in matrimony in the

People's Democratic Republic, were dressed in traditional Lao costumes. They looked adorable. As was the custom, Tukta wore too much makeup and was almost unrecognizable. Despite half a jar of Brylcream, Mr. Geung's hair refused to sit obediently on his head. He looked so handsome in his white jacket and baggy *jongabayn* trousers nobody commented on his hair.

The house, the front- and backyards and half the street were crowded with well-wishers. They were there not only to celebrate the wedding but also to applaud the success of the people-power push that had begun on the first morning after Siri and Daeng's arrest. The customers had arrived at the noodle shop as usual only to find it shuttered. There were no sounds of movement from within. On the door was a poster-sized note, beautifully written, which read:

> *Madam Daeng, Dr. Siri, Chief Inspector Phosy, Nurse Dtui, Comrade Civilai, Mr. Geung and Tukta have all disappeared. Something terrible has happened to them. I love them. So do you. We know they are good people. The customers of this restaurant come from many places: from ministries and offices and hospitals and from the markets and stores. Individually, we have no power. But together there is nothing we cannot discover or achieve. Let us unite to find our friends.*

Thus, the noodle revolt had begun. It was unclear whether there would have been such a tide of indignation had the customers been aware of who wrote that poster.

But it had been so eloquently composed it was as if the giant naga of the Mekhong itself had called the noodle customers to arms. At lunchtime, a huge crowd gathered, suggestions were voiced and assignments were handed out. By evening the crowd had doubled and already they knew where Siri, Daeng and Civilai were being held. Someone's nephew had been charged with trucking them to work camps the following day. It did not take long to work out what was going on at the Ministry of Justice. The crowd did not exactly march upon the ministry training school. That would have been treasonous. Rather, in a very Lao way, they merely dropped by, one by one, to say hello. See how things were going. Hundreds of them filled the tiny complex. Someone might have inadvertently sheered through a telephone line with their scythe. This left the young lads entrusted with the prisoners' care no way of reporting this casual intrusion. There was no violence.

The most senior of the noodle connoisseurs explained that there had been a mistake and that a committee of some two hundred people had been set up to right it. Thus, Siri, Daeng and Civilai were freed. But, until they could locate Phosy and Nurse Dtui, there could be no word of this rescue. Not wanting to get into or cause any trouble, the young jailers—two of whom were related to members of the crowd—volunteered to take the place of the prisoners. Should things go badly, they would claim to have been overwhelmed by armed aggressors and locked up. Madam Daeng told them she'd have noodles sent over for supper and perhaps a bottle or two of something refreshing.

By morning, everyone was aware of Judge Haeng's intentions. Ministry clerks were spilling their guts to anyone who'd listen. By the second day, word of mouth had spread and witnesses stepped forward without coaxing. Someone had seen a man drive a lilac Vespa from a lockup. Ex-girlfriends of Haeng told of the parties at the airport. Someone had seen Haeng and Maysuk leaving a coffee shop. The court stenographer was only too pleased to hand over transcripts from the tribunal. The momentum of the noodle revolt was already rolling too fast to be stopped. They would probably have taken over the ministry sooner were it not for the rational arguments of the threesome they'd released. Siri told the crowd that there was no hurry. Phosy's trial was scheduled to go to a fourth day. The noodlers had the time and the resources to refute the judge's charges by gathering evidence to the contrary.

They had been too late to prevent the banishment of Mr. Geung and his fiancée. That rescue had to wait. But by the time the couple arrived back in Vientiane, they heard the stories over and over. They heard of the peaceful noodle revolution. They learned how lovers of good food might get together and achieve in a few days what the government had been unable to manage in five years—unity. And as noodle makers, Mr. Geung and Tukta were key members of the movement. They were the Marx and Engels of pasta. And everyone knew their wedding would go ahead because everyone wished it to happen. And that was why the street was crowded outside Siri's official residence. Success had been a rare commodity in Laos and once found, it was addictive.

Mr. Geung and Tukta were walking from guest to guest holding a silver tray with a crystal glass on it and a bottle that seemed magically to be always full. They would insist that each partygoer throw back a glass of spirit for luck, and the guests were happy to do so. Chief Inspector Phosy, still in his dress uniform minus shoes, was looking down at the scene from the neighbor's roof. To his left sat Siri and Daeng nursing a fat pot with two cane straws sticking out of the top. It was perched precariously on the tiles between them, and they took it in turns to suck up the sweetest of rice whiskies. To Phosy's right sat his wife, more lovely than ever in her embroidered blouse and handwoven skirt. Malee, desperate for sleep but too entranced by the show below, sat watery-eyed in her mother's lap. She watched Civilai below dancing with his wife to a waltz only they seemed to hear. The band was playing Lao country.

"Are you sure Comrade Vong doesn't mind us occupying her roof?" Dtui asked.

"I'm absolutely certain she'd mind," said Siri, "if she knew. She's the type of person who minds. It's in her blood. She minded greatly when I mentioned we'd be having this little party at my house. She minded even more when I suggested it might be to celebrate an illicit wedding. But when I told her who was getting married, she minded right down to police headquarters and onto a bus to her cousin's place. We won't see her again for a day or two."

"I have her official complaint right here in my breast pocket," said Phosy. He ripped it into little pieces and let it snow down on the revelers.

"I'd like her to play the wicked necromancer in our movie," said Siri.

"What news of that?" Dtui asked.

"We have located a cinematographer," said Siri. "He's the cousin of the Fuji Photo shop owner. He's worked as

a grip on films in Thailand. He'll be back next month to
teach us how to turn on the camera."

"We now have three scripts to work from," said Daeng,
"Siri's original, the women's union rewrite and the Ministry of Culture disaster."

"Of course, we'll use mine," said Siri. "We have a number of competent actors and actresses and the promise
of funding. I have also been looking through my French
tourist brochures to select which hotel I'll be staying in
when we get to Cannes."

"Assuming we live that long," Daeng added.

"And Phosy, what do you plan to do with your dark assas-
sin, Sergeant Wee?" Siri asked. "Toss him in the dungeons
and beat him senseless?"

"No," said Phosy, "we'll send him to Huay Xai to one of
our secure camps."

"That doesn't sound much like a fitting punishment for
a man who turns killer on you," said Madam Daeng before
taking a deep draft of spirit.

"I know," said Phosy. "I really had no idea what to do. I
left it up to his unit. They agreed he was undisciplined and
needed reeducation. I am in the position where I have to
uphold the law. I couldn't let him get away with what he
did. But nobody wanted to see him executed for doing
something they'd all considered doing themselves."

"Phosy and I have already had words on this subject,"
said Dtui.

"I know," said Phosy. "But in a way, I was responsible."

"You told him to kill bad guys?" asked Daeng.

"No, but I left their fates flapping about in the wind. I
said we'd think of some kind of punishment. That wasn't
good enough for a group of officers who were risking

their lives to arrest them. They needed to know the felons wouldn't be let off with a fine. That doesn't condone what Wee did, but it makes me less inclined to have him shot."

"What do you think will become of him?" Dtui asked.

"I don't know," said Phosy. "He's a resourceful fellow. He'll probably escape and vanish."

"You're not afraid he'll come gunning for you?" said Daeng.

"No."

Down below, Mr. Geung and Tukta were posing for photographs and, although the four musicians had stopped playing, Comrade Civilai was still slow dancing with his wife in the garden. Guests came and went but the crowd didn't seem to thin out at all. They'd put up metal frames to be covered in canopies in case of rain but the night sky was cloudless and the moon bathed the crowd in a mystical glow.

"I don't see our poster-writing hero," said Dtui.

"Rajhid stayed long enough to put up the decorations and blow up a few balloons and he was off," said Daeng.

"The attention would have freaked him out," said Siri. "And he had more important things to do."

"Impersonating frogs and running naked along the riverbank," said Daeng.

"No rest for the mental," said Siri.

The time had come for Mr. Geung to make his speech. They'd connected a microphone to a portable speaker in the front yard. Given Geung's stutter, Civilai had suggested they break with tradition and have Tukta give the wedding speech. But Nurse Dtui would hear of no such thing. For a week, she'd been coaching her friend, working on his breathing and his confidence. She had him practice in front of the hospital lab goats, then progress to small groups of nurses. He'd surprised them by achieving a level of competence they hadn't expected. But, just to make sure, she'd slipped a marijuana cigarette into his pocket and recommended he have a few puffs before showtime. He'd obviously taken her up on that suggestion because he swaggered up to the stage platform and raised two thumbs to the onlookers. When he grabbed the mike, there was a swathe of speaker feedback that instantly silenced the crowd. Dtui crossed her fingers.

"Brothers and sisters," Geung began without so much as a b-b-b or a sis-sis, "I am Geung Wattajak and I am an animal."

There were a few embarrassed chuckles. Geung went to the corner of the platform, took his bride by the hand and led her to the microphone.

"This is my wife, Tukta," he said. "She is an animal too."

Tukta had heard the speech many times over. She wasn't offended. She bowed her head and gave a deep, respectful *nop* to the audience. Geung looked up at the neighboring roof and pointed.

"There is my friend, Nurse Dtui," he said. "She is an animal. And all of you are animals."

There was a belt of silence before one drunk shouted out, "I'm not."

"Yes, you are," shouted his wife to gales of raucous laughter.

Ugly the dog, who'd been waiting in the wings for his cue, walked onto the stage and sat.

"This is Ugly," said Geung. "He's a different animal. He's an animal called a dog. People call him a dumb animal because he can't speak and because he licks his arse."

More laughter.

"But he can rec . . . recognize hundreds of different scents and he can run fast. So in many ways, he's better than us. People call me and Tukta dumb animals too. We speak and we don't lick our arses, but most people think they're better than us. They can be unkind. Our bodies are clumsy and we won't live very long and our brains work more slowly than yours. We can't be doctors and we can't be prime ministers, but we work hard and we're kind and funny and we say what we believe. So, my wish on this day, this happiest day of my life, is that we stop thinking we're better than other animals and start to believe that we all con . . . contribute something different and wonderful to our planet. The tiger teaches us d-d-dignity and how to control our power. The pig gives us compost that grows our vegetables. The lizard eats mosquitoes that give us dengue fever. The fish cleans our rivers and gives up its life to feed our children. If I can have one one one . . . wish this day, it is that we all stop comparing the size of our brains and learn to see the size of each other's hearts."

Even the evening cicadas had fallen silent.

AFTERWORD

The Siri series is set in the not-too-distant past. One would like to think that the world has progressed since then and is addressing its mistakes. One would most certainly hope that cruelty had been eliminated. But all of the circumstances I described in this book are true and—because I didn't want to thoroughly depress you—vastly understated. You might hope that countries like Laos or Vietnam or China would have learned compassion but far from it. The trade in animals and their parts is more organized, more profitable more widespread than it was forty years ago. As there aren't enough creatures left in the wild to satisfy the idiots, tigers and bears and pangolins and all their relatives are being farmed in inhumane conditions. Wild beasts are still being shipped around the world to zoos and private collectors, but now they have legal documents. Those documents don't stop the savagery and wickedness. It's not all right to take your kids to a zoo because all you see there are the survivors. And even they have a limited shelf life.

It's not literature, but try to get ahold of a copy of *The Animal Connection* by Jean-Yves Domalain. To see what's happening in Laos and the region more recently take a look at *Wildlife Trade in Laos: The End of the Game* by Hanneke Nooren and Gordon Claridge. For us tiger fans there's *Tigers Are Forever* by Steve Winter and Sharron Guynup. There are hundreds of articles. All we really need is Google and the will to do something about it.

Continue reading for a preview from the next
Dr. Siri Paiboun Mystery

The Second Biggest Nothing

CHAPTER ONE
A City of Two Tails

Dr. Siri was standing in front of Daeng's noodle shop when she pulled up on the bicycle. It was a clammy day, but his wife rarely raised a sweat even under a midday sun. She leaned the bike against the last sandalwood tree on that stretch of the road and patted Ugly the dog. Siri shrugged.

"So?" he said.

"So what?"

"What did she say?"

Daeng pecked him on the cheek and walked past him into the dark shop house. He trotted behind.

"She said I have the body and constitution of a sixty-nine-year-old."

"You are sixty-nine."

"Then I have nothing to be disappointed or smug about, do I? I'm fit and healthy. I'm a nice, average Lao lady with supposed arthritis. She did, however, mention that most people my age in this country are dead. I think that's a positive, don't you?"

"But what about . . . ? You know?"

"She didn't say anything," said Daeng.

"She what?"

"Didn't mention it at all. She obviously didn't notice it."

"What kind of a doctor doesn't notice that one of her patients has a tail?"

"I've told you, Siri. You and I are the only people who see it."

"What about the shamans in Udon?"

"They didn't see it, Siri. They visualized it. Not the same thing."

"It's a physical thing, Daeng. You know it is. I can feel it."

"I know. And I like it when you do."

"But now Dr. Porn would have us believe that it doesn't exist, which means I must be senile," said Siri.

"It means we're both senile."

"Then, by the same account, if you don't have a tail, then obviously my disappearances are a figment of my imagination."

"Not at all," said his wife dusting the stools to prepare for the evening noodle rush. "All it tells us is that nobody else notices you're gone."

"I've disappeared in public before," said Siri with more than a touch of indignation. "Haven't I disappeared in the market? At a musical recital? In a crowded—"

"Look, my love," she said, taking his hand, "there is no doubt that you disappear. There is no doubt you cross over to the other side and learn things there and return and tell me of your adventures. There is no doubt you are possessed by a thousand-year-old Hmong shaman and communicate through an ornery transvestite spirit medium. There is no doubt that you see the souls of the dead just as there is no doubt that I have a tail that I received from a witch in return for a cure for my arthritis. But, for whatever reason, nobody else bears witness to our little peculiarities. And perhaps it's just as well. The politburo would probably have us burned at the stake for occult practices if anyone reported us. Even Buddhism makes them queasy. Imagine what they'd do if Dr. Porn wrote in her official report, '. . . and, by the way, Madam Daeng appears to have grown a tail since her last checkup.'"

"You're right," said Siri.

"I'm always right," said Daeng. She squeezed his hand and smiled and returned to the chore of readying her restaurant. She was startled by the sound of hammering from the back room.

"What's that?" she asked.

"Nyot, the doorman," said Siri.

"He's still here?" said Daeng. "How long does it take to put in a door?"

Mr. Nyot, the carpenter, was busy hanging. Following the previous monsoons, the door had changed shape and would no longer close. Daeng was not afraid of intruders. Ever since it was installed when the shop house was rebuilt, that door had never been locked. Nobody could remember where the key was. There were no security issues in Vientiane. The Party wouldn't allow such a thing. All the burglars were safely behind bars on the detention islands. The ill-fitting door banged in the wind and Mr. Nyot had promised them a nice new door at a special price. But it was also a special door. Daeng went to inspect the work.

"What's that?" she asked, pointing at the missing rectangle of wood at the base.

"It's a dog entrance," said Nyot.

"It's a hole," said Daeng.

"Right now it may look like a hole," said Nyot, "but over there I have a flap with hinges that I will attach shortly."

"That's not what I ordered," said Daeng.

"Maybe not. But this door is five-thousand *kip* cheaper

than the next in the range. And I did notice that you have a dog outside that seems unable to enter the building."

"That dog has never entered a building," said Daeng. "Not because it's unable to but because it has some canine dread of being inside."

"Well, when it gets over its fear this will be the perfect door for it."

She couldn't be bothered to argue and the saved five-thousand *kip* would come in handy even though it was a tiny sum. But she was sure that when the wind blew from then on, the dog flap would bang through the night and the hinges would creak and they would miss their old one. She was very pessimistic when it came to doors.

Siri laughed at their exchange as he wiped the tabletops with a dishcloth and thought back to his last contact with Auntie Bpoo, his unhelpful, unpleasant spirit guide. It had been a while. She had him on some kind of training program. He'd passed "taking control of his own destiny" and "awareness," and he was ready for the next test but for some reason she'd gone mute. He attempted to evoke her often, but the channel was off air. Often, he wished his life could have been, not normal exactly, but more under his own control. Daeng was saying something behind him.

"What was that?" Siri asked.

"I said the ribbon was a nice touch," said Daeng.

"What ribbon's that?"

"You didn't decorate the dog?"

"Not sure I know what you're talking about."

"The ribbon, Siri. You didn't see him out there? Ugly has a rather sweet pink bow on his tail."

"Nothing to do with me," he said walking to the street.

Ugly was under the tree guarding the bicycle. Sure

enough, he was wearing a ribbon with a silk flower, and from the rear he looked like a mangy birthday present.

Siri laughed. "This looks like the work of a certain Down syndrome comedian I know," he said.

"Can't blame Geung and his bride this time," said Daeng. "In case you haven't noticed, we're doing all the noodle work here. He and Tukta won't be back from their honeymoon for another week. And Ugly was not so beautifully kitted out when I left this morning. Don't take it off. He looks adorable."

Siri was bent double inspecting the dog's rear end. There was more of a sausage than an actual tail so it was surprising the decorator had found enough length to tie on the bow and that Ugly would allow it.

"It appears to have a message attached," Siri said. "There's a small capsule hanging from it. Lucky he didn't need to go to the bathroom before you noticed it."

"A message?" She smiled. "How thrilling."

Never one to pass up a mystery, Daeng joined her husband on the uneven pavement. Ugly seemed reluctant to give up his treasure. He growled deep in his throat.

"Come on, you ungrateful mongrel," said Siri. "Who do you think pays for your meals and applies ointment to all your sores and apologizes to the neighbors for your indiscriminate peeing?"

It was a compelling argument and one that Ugly obviously had no counter for. He held up his haunches for his master to remove the capsule. It was a silver cylinder about the size of a cigarette. Its two halves could be pulled apart. Siri had seen its kind before but he couldn't remember where. Inside was a tight roll of paper, which he unfurled.

"Unquestionably a treasure map," said Daeng.

"Only words, I'm afraid," said Siri. "And handwritten."

Still pretending that his eyesight was as good as it had always been, he held out the slip at arm's length and squinted at the tiny writing. He would blame that arm for its shortness rather than admit to any deficiency in his eyesight. The note was just within range.

"It's in English," he said.

"What a shame," said Daeng.

He read it aloud with what he considered to be an English accent.

> "My dear Dr. Siri Paiboun, it has been a while. By now I'm sure you have either forgotten my promise of revenge or have dismissed it as an idle threat. But if you had known me at all, you would have realized that my desire to destroy you and your loved ones is a fire that has burned in my heart without end. After such a long search I have found you and I am near you. I have already deleted one of your darlings. Before I leave I will have ruined the life you have established just as you did mine. I have two more weeks. That should be more than sufficient."

It would be several hours before Siri and Daeng could fully appreciate the seriousness of their note because neither of them understood English. They knew French and could read the characters and they could guess here and there at meanings. But the languages were too far apart to cause either of them to panic. That would come later.

CHAPTER TWO
The Glory of Totalitarianism

At the end of 1980, Vientiane was a city still waiting for something to happen. It had waited through the droughts and floods, through the flawed policies, the failed cooperatives, the mass exodus of the Hmong and lowland Lao and, more recently, ethnic Chinese business holders across the Mekong. It had waited for inspiration, for good news, for a break. It had been waiting for five years but still nothing of any note had happened. So, what better way to celebrate five years of Communist rule than by inviting a large number of foreign journalists to observe the results of all those things that hadn't happened? There were those who argued that *nothing* was a good thing. For thirty years the Lao had been waging a war against their brothers and against the foreign powers that put them in uniforms. Wasn't *nothing* better than that?

It was what they called "a cocktail reception" even though none of the glasses being carried around on silver trays contained anything more exotic than weak whisky sodas and room temperature white wine. The hostesses who carried the trays wore thick makeup, military uniforms and uncomfortable boots. They smiled in a way that suggested they were under orders to do so. They did not enter into conversation with the already soused foreign journalists because they could not. They were from villages in distant provinces and even fluency in the Lao language was beyond their linguistic ability. And they had been warned by their superiors about these men from the decadent West and the shady East who bit the heads off babies and had sexual organs the size of ripe papayas. The girls trembled at every flirtatious glance, each beckoning whistle.

In its day, the nightclub of the Anou Hotel had been a gloomy cavern of nefarious goings on. When first the French, and then the American soldier boys played there, it was a mysterious grotto, so dark you couldn't see the age of your dance partner, so heavy with marijuana smoke you couldn't smell the fluids that had soaked into the carpets the night before. But on this evening, this glorious evening that marked the fifth anniversary of the founding of the People's Democratic Republic of Laos, the lights were all on, and there were no secrets. The gaps in the parquet tiles on the dance floor had been filled with cement and painted brown. The table vinyl curled up at the edges, and the light-blue paint peeled from the beams.

But, as Comrade Civilai said, perhaps this was the symbolism the Party wanted to pass along to the world. The decadent past had fallen into ruination. The last altars to the gods of depravity were crumbling and turning to dust.

"Or," Civilai added, "perhaps there was no other venue with a functioning sound system and a full bar."

Since he left the politburo he'd not been sure of the motives behind Party policy. Perhaps he never had.

Intimacy was obviously another government plot to

endear itself to the outside world. There really wasn't a great deal of space in the Anou. Sixty-four foreign journalists—all male—were shoulder to shoulder with Russian interpreters, most of the resident diplomatic community, selected aid workers and donors and the UN, even though nobody was ever really sure what the latter did to earn their living in Laos. All of the ministries were represented, each minister and vice minister with his own aide to help carry him back to the Zil limo at the end of the night.

Comrade Civilai—wearing cool, *avant garde* sunglasses—was there because of his distinguished service to the cause of communism in Laos and his apparent undying loyalty to the politburo. Chief Inspector Phosy was there because, despite several attempts to oust him by those who had become accustomed to graft and corruption, he was still the head of the police force. His wife, Nurse Dtui was there because it was a perfect opportunity to practice the foreign languages she'd taught herself with little or no benefit thus far. And Dr. Siri and Daeng were there because it was walking distance from their restaurant and a nice evening. They hadn't been invited, but no scruffy sentry with an unloaded AK-47 was going to turn away such a distinguished white-haired couple.

This small group of friends and allies sat at a table near the exit. They'd tired of attempting to snare any of the reluctant hostesses and instead had relieved the open bar of a half bottle of Hundred Pipers. With it they toasted anything that came to mind: to the miracle that they were all still alive, to Geung and Tukta on their honeymoon at a small vegetable cooperative outside Vang Vieng, to the peaceful, almost ghostly quiet streets of Vientiane, to the dizzying figure of 15 percent Lao literacy announced that afternoon, and, finally, to friendship. The bottle was approaching empty. Civilai had made more than his usual number of bladder runs to the bathroom because he'd hit a bad patch of stomach troubles following experiments with Lao snails in fermented morning glory sauce. The comrade was a pioneer in the kitchen and pioneers stepped on their own rabbit traps from time to time.

"What I don't understand . . ." said Siri.

"There must be such a lot," said Civilai, returning from the crowded toilet.

"I'm serious about treating this condition of yours," said Siri.

"I'm not letting you and your rubber glove anywhere near my condition, thank you, Doctor," said Civilai.

"Then, what I don't understand," Siri tried again, "is the significance of five years. Nine I can appreciate. Always been a lucky number. And ten has some decimal roundness to it. But five?"

"Well, young brother, it's quite simple," said Civilai. "The government is celebrating five years because, despite all its mismanagement and false hopes and poor judgment, it's still here. They never expected to make it this far."

"Who's going to kick them out?" said Daeng.

"Exactly," said Civilai. "That's the glory of totalitarianism. You can screw up for five years and admit you have no idea what you're doing and you wake up the next morning and you're still in power. You can experiment all over again."

"If you weren't suffering from dementia I'd arrest you for treasonous rhetoric," said Phosy.

"Look around, young chief inspector," said the old

politburo man. "Point me out one minister or vice minister here who isn't demented. All those grenades exploding too close to their brains."

"Uncle Civilai, you seem particularly nasty tonight," said Nurse Dtui. "Is it the snails?"

They charged their glasses and toasted to the snails.

"In a way, yes," said Civilai. "I'll tell you, sweet Dtui. Today, with no warning, no request, no discussion, I received a copy of the speech they expect me to give to all these pliable journalists at the end of the week."

"You could always say 'no,'" said Siri.

"And then what? They'd give the same script to some other doddery old fool to read the lies."

"So what are you planning to do?" Daeng asked.

"Harness the power of redaction," said Civilai.

"You'd get two minutes into the speech and they'd drag you from the podium," said Phosy.

"But what a glorious two minutes they would be," said Civilai.

"Except the simultaneous interpreters will be reading the original script," said Daeng. "The old king tried to change his abdication speech, and the radio station brought in an actor to read the Party version."

"An actor we could sorely use right now," said Siri, anxious to change the subject.

"I still have the floor," said Civilai.

"Oh, right," said Nurse Dtui, ignoring him, "your movie. I was going to ask about that. Don't you have a cast yet?"

"I feel nobody takes me seriously anymore," Civilai grumbled.

"The Women's Union has brought together a vast gaggle of would-be performers," said Siri.

"All we're missing is a functioning camera," said Daeng.

"The camera is functioning," said Siri, "and we are on the verge of acquiring a world-class cinematographer to operate it."

"Here I am about to re-educate the planet," said Civilai, "and you dismiss my plan out of hand."

"Perhaps we aren't yet drunk enough to take you seriously," said Daeng. "Another bottle might persuade us."

Civilai huffed and the hairs in his nostrils flapped. He walked off to the bar with a heavy smattering of umbrage and a noticeable stagger.

"He's not really going to sabotage the speech, is he?" Nurse Dtui asked.

"He's a politician," said Siri.

He'd planned to say more but realized that short phrase said it all.

"And the camera story?" asked Phosy.

The camera in question was a very expensive Panavision Panaflex Gold which had become 'lost' during the shooting of a film called *The Deer Hunter* in Thailand. Through the rice-growing underground it found its way to Laos and into the spare room on the upper floor of Madam Daeng's restaurant. Until then, all it lacked was someone with the ability to turn it on. But that small setback to the filming of Dr. Siri's ambitious Lao spectacular was apparently resolved.

"Our cinematographer has arrived and will begin his duties this weekend," said Siri with a smile. "Daeng and I and various relatives went to the airport to greet him and make sure he didn't change his mind and get on the return flight."

"And by 'cinematographer,'" said Daeng, "what Siri

means is a young boy with a certificate in film production and no experience."

"Yet more experience than all of us in the operation of a camera," said Siri. "I was born into a generation of candles and beeswax lamps. Electricity entered my life late. It wasn't until I arrived in Paris that I discovered the magic of *volts* and *ampères*. But by then I had decided to dedicate my life to medicine. If I had not, who's to say by now I wouldn't have been the one to invent the cassette player and the Xerox machine?"

"Is he legal, this camera person of yours?" the chief inspector asked.

"He's Lao," said Siri, "the cousin of Seksak who runs the Fuji Photo Lab. He's harking the call of the Party for its lost sons to come home to the motherland to share their new skills and savings."

"He left in the '75 exodus?" Dtui asked.

"Before," said Siri. "He made an orderly exit about ten years before with his father. Dad had a scholarship from the Colombo Plan. His wife died in childbirth, so it was just the two of them. They moved to Sydney. Bruce went to—"

"His name's Bruce?" said Dtui.

"His father renamed him when they got there," said Siri, "perhaps in an attempt to hide him amidst all the other Bruces. The boy had studied with the Australians here and become proficient in English. He sailed through high school and entered college."

"Why would he ever want to come back?" Phosy asked.

"His cousin believes he was disillusioned with the decadent West. His father had been killed in a car accident in Australia and Bruce was homesick. Missed his distant family. When our government announced we'd welcome expatriate Lao with no hard feelings, he was only too keen. His cousin told him about our film. He read my script and was delighted to join us."

"Can you afford him?" asked Dtui.

"Said he was happy to do it for nothing."

"Must be mad," said Civilai, returning with another half bottle of whisky, which he plonked down on the table like a memento of war.

"You could talk the crutches off a legless man," said Daeng. "How do you do it?"

"Those young fellows just need to know who's boss," said Civilai. "Look important. Don't say anything. Walk behind the bar. Pick up the bottle. Simple."

He sat at the table, his revolutionary fire apparently doused.

"And speaking of who's boss," said Daeng, "where's Madam Nong this evening?"

"My wife does not enjoy watching me drink," said Civilai. "She seems to think I devalue myself when I allow alcohol to make decisions for me."

"Whereas Madam Daeng here knows only too well that I am at my brightest and most perceptive with the Hundred Pipers playing the background music," said Siri.

"Sadly, as the music grows louder and the perception reaches a crescendo, the passion is known to wane," said Daeng.

There was a long silence at the table.

"We all know this is Daeng making a joke, right?" said Siri.

"I'm not so sure," said Dtui.

"Daeng, tell them," said Siri.

Daeng looked around the room.

"Daeng?"

The embarrassment was blurred by the voice of some-body leaning too closely into a badly wired microphone. Like announcements at the national airport, nobody knew exactly what had been said. But it was the signal for Siri's crew to down their drinks and head to the exit. It was speech time and their finely tuned instincts naturally sent them in the opposite direction.

It was only a short walk to the noodle shop, but Siri must have told them a dozen times that his wife was joking about his waning ardor. Still she kept mum and they were all shedding tears of laughter by the time they reached the closed shutter. High in a tree opposite perched Crazy Rajhid, the Indian. They could only see his silhouette against the moon, but it was obvious he was as naked as on the day he was born. They waved. He ignored them. He still believed that if he kept perfectly still he was invisible.

It was the time of the evening when the dusty streets were usually deserted and no other sound could be heard: no television, no radio, no hum of air-conditioning. But on that evening their drunken voices were carried across the river to Thailand to show the enemy that socialist Laos could still have a good time once in a while. In an hour, when the curfew took hold, their voices would be silenced too, but right now was as good a time as any to stand on the riverbank and yell abuse. It was nothing personal, just a friendly diatribe against a nation with an ongoing ani-mosity toward their inferior northern neighbors. It was therapy.

Once in the restaurant, Madam Daeng made a batch

of noodles to soak up the whisky and put something in everyone's stomach for the ride home. Only Civilai, still blaming the snails, forwent the meal.

"I think we need to approach the girl," he said.

"What girl's that?" Phosy asked.

"The blonde," said Civilai. "Acting second secretary at the American embassy. Looks gorgeous. Speaks fluent Lao. She was standing at the bar. I've met her at a few functions recently."

"He has these hallucinations," said Siri.

"In a room with two hundred men you really didn't notice one attractive woman?" Civilai asked.

"Even in a room with two hundred women I'd only notice Daeng," said Siri.

Daeng smiled and squeezed his hand.

"I was making all that up about his ardor," she said.

"At last," said Siri. "Why do you feel the need to approach the blonde, Civilai?"

"She has acting experience," said Civilai. "We need her for the film."

"In what role?" Siri asked. "Ours is the story of the nation through the eyes of two young revolutionaries not unlike ourselves. How many pretty blonde Americans featured in the birth of the republic?"

"We could write in a part for her," said Civlilai.

"As what?"

"I don't know. She could be the CIA."

"All by herself?" asked Siri.

"Why not?"

"I think you'll find most women in the CIA back then were making coffee and typing," said Madam Daeng.

"Look, it doesn't matter what she does," said Civilai.

"How many commercially successful movies have you seen that didn't have a glamour interest?"

"I believe we have one or two beautiful Lao women in major roles," said Dtui.

"That is admirable," said Civilai. "But if we're aiming at the international market . . ."

"Lao women aren't attractive enough?" said Daeng.

"They . . . you are lovely in the domestic sense," said Civilai, "but we need sexy. We need . . . we need a Barbarella."

Only Siri and Civilai knew who Barbarella was, and Siri wasn't about to disagree with his friend's choice. There followed a testy five minutes as the old boys tried to define sexy and explain why even the most attractive Lao in her finest blouse and ankle-length *phasin* skirt would not qualify. They dug themselves deeper into the muck with every comment. The discomfort was only eased when Civilai felt the need for one more visit to the toilet.

"Time for us to go pick up Malee," said Dtui. She stood to leave. "She's with a neighbor and they'll want to get to bed."

Despite his lofty position, Chief Inspector Phosy and his wife were still billeted at the police dormitory until their modest government house was completed. To his wife's mixed disappointment and admiration, he'd refused to move into the palatial two-story abode of his predecessor.

"Come husband," she said.

"I'm fine to drive the Vespa," said Phosy.

Dtui twiddled her fingers and he handed her the key. She knew that if he felt the need to tell her he was fine there had to be some doubt. Even in the carless streets of the capital there were potholes and sleeping dogs, and her husband had worked thirteen hours that day. He'd be safer on the pillion seat. They'd started toward the street when Siri remembered his letter.

"Oh, wait," he said, and pulled the folded paper from his top pocket. "A quick translation and you can be on your way."

He explained how the note had been attached to Ugly's tail sometime that morning. Nurse Dtui, hoping for a study placement in America, had put in many hours to learn English. In '75, armed with a scholarship and high hopes, she'd watched the Americans flee, and, like their Hmong allies, Dtui was stranded. She looked up from the words with an expression of horror on her face. Her English was competent enough to read Siri's letter and good enough for her to realize the menace it contained. She called Phosy back from the street and had the team sit once more around the table beneath the buzzing fluorescent lamp while she translated. Siri and Daeng appeared to be unmoved by the content.

"You don't seem that concerned," Phosy told them.

"It wouldn't be the first threat we've received," said Siri.

"Almost a weekly event," said Civilai.

"Well, I'm your friendly local policeman," said the chief inspector, "and I'm not going to let you laugh this one off. It isn't just a threat to you, Siri. The writer is promising to hurt your loved ones and that includes everyone at this table."

"I don't love him," said Civilai. "I'm not even that fond of him. That should let me off the hook."

"Ignore him," said Daeng. "He's having one of his difficult years. Go ahead Phosy. What do you suggest?"

"First, I suggest we look at the letter for what it does, not just for what it says."

"What's that supposed to mean?" said Civilai.

"Well," said Phosy, "the fact that it's in English sends a message in itself. As Siri doesn't speak the language I doubt he's antagonized too many English speakers in his life. And, even if the writer knows more than one language, why would he choose English for this particular threat?"

"I'm assuming you'll just be asking a batch of questions and have us fill in the answers later," said Civilai.

"I think that's a splendid system," said Madam Daeng. "Continue, Phosy."

"Secondly," said Phosy, "why does he only have two weeks to complete his mission? If he lived here there'd be no restriction."

"So, he's a visitor," said Nurse Dtui.

"On a visa," said Siri. "We aren't that generous in the immigration field."

"And we just left a room full of foreign journalists who are in town for exactly two weeks with nice fresh corre-spondent visas in their passports," said Phosy. "Any one of them could be our writer. Even the Eastern bloc boys would have a grounding in English."

"We can't interrogate all sixty-four of them," said Daeng. "We need to eliminate some."

"Well, he's certainly not Vietnamese," said Dtui.

"How do you know?" Siri asked.

"He gave Ugly a break," she said. "They still eat dogs over there. No Vietnamese is going to balk at slicing up a flea bitten mongrel if it serves a purpose."

They heard a low howl from the street. It might have been a coincidence but Siri doubted that.

"Okay, there are four Vietnamese journalists," said Daeng. "That takes us to sixty."

"Not much of a help," said Civilai.

"We need to start with the threat itself," said Phosy. "Siri, the writer made a promise that he would have his revenge. That his lust for vengeance is still burning inside him. I'm guessing that when he made that threat initially you would have sensed that it was more than just words. You would have seen him as capable of following through with it. It would have frightened you. For some time you would have been looking over your shoulder. On how many occasions have you experienced that type of fear in your life?"

All eyes turned to Siri. He looked up at the lamp and seemed to be fast-rewinding through his seventy-six years. He sniffed when he reached the end.

"Twice," he said.

"Then, that's—" Phosy began.

"Better make it three times," said Siri. "Just to be sure. Three times when I truly believed the nasty bastard meant what he said and had the resources to keep his promise. I'm not given to panic, but I confess to missing a few heart-beats on those occasions."

"Then that's where we start," said Phosy. "Who's first?"

CHAPTER THREE
Paris, 1932

I was sitting at an outdoor table in front of the Café de la Paix. I was alone, but I told the waiter in his long white apron that I was expecting someone. He was surprised to hear French from my lips. They usually were. He was unnecessarily polite. All the other tables were occupied by French sophisticates. White people as far as the eye could see. Dapper men with pencil mustaches and straw boaters. *Vogue* magazine women with bangs that restricted their vision to lap level. White silk dresses billowed in the wind. Champagne bubbled. You'd never have guessed France was in the middle of the Great Depression.

There was a sort of upside down racism in Paris those days. The French military had recruited thousands of Chinese for the war effort, and most of them had been killed in battle: ravaged by Spanish flu or just left to die slowly from neglect and hunger. They were expendable and soon forgotten. Their story would never have been released by the government but the bolshie French press got wind of it and exposed the disgrace in its national newspapers. The government had no choice but to apologize and thank the Chinese for their contribution to the Allies' victory over the Germans.

As I had an Asian face I got a lot of looks of remorse during that period. Those "we're sorry for what we did to you" looks. The looks never became words or actions, but I did get the odd smiles from pretty ladies in white. It was May and *la mode* of spring was the tennis look. The temperature was taking its time to catch up to the season. Hundreds of inappropriately dressed people sat shivering at their tables or walking briskly along the boulevard. Three ladies at the table beside me were cradling their coffee cups to keep their fingers warm. I smiled at them. They looked at one another before smiling back. As I was no slave to fashion, I wore mittens and a muffler.

I'd arrived in Paris on a steamer in 1924 at the age of twenty. Unlike the other Asians on board, I didn't have to shovel coal or stagger from the galley to the state rooms with trays of canapés and champagne buckets. I had a ticket. My cabin was small but comfortable. I was in the enviable position of having a sponsor who had taken it upon herself to turn me from a shoeless waif into a young man of letters. Madam Le Saux, more commonly known as Loulou, had first met me at a temple in Savanakheth. I had been dumped there at the age of ten by an uncaring relative who instructed me to learn all I could, then disappeared from my life. I learned everything the monks had to teach and read the French books in the small library over and over again. By the age of twelve I was bored.

Madam Loulou arrived one day in a yellow Peugot with a driver in a cap. She was tall and slim but for her midriff, where fat had gathered unkindly. She reminded me of a python I'd once seen digesting a pig. Hers was the first

French I'd heard spoken by a native speaker. My initial reaction was amazement at how clever she was to have mastered such a difficult language. Her face was so heavily cased in makeup it took some time for her expressions to match her words.

"Does anybody here speak French?" she called out. Her voice was manly, crumbly at the edges.

Nobody answered, not even the abbot whose French was by far the best at our temple. He slunk back into the prayer hall, took up a broom and started sweeping.

"My word," she said. "They sent me here because your temple has such a fine reputation. Yet I cannot find one person who understands me."

I don't know what possessed my skinny legs to walk me forward, nor how I dared look her in the eye.

"We all speak French, Madam," I said, "but we are embarrassed to attempt it in front of you."

She walked toward me, her heels sinking into the dirt with each step.

"And why would you be embarrassed?" she asked.

"Because we are not perfect," I said.

Despite the tightness of her dress, she crouched and wiggled her index finger in my direction.

"Come here, Little Prince," she said.

I shuffled forward close enough to see the wrinkles under her makeup.

"Only in nature can we find perfection," she said. "Man must settle for 'good enough.' And you are good enough for me. I choose you."

And, just like that, I became her project. She made donations to the temple for extra tuition. She produced excellent counterfeit documents proving my links to the

Lao royal family that gained me entry into the *lycée* in Saigon where she paid my fees. She attended my graduation and presented me with a second-class ticket on the *Victor Hugo* to France. In my pack, I had a letter of introduction from the governor general in Saigon to the director of Ancienne University and enough funds to cover my first-year expenses in Paris. Madam Loulou guaranteed me funds for every year that I achieved excellent grades until the day I became a doctor.

What she didn't guarantee was that she would stay alive long enough to honor that promise. Even as I was journeying across the Atlantic my sponsor succumbed to consumption and was dead by the time I docked in Marseilles. It wasn't until several years later that I learned of the background of my dear Madam Loulou. For many years, my sponsor had been the proprietor of one of the most popular whore houses in Saigon. She had amassed a small fortune mainly from the patronage of French army officers, one of whom was the aforementioned governor general. She had arrived in Vietnam early in the French campaign and in a city with more brothels than drain holes, she quickly made a name for herself. This was achieved, not from the beauty of her girls but from their unique skills. Madam Loulou had trained each one in the ancient art of fellatio. You might say she'd become a celebrity by word of mouth.

Loulou had never married nor produced offspring. She had nobody to share her wealth with. Somewhere along the line she got it into her head that she was on her way to hell: a belief loudly supported by the wives of the officers she serviced. A Catholic priest in Saigon—also a customer—suggested she might readjust her trajectory by saving poor orphans. And, in the shell of a nut, that's what led her to me and twenty other young boys. I still look for her in the back alleyways of the Other World, but I never see my darling Madam Loulou. And that, omitting several years of struggles and humiliations, of poverty, of retaking high school courses and accepting disgusting jobs to keep myself alive in France, explains why I was sitting in front of the Café de la Paix that chilly May morning. I was in my third year of medicine at Ancienne and doing moderately well, "for an Asian." But I'd run into a bad patch of my own doing and I needed counsel.

"Anybody sitting here?" came a voice.

The young fellow leaning over me was dark-skinned with a fine head of black hair greased back. He was dressed like half the men there at the café, and he grasped a tennis racket in his left hand. His right hand he held out to me. I grabbed it, laughed, and shook the hell out of it.

"Sit down, you fool," I said, "before someone challenges you to a game."

Civilai pulled out the chair and apologized in charming French to the three ladies behind him who needed to shuffle slightly to allow him to sit. They smiled. He gestured to the waiter, pointed to my cognac and held up three fingers.

"What makes you think I couldn't beat them?" he said.

"I doubt that racket's ever kissed a ball," I said.

"You're right. But see how impressed everyone looks. A Chinaman trained in the fine art of tennis. They'll go home and tell all their friends we can count to forty."

Civilai was, in many respects, my cultural savior in those tough years. We'd met at the Louxor, a small cinema in La Chapelle, where I worked as an usher and confectionary seller. I'd been there so long most of the patrons knew me by name. Civilai was from a wealthy family and never really had to work for a living. Our backgrounds were so different we really had no right to have become friends, but our love for the cinema drew us together. He told me that he was a Communist. At the time, I really didn't know what that meant. It seemed everyone in Paris had to have a cause. You had to be something other than your-self: a fascist, an anarchist, a poet. So I paid little heed to Civilai's constant references to Karl Marx and Lenin. He told me about his pal, Quoc, a Vietnamese who had great plans to go back to Indochina and rescue the slaves in the French colonies. Together they would establish a Communist state, just as soon as Quoc got out of jail in Hong Kong. He seemed, to my mind, to be spending a lot of time in jail.

As a child at the temple in Savanaketh, I hadn't had many dealings with the French administrators. In fact, I probably viewed them as great white gods educating us natives—through armed force—how to be civilized. I liked their uniforms. It didn't occur to me they were raping our land. We didn't have anything when they arrived and sev-eral decades later we had even less and were paying taxes on it. But, to a ten-year-old boy, that seemed to be the way of the world. If you had a big gun you had the right to do what you wanted.

But then, in France *entre deux guerres,* Civilai had become my grapevine to a country I had no other means to com-municate with. I had no friends or family back in Laos. Like all the bemused tribesmen and women, who had been corralled together under a Lao flag, I'd been born in a country that I still knew very little about. I'd written

'Buddhist' on the application to Ancienne, but the religion of my birth made no more sense to me than the Catholicism drummed into me at school. At 23 I'd already seen more of France than I had of Laos. Without Civilai I would probably have swallowed the colonial line that the country was working in the tropics to improve the lot of ignorant savages. Were it not for a generous fellationist, I would have been one of them.

"Do you ever order just one drink?" I asked my young friend.

He placed the newly arrived drinks like chess pieces on the checkered tablecloth and pushed one toward me: cognac to queen's pawn two.

"Monsieur L'Usher," he said, "one never knows when one's waiter might be struck down with a heart attack, leaving all those at the tables around his prone body deprived of their rightful *digestifs*. Always order as if these drinks might be your last."

"At these prices they undoubtedly will be," I said.

"Then consider yourself lucky that this very morning a handsome filly at Longchamp caught my eye. She almost begged me to put a hundred francs on her to win. And she did not disappoint me. Consider this afternoon my treat."

I knew there were no races at Longchamp in the morning. With Civilai, there was always a horse, a greyhound or a roulette table keen to cover the costs of our outings. He never once belittled me over my poverty nor offered to pay for my courses or keep up with the rent. My pride remained intact, but I was certain that if a disaster befell me, my friend would be there to help me out. I just had to ask. I never did.

"*Salut,*" he said and clinked my glass with his. We drank

to nothing in particular. "Shouldn't you be in school?" he asked.

"I don't go to as many classes as I used to," I said. "I work better from books. I tend to pick out the best lectures to attend. I went to one this morning on diacetylmorphine."

"Sounds fascinating."

"It was," I said. "It was one of those moments when you can be sure the world has just made another one of its serious mistakes."

"Like assassinating Archduke Ferdinand?"

"Potentially much worse than that," I said.

"Then tell me all about dicey mental morphine," he said.

"Diacetylmorphine is a pain reliever ten times more powerful than morphine. Morphine was first extracted from opium in 1805. It served us well medically, but it tended to be addictive. Scientists, searching for an alternative, synthesized diacetylmorphine, and it was an immediate success. The Bayer Company began mass production. Countries around the world hastily approved this new 'non-addictive' painkiller, and soon it was more popular than sex. And for good reason. A year after its launch in North America, 200,000 people had become addicted to this super drug that Bayer had named heroin. It was immediately banned worldwide for anything but medical or scientific use.

"But, of course, as soon as the drug became illegal, all the criminal networks went up a gear. The Chinese gangs already have refineries. The Corsicans are building labs right here in France under the noses of the *gendarmerie*. The lecturer believes that in the next decade heroin will outperform opium as the addiction of choice worldwide. It's less bulky and easier to hide."

"And this is what they're teaching you at medical school?" Civilai asked.

"You can pass on the information to your boss."

"Quoc? Why would he be interested?"

"Some of the most successful revolutions and coups in history have been funded by the drug trade. It's how the French maintain their presence in Indochina. You and your Communist buddies could get in on the ground floor."

"Siri, communism is all about empowering the workers, not debilitating them. When we take over from the French, the first thing we'll do is burn their opium crops."

"I admire your faith," I said, even though I didn't give it much of a chance.

"So anyway, what brings me here?" he asked.

"My postcard, I presume."

"It gave up so little information."

"I didn't want the French postal service to be the first to know."

"Excellent. I have an exclusive, and you want my advice."

"More, your blessing," I said.

"Oh, no."

"Oh, no, what?"

"I sense a liaison."

"More than a fling," I said. "I've asked her to marry me."

Civilai whooped and held up four fingers to the waiter.

"Does she know you have fifty centimes to your name?"

"She does. But she also has fifty centimes to hers. So between us we have one franc, which is the beginning of a fortune."

"Have I met her?" he asked.

"Yes, on your last trip to Paris. You and your Mademoiselle Nong joined us for the matinee of Mata Hari at the Louxor."

"Not the Lao beauty with the tight sweater?"

"The very same: Bouasawan."

"Why would a girl whose figure outperforms every erotic postcard on sale along the banks of the Seine agree to marry you?"

"I'm a catch," I said.

"You do know she's a Communist?"

"So are you."

"No, I mean she's a *Communist* said very loudly. I recall she discussed her motivation with Nong that day. She came to Paris for the sole purpose of joining the Party. She'd already memorized the manifesto before she arrived. She signed up with the CPF even before she registered at Ancienne. Nong believed she was a fanatic."

"Passion is a wonderful thing."

"I hope she can find time for you amid her obsession."

"This from a man who's leaving in a week to muster a proletariat and turn Indochina red?"

"I'm enthusiastic," he said, "not fanatical. I like to call myself a middle-path socialist. I appreciate the concept and the potential of communism. I think it could work to unite our people against the French. But I don't decorate my apartment with hammer and sickle wallpaper. I don't send photos of myself in a swimsuit to Lenin."

"You know she doesn't do any of that."

He was starting to irritate me.

"Don't get defensive, little brother," he said. "I'm just offering my opinions."

While the waiter was putting the new glasses on the table, Civilai knocked back the drinks he already had.

"How can I not be defensive when you disparage my choice of bride?" I said.

"Look, Siri, she's gorgeous. She'd make any man's heart turn somersaults. And there is no doubt she's intelligent or that she loves her country. I see no problem with her whatsoever. The only problem I see is you."

"I'm not good enough for her?"

"Like me, she obviously recognizes just how good you are. You are unique and supremely talented. But you don't believe in what she believes."

"I believe."

"You don't."

"I do."

"Convince me."

"What?"

"Convince me that you share her passion."

The cognac had warmed my blood and was making me disagreeable. I took off my muffler. I hadn't been planning to tell him but he'd left me no choice.

"I've joined," I said.

"Joined what?"

"The Party."

"Nonsense."

"It's true. I went to a few meetings with Boua and thought, well, this isn't so bad, is it? And I decided that, with a bit of work, this communism thing has a chance. So I paid my dues and got my card. I can show it to you if you like."

"I don't want to doubt your motives . . ." he said.

"I love her, Civilai. I've loved her since the first day I saw her in class. She's the most . . . the most substantial Lao woman I've ever met. She has dreams. She has unselfish ambitions. She smells nice. She can change the world, and I want to be beside her while she's doing it."

"Then all I can say is congratulations," said Civilai, and,

as a fitting subject break, a coal cart was pulled over by a fat policeman right in front of us because the horse wasn't wearing blinkers. In protest, the horse shat all over the boots of the policeman who arrested the driver. He in turn protested that it was the horse that did the damage, not he. Some of the more intoxicated onlookers applauded the horse.

To my mind, our conversation became a little less amicable after that. We didn't part on the best of terms. If we'd known how long it would be before we'd meet again, we'd probably have drunk one more glass for the road, said *au revoir* with a handshake and wished each other luck. In retrospect, I wish we had because then I would have been late for my appointment and not become embroiled in one of the most unpleasant events in French history. Instead, still miffed about his comments, I told Civilai I had to leave in a hurry to pay a visit to the Hotel de Rothschild, where there was a sale of secondhand medical textbooks. But I made the mistake of mentioning that the main event of the book exhibition was its opening by the president, Paul Doumer, himself. I knew that would irritate him.

It was as if I'd pushed down on the detonation plunger of Civilai's personal TNT. He launched off on a tirade against the fuzzy-bearded gentleman that, were it not in Lao, would have shocked and offended all those around us. Drinkers tutted their disapproval at the volume, but Civilai ranted on. Doumer had been the Governor General of the colonies in Indochina. His were the taxes that drained the lifeblood out of the villages. His were the laws that favored the French over the natives; favored the lowlanders over the tribes people. His were the policies that made a success of their investments for the first time, all on the back of local suffering. More investors came to take the gamble that led to more pillaging and looting. When the Lao proved too backward and lazy to absorb this development, Doumer carted in Vietnamese administrators and laborers by the thousands. There were probably more Vietnamese in the country than Lao at that time.

And what funded all these grandiose projects? *La grande comtesse d'O.* Doumer took over the opium monopoly and used the profits to supplement the modest funds he received from France. It was not a new policy. He was merely continuing a historical precedent in the third world. But he was good at the game. His chemists processed raw Indian resin using a technique that made the opium burn faster, thus increasing the demand. He imported impure opium from China for the poor addicted coolies. While the world was seeking bans on the opium trade, Doumer was embracing it. So successful was his policy in the Far East that he returned to France a hero, and his rise through the political ranks was inevitable.

And in Civilai's mind, I was on my way to stand meekly in a chilly street alongside the type of people who adored celebrity. We would applaud as he arrived and applaud as he left, and we would go home and tell our loved ones how close we'd been to the great statesman. That could not have been further from the truth.

"I hope you two have a very good time together," said Civilai, throwing down his last cognac and leaving me with three untouched glasses of my own. His chair bumped our neighbors' table as he stood and he bowed in apology. He picked his way through the diners and stood at the border of the sidewalk. He looked back at me, winked and smiled before joining the passersby. On the table he'd left some bank notes and an unused tennis racket.

Other Titles in the Soho Crime Series

Michael Genelin
(Slovakia)
Siren of the Waters
Dark Dreams
The Magician's Accomplice
Requiem for a Gypsy

Timothy Hallinan
(Thailand)
The Fear Artist
For the Dead
The Hot Countries
Fools' River

(Los Angeles)
Crashed
Little Elvises
The Fame Thief
Herbie's Game
King Maybe
Fields Where They Lay
Nighttown

Mette Ivie Harrison
(Mormon Utah)
The Bishop's Wife
His Right Hand
For Time and All Eternities
Not of This Fold

Mick Herron
(England)
Slow Horses
Dead Lions
Real Tigers
Spook Street
London Rules

Down Cemetery Road
The Last Voice You Hear
Why We Die
Smoke and Whispers

Reconstruction
Nobody Walks
This Is What Happened

Stan Jones
(Alaska)
White Sky, Black Ice
Shaman Pass
Frozen Sun

Stan Jones cont.
Village of the Ghost Bears
Tundra Kill
The Big Empty

**Lene Kaaberbøl &
Agnete Friis**
(Denmark)
The Boy in the Suitcase
Invisible Murder
Death of a Nightingale
The Considerate Killer

Martin Limón
(South Korea)
Jade Lady Burning
Slicky Boys
Buddha's Money
The Door to Bitterness
The Wandering Ghost
G.I. Bones
Mr. Kill
The Joy Brigade
Nightmare Range
The Iron Sickle
The Ville Rat
Ping-Pong Heart
The Nine-Tailed Fox
The Line

Ed Lin
(Taiwan)
Ghost Month
Incensed
99 Ways to Die

Peter Lovesey
(England)
The Circle
The Headhunters
False Inspector Dew
Rough Cider
On the Edge
The Reaper

(Bath, England)
The Last Detective
Diamond Solitaire
The Summons
Bloodhounds
Upon a Dark Night

Peter Lovesey cont.
The Vault
Diamond Dust
The House Sitter
The Secret Hangman
Skeleton Hill
Stagestruck
Cop to Corpse
The Tooth Tattoo
The Stone Wife
*Down Among
the Dead Men*
Another One Goes Tonight
Beau Death

(London, England)
Wobble to Death
*The Detective Wore
Silk Drawers*
Abracadaver
Mad Hatter's Holiday
The Tick of Death
A Case of Spirits
Swing, Swing Together
Waxwork

Jassy Mackenzie
(South Africa)
Random Violence
Stolen Lives
The Fallen
Pale Horses
Bad Seeds

Sujata Massey
(1920s Bombay)
*The Widows of
Malabar Hill*

Francine Mathews
(Nantucket)
Death in the Off-Season
Death in Rough Water
Death in a Mood Indigo
Death in a Cold Hard Light
Death on Nantucket

Seichō Matsumoto
(Japan)
*Inspector Imanishi
Investigates*

Magdalen Nabb
(Italy)
Death of an Englishman
Death of a Dutchman
Death in Springtime
Death in Autumn
The Marshal and
the Murderer
The Marshal and
the Madwoman
The Marshal's Own Case
The Marshal Makes
His Report
The Marshal
at the Villa Torrini
Property of Blood
Some Bitter Taste
The Innocent
Vita Nuova
The Monster of Florence

Fuminori Nakamura
(Japan)
The Thief
Evil and the Mask
Last Winter, We Parted
The Kingdom
The Boy in the Earth
Cult X

Stuart Neville
(Northern Ireland)
The Ghosts of Belfast
Collusion
Stolen Souls
The Final Silence
Those We Left Behind
So Say the Fallen

(Dublin)
Ratlines

Rebecca Pawel
(1930s Spain)
Death of a Nationalist
Law of Return
The Watcher in the Pine
The Summer Snow

Kwei Quartey
(Ghana)
Murder at Cape
Three Points
Gold of Our Fathers
Death by His Grace

Qiu Xiaolong
(China)
Death of a Red Heroine
A Loyal Character Dancer
When Red Is Black

John Straley
(Sitka, Alaska)
The Woman Who Married
a Bear
The Curious Eat Themselves
The Music of What Happens
Death and the Language of
Happiness
The Angels Will Not Care
Cold Water Burning
Baby's First Felony

(Cold Storage, Alaska)
The Big Both Ways
Cold Storage, Alaska

Akimitsu Takagi
(Japan)
The Tattoo Murder Case
Honeymoon to Nowhere
The Informer

Helene Tursten
(Sweden)
Detective Inspector Huss
The Torso
The Glass Devil
Night Rounds
The Golden Calf
The Fire Dance
The Beige Man
The Treacherous Net
Who Watcheth
Protected by the Shadows

Hunting Game

Helene Tursten cont.
An Elderly Lady Is Up to
No Good

Janwillem van de
Wetering
(Holland)
Outsider in Amsterdam
Tumbleweed
The Corpse on the Dike
Death of a Hawker
The Japanese Corpse
The Blond Baboon
The Maine Massacre
The Mind-Murders
The Streetbird
The Rattle-Rat
Hard Rain
Just a Corpse at Twilight
Hollow-Eyed Angel
The Perfidious Parrot
The Sergeant's Cat:
Collected Stories

Timothy Williams
(Guadeloupe)
Another Sun
The Honest Folk
of Guadeloupe

(Italy)
Converging Parallels
The Puppeteer
Persona Non Grata
Black August
Big Italy
The Second Day
of the Renaissance

Jacqueline Winspear
(1920s England)
Maisie Dobbs
Birds of a Feather